PRAISE FOR

Anahita's Woven Riddle

ALA/YALSA TOP 10 BEST BOOKS
FOR YOUNG ADULTS

BOOK SENSE PICK

ALA AMELIA BLOOMER PROJECT
FEMINIST BOOK SELECTION

"The exploration of another culture in an earlier time
with a side of almost fairy-tale romance results in a
satisfying read." —*VOYA*

"An engrossing story." —*School Library Journal*

"Richly textured novel of a young girl's quest for the perfect
husband in [19th]-century Iran . . . Romantic
[and] delightful!" —*Kirkus Reviews*

"It's Anahita's warm heart and bold intelligence that linger as
readers imagine her future." —*The Sacramento Bee*

"Offers a glimpse of a world not many books enter . . .
tugs at the heart." —*Historical Novels Review*

Amulet Books

New York

Anahita's
WOVEN RIDDLE

MEGHAN NUTTALL SAYRES

Proceeds from the sale of this novel will go to development enterprises for women and children who have been the victims of earthquakes in Iran.

Cataloging-in-Publication Data
for the hardcover edition of this book is available from the
Library of Congress.

Hardcover ISBN: 978-0-8109-5481-6
Paperback ISBN: 978-0-8109-9548-2

Printed and bound in U.S.A.
1 3 5 7 9 10 8 6 4 2

HNA
harry n. abrams, inc.
a subsidiary of La Martinière Groupe

115 West 18th Street
New York, NY 10011
www.hnabooks.com

For
Mojdeh, Farhad, Nanaz,
and Anahita

To

weavers everywhere

And to
those who—like nomads
—seek greener pastures

Contents

Characters   viii

Place Names   ix

PASHME CHINIE BAHARE
Spring Shearing

1. Riddles   1
2. A Few Quick Stitches   7
3. A Test of Wit   19
4. A Scholar, a Gentleman, and a Foreigner   31
5. A Yomut Nomad, a Gentlemen, and a Prince   39
6. A Shepherd, a Gentleman, and a Friend   47
7. The Caravan   51
8. The Magic of Mashhad   59
9. The Migration Trail   70

TAUBESTAN NAKHRISI VA GUL CHINI
Summer Spinning and Wildflower Gathering

10. Princely *Dayn*, Duties   82
11. A Khan, a Gentleman, and a Diplomat   97
12. High Pastures   104
13. Mating Calls   118
14. The Ultimatum   129
15. Autumn Market News   142
16. Leaving Mashhad   161

PAIZ RANG RAZI
Autumn Dyeing

17. Earthen Pigments   174
18. Fatima's Fire   185
19. Weaving a Plan   191
20. A Lesson of Her Own   198
21. Bride Price   208

ZEMESTAUN BAUFTAN
Winter Weaving

22. Warp, Weft, and Wishes   220
23. A Riddle in the Weaving   232
24. An Alchemy of Color   239
25. *Aub*, Water   246

PASHME CHINIE BAHARE
Spring Shearing

26. Spring Fever   256
27. Wounds   265
28. The Riddle in the Weaving   278
29. Sandstorm   285
30. Unweaving a Tale   289
31. Surprises   297
32. May the Fated Gentleman Win   305
33. A Twist of Fate   315
34. Weaving a Mate   327
    Glossary   334
    Reader's Guide   342
    Author's Note   350
    Acknowledgments   356
    References   360

Characters—IN ORDER OF APPEARANCE

Anahita (Ah-na-hee-ta)—a semi-nomadic weaver who lives in the village of Hasanabad, Iran, and belongs to an Afshar tribe

Baba (Bah-bah)—the word for father; Anahita's father, whose first name is Farhad

Farhad (Far-hod)—Anahita's father, the *kadkhuda* of the Afshar tribe

Kadkhuda (Kad-khoo-da)—Farhad's title; a tribal wise man and leader who resides with a branch of the Afshar tribe and is appointed by the khan

Maman Bozorg (Maa-mon Ba-zorg)—the words for grandmother; Anahita's paternal grandmother

Maman (Maa-mon)—the word for mother

Mojdeh (Moje-day)—Anahita's mother, Farhad's wife

Mullah (Moo-la)—a Muslim religious practitioner

Shirin (Sheer-een)—Anahita's female cousin

Granduncle—a dyemaster; Anahita's grandmother's brother

Ali (Ah-lee) and **Fatima** (Fat-ee-ma)—husband-and-wife villagers who own a teahouse

Reza (Ray-za)—a schoolmaster

Arash (Awe-rash)—a Qajar prince and governor of Marv whose mother belongs to a Yomut tribe

Dariyoush (Dar-y-oosh)—Anahita's family's hired hand and village neighbor

Khan (Khawn)—chieftain of the entire Afshar tribe who represents the tribe with the shah's government

Jaleh (Jaw-lay)—a woman in Arash's tribe

Ismail (Iss-mail)—Farhad's trusted subject and adviser in Marv

Pirouz (Peer-oose)—a street kid/orphan in Marv whom Arash befriends

Place Names

Abadi-eh-Golab (Ah-baa-dee-a-Go-lob)—a fictitious village on Anahita's migratory route

Hasanabad (Ha-san-a-baad)—a fictitious village; Anahita's winter village

Kemesh (Kem-esh)—a fictitious village near Hasanabad

Khurasan (Coor-a-zan)—a northeastern province of Iran

Mashhad (Ma-shad)—a holy city in northeastern Iran with shrines, caravansarais, and a marketplace that was part of the ancient Silk Route

Marv (Marv)—a city in present-day Turkmenistan that once belonged to Iran and was part of the ancient Silk Route

Tehran (Tear-an, Teh-ran)—the capital city of Iran, south of the Caspian Sea, home of the shah and his court

*H*ere in this carpet lies an ever-lovely spring;

Unscorched by summer's ardent flame,

Safe too from autumn's boisterous gales,

Midwinter's cruel ice and snow,

'Tis gaily blooming still.

The handsome border is the garden wall

Protecting, preserving the Park within

For refuge and renewal: a magic space.

—unknown Sufi poet

MORE THAN ONE HUNDRED YEARS AGO

in the ancient land of Persia, a great change had begun. Railroads raced across the desert replacing the camel trains that had walked the sands for thousands of years. Wealthy landowners, eager to protect their property and its precious supply of water, no longer agreed that nomads should be free to cross the desert with their sheep. Many tribes were being forced to settle. In his luxurious court in Tehran, the shah heard whispers of discontent. Landowners and merchants alike called for a different kind of government, an assembly of men to help make the laws for a country that would soon become known to the world as Iran.

Sensing weakness in its neighbor, Russia sent soldiers to nibble at the borders of the land like moths on the fringe of a saddlebag. Bandits followed in their wake, preying on villages and the newly settled nomads.

Yet there were those who lived as they always had, spending summers in the mountains with their herds and winters in the villages where they wove sheep's wool into beautiful carpets, coveted for their intricate patterns and ever-bright colors. But even this old and envied craft was changing. In the spice markets of the city of Mashhad, new man-made dyes were for sale, tinctures made without the traditional ingredients of roots, insects, and wildflower petals or the careful hand of the nomadic weavers . . .

PASHME
CHINIE
BAHARE
Spring Shearing

Riddles

"Baba, I have a riddle for you," Anahita said, standing among the pregnant ewes corralled for an early spring shearing. "What gives us flavor, color under our feet, and brings sunlight indoors?"

"Hmmm. How about a hint?" her father, Farhad, asked. His smile softened his rugged features, stretching the close-clipped beard on his chin.

"No hints!"

"Your riddles get harder each year, my sweet," he said, leaning over the sheep that lay in front of him with its feet toggled. "Just one clue for your poor father?"

"Well, perhaps. Let me see . . ." Anahita put her hands on her hips. The birds embroidered on her full skirt seemed to flutter their wings as she moved. "All right, Baba, I've got one: too large a dose may cause uncontrollable laughter."

Farhad dug his shears into the wool under the sheep's chin. "Ah, it must be *zafaran!*" He chuckled as he clipped a straight line down the sheep's large belly. "It seasons our rice, dyes yarn for our carpets, and is the color of the setting sun."

Anahita narrowed her eyes, pretending to be angry. "You didn't need a hint."

She gathered the fawn-colored fleece as it fell in one piece from the ewe and spread it on a woven blanket. Removing the locks stained with urine and dung, she kept the finest fiber from the animal's shoulders and back, which she placed in a basket. Her father would allow her to use some of this wool for her weaving.

Anahita wiped her brow with the hem of her bright orange tunic. The mid-morning sun already burned. She watched her father as he clipped the sheep's hooves before releasing the shorn ewe. She always looked forward to spring, when she could work outdoors with him. Many in her tribe liked to work with her father, too. She thought how his quiet strength—*his leopard-strength*—drew people to him. Although he rarely spoke about it, it was well known that he had once single-handedly scared away a snow leopard, the elusive creature that sometimes threatened their herds. Perhaps for this reason, their khan had appointed him *kadkhuda*, wise man and leader of their branch of the Afshar tribe.

Anahita searched among the jittery flock for another healthy, four-legged fleece—one of hundreds of sheep her family owned. As she brought her father a new ewe to shear, she said, "Pose me a riddle, Baba!"

"This shall be my toughest yet. Are you ready?"

Nodding with delight, Anahita scratched behind the ear of the sheep, which Farhad had wrestled to the ground. Turning her face, full and round like the moon, toward her father, she waited for his riddle.

"What, like a garden, never stays the same?"

Anahita wrinkled her brow.

"My sweet daughter, while you contemplate this riddle we must discuss another matter," Farhad said. He braced the sheep's head to shear its neck. "Next year at this time you will be old enough to wed . . ." Clearing his throat, he continued with a lighter tone, in his is-this-not-the-greatest-news? voice. "The khan tells me he is fond of you. It would be a very prosperous arrangement."

Anahita stared at her father as he worked the long blades of the shears. *The khan? Marriage? Never!* She pulled her head scarf forward to cover more of her hair, an anxious habit. Her mind raced to remember how old her cousins had been when they married. Soheila couldn't have been less than seventeen. Farahnaz? Eighteen. Shirin? Anahita's heart sank. Shirin married at fifteen and so did her sister. Gathering the newly clipped wool, she said, "Baba, I cannot marry next year. I want to apprentice myself to the dyemaster."

"What?"

"Granduncle needs help," she said. "He's absent-minded in his old age . . . and always running out of indigo. He forgets to ask someone to buy it for him at the bazaar in Mashhad. He mixes up the village women's yarn. Last time I went for mine, he gave me a dozen green skeins I hadn't asked for."

The sheep gave an uncomfortable groan. Anahita stroked its neck.

3

"And for this reason you cannot get married? Because your granduncle is sometimes confused?"

"Baba, you don't understand. The colors of our tribe's carpets are the most beautiful at the market. I want to learn the dye-master's secrets. They'll be lost otherwise."

Farhad looked at his daughter. *Mature thoughts for a girl of her age*, she would later hear him say to her mother, Mojdeh.

"Baba, you know I've always wanted to be a master dyer."

"Surely it is possible to be a dyer *and* a wife."

Anahita cast her eyes to the ground. "I don't know any men. And I *won't* marry a stranger."

"You know the khan."

"He's older than you!"

"Age does not matter in marriage, or love." Farhad looked up and smiled.

"Love? He knows nothing about me aside from my looks." Frowning, she held her father's gaze. "He's no longer one of us. He's a diplomat. He spends most of his time in the city."

"I thought you liked Mashhad."

"I do. But I don't want to live there. I'd have to wear the *chador* all the time. I would suffocate under all that black cloth! And who will take care of Maman and Maman Bozorg if something happens to you? Who will bargain for good prices in Mashhad for our animals?"

"Anahita, I have plenty of brothers and cousins in this tribe who will look after the women in my life. This is not your concern."

Anahita stiffened. *So, I am good for nothing.*

After Farhad finished with the sheep, it scurried to the far side of the corral with the others. Following it, he singled out another ewe.

"Remember, Anahita, a good Muslim man may keep four wives if he has the means to support them. The khan can afford this, yet he waits for you."

Silence, like the thick lanolin scent in the air, lingered between Anahita and her father.

"His only good quality is that he's nice to cats," Anahita said at last. An image of the bearlike khan climbing the oak tree in the village square to rescue a kitten flashed to mind. It was followed by another image of them both falling to the ground, the khan's garbs torn, the cat mewing as it clung to his turban. The village children had imitated him for weeks, stuffing kittens in their fathers' turbans, plunking them on their own heads, and prancing around.

Farhad gathered up another freshly shorn fleece and tossed it to Anahita. "This wool will provide you with enough yarn to weave a fine carpet for your dowry. When the *qali* is complete, you must prepare to marry."

Anahita straightened, throwing her shoulders back. *"Na!"* she said. She was taller than her mother and still growing; she had inherited her father's height.

Farhad grabbed ahold of her arm. His eyes never left hers as he said, "Marriage is what gives women value. Don't ever forget this. To be unwed in this world is to be nothing!"

Anahita shrank away. Her father rarely spoke to her with such anger.

Farhad let go of her arm and turned toward the next ewe. Shaken, Anahita threw the wool into a basket with the other fleeces and carried them to a grove of silver poplars by the stream. Sitting in the shade, she picked at handful after handful of the beige fiber until she had removed every bur. *I do not want to marry. I wish to work with the dyemaster. How can I make Baba understand?*

A Few Quick Stitches

*S*urely Maman is not ready for me to marry, Anahita thought as
she walked home to find her mother. Her dome-roofed
house sat near the village square—a collection of sun-soaked
stones that consisted of a fountain, a bathhouse, a bakery, and a
modest mosque. Like the other dwellings in the village, hers was
made of mud mixed with straw (and a few dead camel spiders),
and it faced south to catch the warmth of the sun in winter. From
the square, her village wiggled in all directions—down dirt paths
lined with high walls that concealed courtyards, sheds, and old
wells.

A group of boys and girls ran in a pack near the mosque, leaping over camels resting in the midday sun. Anahita smiled as she
walked past the children; she'd played the same game years ago
with her cousin Shirin, she the one with the long legs, taller than
the boys, Shirin the one racing to keep up, light brown hair flying.
In some ways she missed those days. Or maybe it was her cousin's
company she missed. The before-she-was-married Shirin. The fun

Shirin. The Shirin who used to say that she would never marry a man she did not choose.

Anahita recalled the times when the two of them had enjoyed sleepovers, talking until sunrise, pondering the notion of getting married, but not to just *anyone*. They even spied on the village widow, unaware that someday Shirin would become the woman's daughter-in-law through an arranged marriage.

One day while standing on tiptoes to peer over the widow's courtyard wall, Anahita had whispered to Shirin, "With only one son to cook and weave for, what does she do with her spare time?"

"Were I never to marry, I would work with the bonesetter, Dariyoush's father," Shirin said as she held the crate on which Anahita stood steady. "My patients would be family enough for me."

"The widow is sipping a drink with her feet up!" Anahita reported. "She has time to rest in the middle of the day."

"Let me see," Shirin said, but just then the widow looked up. Anahita ducked, and the two giggled as they ran away.

Anahita stopped at the large loom, which stood beside her house in the shade of cypress and poplars, its wooden structure as upright as the trees. Her mother and grandmother hauled the loom outside when the warm weather arrived each spring. Anahita examined the completed, room-sized carpet, which she, her mother, and grandmother had made over the winter to sell at the market in Mashhad this spring. She liked how the white floral pattern popped out of the gold-and-turquoise background. With a critical eye she focused on the sections she had knotted, the cluster of leaves she had unraveled and rewoven. She wondered when her mother planned to cut the carpet from the loom. She always looked forward to the small gathering with which village women celebrated the completion of a weaving, and the accompanying song and sweets.

But thoughts of completed carpets only reminded her of her father's marriage plan and she looked around anxiously for her mother. Instead, she found her grandmother, Maman Bozorg, working in the courtyard behind their home. With small, strong hands she was wringing out Anahita's favorite cream-colored scarf, the one on which Anahita had sewn tiny tassels dyed red with madder root. As her grandmother hung the dripping scarf on the clothesline, Anahita could smell rose water and jasmine. She kissed Maman Bozorg on both cheeks, then spotted her mother, Mojdeh, behind their red donkey cart, milking a goat. "Maman," Anahita said, crossing her arms, "Baba tells me I must marry next spring. He says the khan is fond of me. But I am not fond of him, nor any man."

Mojdeh stood up. She was a delicate-featured woman who spent little time fussing over her appearance. "Marriage is not something to be afraid of, Anahita. It is as natural as our migration each spring. *Bia*, please come. Help me prepare our meal. Your father will be hungry after shearing." Mojdeh handed Anahita a goatskin of milk to tie onto a tripod of sticks that they would later use to churn the milk into butter.

"But Maman!" Anahita said as Mojdeh rekindled the cooking fire. "The khan has no sense of humor. He'd be an awful bore!"

"You judge him harshly," her grandmother said.

"He would accept shelter from a tribe whose name he would not bother to learn."

"Anahita," Mojdeh said, "you give him no credit. Have you forgotten that he secures our tribe's water rights from the landowners? And our use of the *qanat*?" She pointed north, in the direction of the Binalud Mountains from which underground irrigation ditches descended and ran across the plains to their village with a supply of water. Her mother continued, "He has brought doctors to our village from Mashhad—and paid for their services."

"Once."

The two held each other's gaze. A vague memory of a rumor came to Anahita's mind, something she remembered hearing as a child. "Maman, wasn't the khan married before? I seem to recall some kind of . . . funeral service?"

"Ah, yes," Mojdeh said, looking away. She poured rice into a pot of boiling water, and wiped her hands.

"So he *was* married," Anahita said. More snippets of a conversation between her mother and aunt surfaced. They were talking on a day long ago, when she still wore a little red skirt and played with tea glasses. *The poor man, he's lost three wives to illness.*

"Maman, did the khan have *three* wives?" Anahita rubbed her arms, feeling rather chilly. "Did they *all* die?"

"Well . . . yes, but . . ." Mojdeh said, then paused and reached for her basket of spices.

"Of what?" Anahita looked to her grandmother, hoping for an explanation.

"Some people in the village believe that his wives were victims of the evil eye—someone envied them, and cursed them all," Maman Bozorg said. "Perhaps this person wanted the khan to marry her own daughter, or herself, even."

"Oh Maman, how could you and Baba even consider letting the man near me?" Anahita said, fists clenched tightly at her sides.

Curling an arm around her daughter, Mojdeh said, "It is a silly superstition. Your father and I believe that the deaths of the khan's wives were purely coincidental." Mojdeh turned Anahita to face her. "Since you are so opposed to the khan, whom, may I ask, would you suggest for your suitor?"

Anahita looked away. No one came to mind.

"How about Dariyoush?" Mojdeh offered. "He's a fine young man. And an excellent help to your father."

When Anahita did not respond, Mojdeh went back to her cooking. She picked up a stick, which she used to lift the lid from the pot of rice, and sprinkled in a teaspoon of saffron water. Then she stirred the rice before adding in raisins and bits of chicken that she had seared earlier in the day.

"Surely you feel comfortable with Dariyoush," Mojdeh said. "Perhaps you are the reason he chose to work for our family."

"Oh stop, Maman. Dariyoush? He thinks of me as nothing more than a sister. He fixes things for me. Tells me when my hair is falling out of my scarf." Anahita crossed her arms. "And besides, don't you think he helps Baba so that he may learn from him? Dariyoush stands to be his successor as *kadkhuda* since I am a woman." Anahita thought about how the women in her village knew as much about livestock as any of the men. "Wouldn't women make fine *kadkhudas!* Isn't it we who pack up the village every spring for the migration? And beat the dust from our carpets and tents?"

"You speak as if we can do without our men, as if we could fight off bandits and the Russians, should they come. Now hush with your senseless talk. Have you forgotten how your views about women got this family into trouble? I'll not have another bathhouse incident."

Leaves on the poplars rustled. A mix of dirt and sand whisked through the courtyard. Anahita covered a bowl of yogurt with a cloth to keep out the dirt and flies. "Still, I do not want to marry," she said softly. "I like my life. I don't want it to change."

Anahita watched her grandmother pin up the last of the washing and walk into the house. Looking toward the barn she saw her father coming and remembered his riddle. *Life. That's it!* she thought. "Baba," Anahita called to Farhad as he approached. "The answer is *life!* Life, like a garden, never stays the same."

"Very good, my sweet. I thought for sure I'd stumped you," he said, tossing his shears on the ground and slipping off his shoes before entering their carpet-covered house. The rugs, piled one on top of the other, kept dust down in the spring and summer and their family warm in the winter.

That evening over dinner Anahita didn't dare talk to her father about the khan's marriage proposal. She didn't want to provoke his bad temper again. She wished she could challenge him with a riddle, and if she baffled him, demand that her reward be never having to get married. But then she had a clever thought. *The mullah! He likes me well enough—he's always been grateful for my help. I'll ask him to talk with Baba, tell him my wish is not to marry . . . that I'm committed to apprenticing myself to the dyemaster.* She would go talk to him after dinner.

When the meal was over, Anahita shook out the indigo and purple dinner cloth—her favorite *sofreh*. It was the first of many weavings she and her cousin Shirin had made together since they were nine years old. Thinking about how many times she had darned this cloth, she wished her friendship with Shirin could be mended as easily, with a few quick stitches. It was Shirin whom she really wanted to talk to about this marriage news, but it seemed that no needle and thread could patch the space that had grown between them. Folding the *sofreh* and placing it in a trunk, Anahita told her mother she was going out to see who might be gathered in the square that evening.

As she walked to the mosque, her mind traveled back to her cousin's wedding week and how miserable it had all seemed, especially the day when she had gone to Shirin's new home to see her cousin's dowry and wedding gifts.

As Anahita had approached Shirin's home (a shed her mother-in-law had emptied of its junk on the day before the wedding), she found Shirin sweeping billows of dust out the front door. Waving a hand to shield her face from the particles, Anahita noticed her aunt inside the shed hanging lace curtains over the single pigeonhole of a window.

"Thank you for inviting me," Anahita said, stepping inside. In an attempt to hide the crumbling walls of her receiving room, her cousin had decorated nearly every inch of it with embroidered cloth and mohair textile trunks. Shirin's anxiety about the humbleness of her home gave Anahita a twinge of guilt since she hadn't helped her cousin with much of her dowry handwork, or her wedding preparations. After all, Anahita had needed to tend to her charity work. Otherwise the mullah would have been disappointed—wouldn't he have?

Fingering the curtains, Anahita started to say, "This is a fine piece of lacework, Shirin. I wish I could have helped . . ." but Shirin's mother interrupted. "Anahita, we can't thank you enough for the clothing cart, what with all the young ones in the village who are forever in need of extra clothes." The clothing cart was a lending system Anahita and the mullah had organized which saved weeks and weeks of labor for every woman and girl in Hasanabad old enough to card wool or thread a needle. Contributing families—nearly every household—sorted outgrown children's garments according to size to store at the mosque. The mullah invited everyone in the village to borrow what they needed. If a surplus of clothing remained, the mullah, accompanied by Anahita or others, delivered it to nearby communities.

"Oh yes, we have our very own little *Hajj Khanom*, here in Hasanabad," Shirin quipped, sneering at her mother and Anahita. "She never fails to think of us all."

Shirin's sarcasm hurt. Such a title was reserved for respected women who had completed a pilgrimage to Mecca. Not for unmarried girls, like Anahita.

Anahita didn't know what to say. She wished her aunt had kept her praises to herself, and instead given Shirin more attention; it was her cousin's wedding week. And thanks about the clothing cart only magnified Anahita's neglect of her cousin.

Now, nearing the mosque, Anahita thought, *Shirin was miserable then and she didn't even have to marry the khan. Imagine how awful my circumstances will be if . . .* She forced herself to stop fretting when she reached the fountain wall, where the mullah sat with his long, white beard resting on his chest. His emerald ring, a gift from the khan—chosen because green is the Prophet's color—glinted in the twilight as she approached.

Smelling of sweat and incense, the holy man clasped his hands and didn't look directly at Anahita as he spoke, his eyes taking in his surroundings. "How are you this fine spring evening?"

"I couldn't be better," she said.

"I am grateful for your service, Anahita. So many of the women are busy with the little ones this spring—Hasanabad is full of life this season!"

"I am happy to be of help. And how are you?"

"I too have been blessed—with this dry weather. My joints feel rather well this week." He held his arms out straight and wiggled his fingers. "See? No pain." Then, patting the wall with one hand, he said, "Please rest a while."

The two sat quietly for a few moments, as was often the mullah's way. Anahita wondered if he had always been comfortable with silence or if it was something he learned from years of being a mullah. Perhaps it came from having only one wish in this life: to serve his very own congregation until sickness or death.

She thought he looked tired. Perhaps from the recent *Nooruz* festivities celebrating the new year. The square looked so bare now, when only last week the villagers had spread carpets on the ground and picnicked. They lit a bonfire, then leapt over it to purify themselves for the coming year—Anahita's favorite part of the spring ritual. The mullah presided over it all. But perhaps he was simply worn out from years of climbing the spiral steps inside the minaret. Five times each day he climbed fifty feet up this round tower to cry out *azan*, the call to prayer.

"Mullah," Anahita ventured now. "Today my father tol— *suggested* . . . that I think about the idea of getting married . . ." She hesitated.

"Ah," the holy man said, turning to look at her. "You will make some man very happy."

This is not what I want to hear, she thought and tapped her headscarf forward. "You see, I was hoping to apprentice myself to the dyemaster this year . . . I—" Something in the mullah's pale eyes stopped her chatter.

He stroked his beard. "And you do not wish to get married?"

Anahita beamed. "Mullah, I am so glad that you understand. Will you please explain this to my father?"

Seconds of silence passed like long minutes. Anahita tucked her hair into her scarf. *Maybe he doesn't understand.*

Finally the mullah responded. "My ambitious one, you are not the first young woman to come to me with such a question. It is very natural to feel overwhelmed at the notion of marriage. But I am sorry to say that you are certainly old enough to get married, and this is not my decision, but your parents'. Look upon the occasion with anticipation rather than dread, and this is what you will experience."

Trying to conceal her frown, Anahita said, "Thank you, Mullah." Adjusting her headscarf once more, she left.

Later that night, Anahita tossed restlessly in her bedroll as she listened to her grandmother's soft snores. Slants of starlight streaked the wall of the room where they slept, the same room in which her family gathered to eat and to receive guests. *I don't want to get married.* She punched her pillow. *And especially not to the khan!* She wondered if Shirin remembered the rumor about his former wives. Angry, she thought she'd never fall asleep. She wished the mullah would have understood. *Others might not have wanted to marry, but they didn't want to become dyemasters—something helpful to all of our weavers, to our tribe . . .*

Before long, her frustration gave way to tears. She relived the sadness she had shared with Shirin when her father had announced that she was to marry the widow's son, and would live in that family's hovel. She and Shirin wept over cups of *chai* in the teahouse, while Fatima, the owner, tried to cheer them up with stories about her childhood in faraway Samarkand and Bukhara, places of legends, glories, and chivalrous romances.

Now it's my turn, and I have no one to weep with. Sobbing, she drew her blanket to her chin. In the back of her mind she knew that she would soon be choosing colors for the yarn she would spin for her *own*—the words didn't feel true—wedding *qali*. The carpet she would keep forever. Even though the thought of marrying now made her so upset, she always looked forward to weaving—losing herself for hours between warp and weft, giving shape, color, and texture to her thoughts, prayers, and dreams. Expressing herself in a tangible way she could never do with words alone. At least this was one consolation, she thought.

Outside, a goat bleated. Then a dog barked in the distance. Anahita usually liked night for its sounds and for the tracks animals left—little riddles under the moon—that she would discover at daybreak, reminding her of all that happened which she could not see.

A Test of Wit

Anahita awoke with a start to the mullah, sweetening the morning with his call to prayer. Normally it was hard to get out of bed before first light, but Anahita was glad that *azan* had rescued her from a nightmare about the khan. In the darkness, Anahita and her grandmother stood, kneeled, and touched their foreheads to their prayer carpets as they recited words from the *Quran*, the Muslim holy book. *"La ilaha illa Llah."* There is no god but God. The chant helped Anahita shake off the unbearable image from her dream of the khan tickling her neck.

She did not want to linger at home that morning, for fear her father would talk more about the marriage proposal. Gobbling some goat cheese and dates for breakfast, she hurried out to collect goods for the clothing cart. Without the mullah's support, she needed to come up with a new idea to convince her father not to make her marry the khan. Work helped her think.

After visiting several families, Anahita carried a huge basket of donations to the mosque: camel-down baby blankets, toddler pantaloons, women's tunics, and fabric remnants. She saw that the village's morning activities had begun: three men slipped into the public bathhouse, and Fatima and Ali, who owned the local tea-house and bakery, rolled up the *gelim* that Anahita and her mother had recently woven them for a door. It featured an image of a *samovar*, a tea kettle, and three loaves of flat bread. Beneath the image they had carefully embroidered the words the mullah had written for them on a piece of parchment:

ALI'S TEAHOUSE: FRESH BREWS AND FLAT BREADS (BOASTING FORTY VARIETIES)
SINCE 1257

Fatima had moved her bread ovens into the teahouse only last year, wanting to keep an eye on Ali and to hear the village gossip firsthand. It was the men rather than the women of Hasanabad who prattled generously, as if time, like sheep's wool, were plentiful. They stirred and sipped tea, saying, "What nonsense is that sign? This is the only teahouse in town. Who could not find it?"

Inside the mosque, Anahita sorted the morning's collection. Throwing one of the last items, a sash, in the direction of the men's basket, she finally thought, *What's the use fighting the inevitable? Every woman has to get married.* But then it occurred to her that she could not live with someone who did not enjoy riddles. *Surely Baba can understand this. I will remind him that the khan doesn't care to challenge himself with even the simplest of riddles, and that he must find me a suitor who does.*

Feeling as if she had come a step closer to her father's wishes for marriage—that she at least was considering it—and bolstered by the fact that he loved riddles himself, she felt more confident about telling him of her own wishes. She resolved to do so at dinner that evening.

"Baba," Anahita said that night, "I've been thinking . . . I will agree to marry when my *qali* is woven." Touching a hand to her heart, she continued, "But I will only marry a man who has wit and likes riddles."

Farhad looked at her and then at her mother.

Maman Bozorg served her son more lamb kabob and said to her granddaughter, "How will you measure the wit of your suitors? Wit is both intelligence and intuition. One serves the mind, the other the soul."

"Suitors?" Anahita blinked. She drew the dinner *sofreh* over her crossed legs.

"My sweet," Farhad said, "you come from a good family. I hear your name on many a man's tongue. They are charmed by your riddles, your weaving skills, your keen interest in sheep. When you are about, men hover like moths around a candle."

Anahita blushed. She pushed the rice around in her bowl with flat bread, but did not take a bite. "Baba, I know not where my heart is. I cannot marry these men."

"You need marry only one," he said.

Anahita stared at her food and a new thought flowered with great clarity. She stole a glance at her grandmother for strength.

"Baba, I will weave a riddle into my wedding *qali*. The man who solves it, I will marry."

A hush swept over the room. Farhad wiped his mouth. Maman Bozorg lowered a piece of flat bread to her lap. Mojdeh stopped chewing.

Anahita looked from face to face.

"But Anahita, whose name would you weave next to your own in your *qali*? We must choose a suitor before your dowry is complete next year—it is the way of our people!" Mojdeh said.

"I will never weave the khan's name into my *qali*, nor the name of a stranger, someone who is not my kindred spirit—my *yar*."

Farhad looked at his daughter for some time. "Even if I were to entertain such an idea, a betrothal such as this could foster bad feelings."

"People won't like that you are receiving special treatment," Mojdeh said. "Jealousy is a powerful emotion."

"Are you referring to Shirin?" Anahita said. Shirin who betrayed herself—*betrayed our dream*—and settled for a husband she did not choose.

"Not only Shirin. There will be others who will not take kindly to this, or to you, or to us, for allowing such an arrangement."

"I'm willing to live with the consequences, Maman."

"Including marrying the one who solves your riddle, whether you know him or not?" Her mother got up and stood beside Anahita. "Do you think your father or I would allow you to marry a stranger who may treat you poorly or cast you off when he tires of you?"

Placing a hand on Anahita's shoulder, her mother continued, "After marriage you will belong to your husband's family. At least with the khan we could watch that he is treating you well."

"I *do not* want to become his fourth dead wife."

Farhad burst into laughter. "Magnificent try, my daughter. But I don't believe we raised you to let superstition dominate your thinking."

Anahita knew her father was right. Normally she was skeptical of such notions. Yet the khan's past luck with love gave her the jimjams.

No one spoke. As the silence grew, the more absurd the riddle idea seemed to Anahita. Looking out the window, she glimpsed the mosque. As if her father had read her mind, he said, "The mullah will not like it."

"Why would he care *how* I choose a husband?"

"Our mullah devotes his life to birth, marriage, and death." Maman Bozorg said. "Mullahs are slow with change, my dear."

Anahita shifted.

Farhad reached for the bread and tore off a piece. "You must remember the khan has already stated his wishes for your hand. He likes to have his way."

"But he has not yet offered a bride price," Anahita pointed out. This was solace, that the khan had yet to formally commit himself.

"We need to be in his favor. He's our tribe's voice with the *divan* in Mashhad," Mojdeh added.

"And with the other landowners, like himself." Farhad pushed back from the table. "Nevertheless, you must understand that if I—or anyone in this tribe—were to allow his daughter to choose a husband, there would be many repercussions."

Anahita's last bite of food stuck in her throat before sliding on. "I am sorry, Baba," she said, trying to keep her voice firm. "I cannot marry the khan. I will marry only the man who solves my riddle."

Farhad leaned into his daughter, his eyes holding hers. "You will marry whomever your mother and I tell you to."

Anahita glared at him, and then at her mother. Mojdeh's expression showed a mix of concern, disapproval, and worry. The same look of a year ago, when Anahita asked why the women of the village couldn't use the men's side of the public bath now and then.

It had happened when she was cleaning soiled rags in the creek. She said to the women washing diapers downstream, "I don't see why the men enjoy a deep pool, while the women's half of the bathhouse contains only shallow basins with trickling fountains. Imagine what it must feel like to float!"

The women had paused in their work, placed their hands on their hips, and stared at Anahita with disapproval.

"At least we don't have to fight for the best bathing hours, like women do in other villages where there's only one bathhouse," Shirin said.

Shirin's mother-in-law had squinted at Anahita, then said, "So your family thinks they can change tradition?"

When the mullah had first heard about the bathhouse discussion, he seemed not to believe it so important as to deserve a sermon. But when the gossiping was not shed with the sandals left just outside his mosque, and each member of Anahita's extended family had been criticized, he changed his mind.

The Friday morning after the incident, Anahita attended prayers with her mother, grandmother, and aunt. Feeling unwelcome, they stood in the very last row of worshipers, near the side door of the mosque, for a quick exit. The mullah, dressed in his black robes and black turban, climbed his pulpit, and raised a hand to greet his congregation. Anahita took a deep breath. *Here it comes*, she thought, expecting to hear a lecture on appreciation for what one has in life. But instead the holy man had addressed only his congregation's immoral behavior.

"I have been overhearing inappropriate comments about Anahita's idea for sharing our bathhouse. I should like to think that my fellow Muslims in Hasanabad would not stoop to such mean-spirited chatter, and were more open to one another's ideas." Anahita had to hide her smile with one hand. She nudged her grandmother. The mullah continued, "When we look with the eye of nonjudgment—that is, with the eye of love—our vision includes tolerance for all of humanity."

Even though the mullah had stood up for her last year, Anahita still winced at the memory—at how awful it had felt to be ridiculed by nearly everyone. She had learned from the bathhouse incident that only in her heart should she voice her ideals.

And I've spoken out again to no avail, she thought. *Baba will never agree.*

Anahita crossed her arms and gazed out the door. She felt a stirring inside, and began to question now if what she had learned by that experience were true. *Surely women should not be afraid to speak out in this man's world. Maman Bozorg must feel this way too. Why else was the first prayer she ever helped me to memorize one of Rabi'a's, a Sufi woman?* A thousand years ago Rabi'a had dared to write poems to Allah, despite the fact that then and even now women were not always allowed in mosques or permitted to attend their own relatives' funerals.

With Rabi'a's prayer, Anahita believed, came also Maman Bozorg's blessings:

> O my Lord
> if I worship you
> from hope of Paradise, bar me from its gates.

> But if I worship you
> for yourself alone, grant me then the beauty of your Face.

I am like Rabi'a, Anahita thought, *a woman wishing to express her inner or outer life to anyone I choose, even to Allah.*

Maman Bozorg poured *chai.* Except for the occasional chime and ting of a tiny spoon against a tiny glass teacup, the family finished their meal in silence. At last, in her soothing voice, Maman Bozorg said, "The old saying is true, Anahita: The earth itself trembles beneath the feet of the unmarried man or woman. But there is no question that the ground rumbles more ominously under a woman's."

* * *

After dinner, Anahita walked all the way around the village to let her thoughts settle. She needed time alone to adjust to the fact that she must indeed get married next year. As the sun set, it left swaths of peach light in the sky. Warmth radiated from the adobe walls of the houses. Anahita realized she would have to tell the mullah that she would not have time to help him deliver clothing to nearby villages this spring. Last year it had taken nearly two weeks, two days here and two days there, right up until her tribe left for the migration. Now that she would be weaving her wedding carpet in the autumn, she needed to begin spinning the yarn for her *qali* and working with the dyemaster to learn his secrets before her marriage claimed most of her time.

Anahita thought about a woman she had met last year in Kemesh village where she, a few of her cousins, and the mullah had delivered donations, someone who received permission to marry a man she loved. *I, too, deserve to choose my own husband!*

When Anahita's stroll brought her to the mosque, she noticed the mullah outside sweeping the flagstones. He dipped his broom into the water gurgling in the *jube*, a shallow trench that ran alongside the lanes in the village.

"Peace be upon you, *dokhtaram*," the holy man said to Anahita. "What a pleasure to have your company two days in a row." He greeted Anahita as he usually did, using the title "my daughter," which he had given her when she began the clothing cart. The honor made Anahita squirm because others had helped with the clothes-lending scheme, too.

She explained why she could not help deliver clothes to the

nearby villages, but still offered him the use of her family's donkey and cart.

"We shall miss your company," the mullah said.

Looking at his kind face, Anahita thought about sharing her riddle idea with him. *Will he become irritated with me? What would my family think of my mentioning this to him?* She adjusted her scarf and rallied her courage. "Mullah," she said, "do you remember last spring when we delivered donations to Kemesh?"

A short-haired cat scurried across the village square and out of sight.

"Yes . . ."

"Do you remember the newly married woman who received our donations? The one who promised to distribute the clothes to her village?"

"I believe so." Droplets of water dripped from the mullah's broom, helping to dampen the dust.

"The one whose house was still decorated with her wedding dowry?"

"Oh yes. She was quite talented, was she not?"

Anahita hesitated, looking down.

The mullah stopped sweeping and turned to Anahita, waiting.

"Didn't she choose her own husband?" Out of the corner of her eye, Anahita could see the mullah staring at her, and she felt as if she had just committed a crime. *I am most certainly in trouble now.* She fidgeted with her head scarf again.

The mullah leaned on his broom. "I'm not certain I know of whom you speak."

Not sure herself whether to continue, Anahita drew lines in the sand with the sole of her sandal, noticing her dirty toes. But having stuck one foot into the forbidden pool, she decided she might as well plunge in all the way. If the mullah accepted what she had to say, her parents might also. If she helped herself, Allah might help her twice.

"You know what I wished for this *Nooruz*?" she said.

"You wished to think of the most clever riddle in the heavenly kingdom."

Anahita smiled. *At least he's on the right path*, she thought. "I wished I could visit the Caspian Sea."

"That would be a treat, indeed."

"But, had I known my father was going to tell me that I must marry next year, I would have wished that I might choose my own husband and marry for love like that woman in Kemesh."

Anahita followed the mullah's eyes to the small birds splashing in the fountain. He was quiet, then said, "I see." Anahita wished herself far away, wandering instead in the Mashhad bazaar. There she could lose herself among the shops, alleys, or hidden alcoves, and forget about what she'd just proposed.

The mullah slowly turned to face Anahita. "Do you have someone in mind?"

Anahita tilted her head back—*no*—and exhaled, realizing she'd been holding her breath.

When the mullah smiled in response, she continued, "I have explained to my parents that I would be miserable if I were to live with someone who doesn't like riddles, and I told them—" she paused to take a deep breath—"that I would marry only the man who could solve the riddle that I will weave into my wedding *qali.*"

Silence fell between them, except for the *shush, shush* sound of the mullah's broom as he resumed sweeping the wet sand over stone. Since she was no longer refusing to get married, as she had yesterday, Anahita hoped he would give his blessings to her idea. Stilling his broom, the holy man said, "*Dokhtaram,* this request . . . is liken to none. A man who can solve your riddle, you say? I shall have to ponder this."

A Scholar, a Gentleman, and a Foreigner

Reza picked up the cage containing his two new love-birds, thanked the merchant for the complimentary sack of sunflower seeds, and strolled down the alley, a shortcut to his school in Mashhad. He stepped carefully over smashed melons, fragments of sheep pelts, and a pile of pistachio shells someone had thrown from a window above.

Inside Reza's classroom, the morning light coming through the window reflected off the tiny mirror dangling inside the birdcage. As he placed the cage by the window Reza caught a glimpse of himself in the glass disc—his red highlights showing more prominently today in his brown hair. His auburn streaks, his family joked, were "gifts in the blood" from some Celtic ancestor who must have traveled down the Volga River to the Caspian Sea, long before the time of the Prophet Muhammad. The same ancestor gave him his blue eyes, too. But his skin, like most everyone else's in Iran, was shaded, as if by the centuries of sunlight that had baked the earth of this land.

Reza knelt next to the cage and said, "My students will be surprised to see you." Sitting side by side, the birds cocked their heads as if listening to him. Reza would talk to his lovebirds this way for several days before he tried to touch them, a method that had worked with the cockatiel he kept at home. Pulling a book, *Winged Pets*, from his shelf, he flipped to the section on parrots, put on his glasses, and read:

> Lovebirds must always have a companion and should be raised in pairs of their own kind. Birds adopted directly from the nest will become finger-trained easily. Adult birds will require patience.

Studying his birds, Reza surmised that they were not newborns. *They'll challenge me,* he thought. Laying the book next to the cage, he gazed out his second-story window, thinking that it was time he should find *himself* a mate.

Reza's birds chirped, reclaiming his attention. The peach-colored one hung upside down from the side of the cage while the yellow one sat still on the perch. "Maybe I'll name you Acrobat," Reza said to the peach one. "You are even sillier than my cockatiel, Genghis, whom I named after the ancient Mongol invader because he believes he rules the roost."

The voices of Reza's students skipped through the window, swinging his mind toward the school day. He turned his calendar ahead and saw he had noted the week of the upcoming public wool and lamb market. He enjoyed visiting this market each spring and autumn to talk with shepherds and *kadkhudas* from miles around. Perhaps he'd bring his schoolboys there again. In doing so, he could expand his curriculum to include the basics of economics without drawing unnecessary attention from the clerics who ran the school. *What better way to teach my students the skills of mathematics and business,* Reza thought, *than from these men at the bazaar who shake profits out of sand-filled wool?*

He looked up to the snap and crinkle of seed-eating coming from his birds' cage. For sentimental reasons, too, Reza liked to visit the market. It reminded him of his childhood and those days in Tabriz as a small boy when he used to mingle among the gold merchants with his father, a jeweler, may he rest in peace with his mother. He thought how his parents never lived to see him become a teacher. *They would have been proud.*

Soon a pack of children, laughing and jabbering, bunched inside the door to his classroom, each vying to enter first. As they squabbled over the low desks in the front row, their books, lunch sacks, and bodies bounced with energy.

"Good morning, my dear friends," Reza said. "What lessons would you like to begin with today?" he asked.

"Bazi tafrih!" they shouted back. "Let's play."

Reza smiled and said, "Does anyone notice something new in the classroom?"

"Birds!" a child with eyes the size of small melons shouted, and they all rushed to the cage.

"Boys, please take your seats," Reza said, ushering one or two students at a time away from the cage. "You will scare them. We will get plenty of chances to visit with the birds, as they will live here in our room."

A dozen smiles settled on a dozen eager faces.

The lovely spring weather and his students' obvious energy inspired Reza to take his class outside. Though the wool market was not yet in session, the city offered daily lessons. "Now, let us go and sit on the front steps and observe our beautiful community coming to life this morning."

"Master Reza? What does *observe* mean?" his youngest student asked.

"It means watching carefully, Kaveh. Now let us see what Mashhad will teach us today."

Reza sat with his students on the sun-drenched stones and watched as Mashhad creaked and moaned like a wheel lurching into motion. From the school steps they could observe all kinds of people—those who came from the east and west to trade, learn, pray, and play, and those who catered to them. Shopkeepers swept sand from their doorsteps, and carried produce—lettuce, green onions, and spinach—from inside their shops to carts on the streets. Butchers sharpened their cleavers and splashed buckets of water on their floors, washing away fat and bones they had missed the night before. Jewelers polished silver and gold. Soon the streets would teem with customers: pinching, smelling, and bargaining for goods—essential or not—with money they had or promised to have.

Reza could spot, nearly without fail, the customers too trusting or too stupid to see a shopkeeper's trick. Grocers in Mashhad were known to cheat their customers shamelessly to make their produce go further. Reza believed the older man standing at the fruit cart across the street—with a tiny kitten in the crook of his arm and a peacock feather sticking up from his turban—would be the merchant's next victim. *Who could resist cheating someone who dressed like that?* he wondered. The man's wide girth and fancy clothing could only mean that he enjoyed a life of excess or privilege. *Probably a landowner, or maybe a diplomat,* he thought.

"Boys," he said. "I want you to keep an eye on the fruit vendor."

"Why?" asked a student.

"Just *observe* . . ." Reza said. They watched closely as the fruit vendor weighed the handful of early-season apricots the man had chosen on a scale beneath the counter. Wrapping the produce out of view, the merchant then handed the customer his purchase with a smile. Reza read his boys' expressions to see if anyone had caught what the merchant had done. The buyer strode off in the direction of the imam's shrine, reaching into his sack as he went. Then he stopped, looked over his shoulder, and raised a fist clutching a rotten apricot into the air. "I'll tell others what you have done!" the man spat, his pudgy face reddening, his feather wiggling.

Reza thought that he hadn't let anyone cheat him like that since he was twelve, and he wanted his students to learn to be cautious, too.

"The merchant switched apricots on him!" a student shouted.

"He did it when he bagged the fruit!" said another.

"It wouldn't have happened to me," little Kaveh said, straightening his back.

The class set off on a walking tour of the streets of Mashhad. Reza pointed out to his students how, like spokes on the hub of a wheel, the streets and alleys of Mashhad stuck out in all directions from the shrine at its center—that of the Imam Reza, the revered eighth imam, holy leader, of Shiite Islam. From any alley they chose, they could find their way to the shrine.

"The architects of Mashhad designed the city according to a circular plan," Reza reminded his students. "The circle is linked with the fundamental principles of Islam. The circumference, or wheel, represents the religious law that encompasses the whole Islamic community. The spokes, or radiuses, symbolize the paths, *tariqas*, that lead to the center, where Supreme Truth, *Haqiqa*, is found."

This walk was one of many Reza had taken with his students so that they would become familiar and comfortable in all parts of the city. Besides the imam's shrine, where thousands of pilgrims flocked year-round, his tours included the provincial government buildings in the north quarter. The *caravanserai*, a caravan shelter in the west beside Reza's *madrasa*, or school. And in the east, the public bath. Reza and his boys also enjoyed strolling south through the quiet neighborhoods of beautifully constructed homes with secluded gardens and tiled fountains.

Sometimes the owners would invite them in and demonstrate the gardening or pottery skills that had produced the healthy trees, flowers, and well-made fountains in their courtyards. Reza also took his students beyond the wealthy homes to the modest, one-storied stone buildings containing single-room tenements with small courtyards, like the one in which Reza himself lived. From there they ventured to the outermost edge of the city, where the dwellings were made of mud and reed. Salt plains claimed the space beyond.

After school, Reza took the cup of *mast*, yogurt, from his satchel that the widow who lived next door had given him on his way to work. His first bite, full of garlic, burst in his mouth. Sitting at his desk, he thought about how his neighbor had smothered him with kindness since he arrived in Mashhad a few years ago. She treated him as if he were her son.

He felt lucky that his community in Mashhad seemed like family. He felt so comfortable in this city, it was as if he'd always lived here. Upon his graduation from Dar al Fonun, an institute in Tehran for young men, he had accepted his position here in the local *madrasa*, which taught mainly Arabic and the rudiments of Islam. He harbored the hope of starting a school like Dar al Fonun in Mashhad, offering a course of study similar to schools in the West, including history, sciences, and philosophy from Austrian, French, and Italian teachers. He felt such a school would be welcome in Mashhad, a city where people from so many places came to trade.

Reza finished eating his yogurt and took an apple out of his satchel. As he sliced it, he realized that his twenty-fifth birthday was coming up. It was by this age that he had long hoped to marry. His career was underway and he was satisfied with the neighborhood in which he lived; perhaps he would ask the widow if she could help him find a wife. He carried this thought over to his birdcage, where he fed his new lovebirds the apple.

A Yomut Nomad, a Gentleman, and a Prince

Arash and his eldest cousin hiked up the gorge above Rudkhaneh Bozorg, the Great River on the northern-most reaches of Iran, which their nomad caravan would cross as soon as the two men returned from their scouting mission. They were looking for Russians. As the caravan had passed though villages on the way to summer pastures, the Yomut tribe had heard tell of Russian troops attacking from the north. With hundreds of goats, camels, horses, and other livestock, the nomads knew they were a tempting target.

As Arash and Sohrab climbed between two large boulders, Arash caught the scent of decay and saw a naked foot jutting out from behind one of the rocks. They peered around the rock and found that the foot belonged to a Russian soldier, a buzzard pecking at the flesh on the side of his face, yellow sand filling the wrinkles of his gray uniform, and sun blisters covering his swollen feet.

"It looks as if someone dragged him here for the shade. He must have died of thirst or maybe dysentery," Arash said, glancing from one rocky outcropping to the next, thinking that the soldier's regiment could not be far away. Noticing deep wagon tracks, he wondered if the Russians were hauling heavy guns and, realizing that they could not pull them down the gorge safely, had turned back.

"I doubt their army is equipped to cross the rapids," Sohrab said, as if reading Arash's mind.

"We can't take any chances. After we help the others across the river, we should come back up here to look for this soldier's troop. I want to see how many we're up against."

Clink. Arash spun toward a sound coming from above. A Russian soldier leaped from the top of the boulder onto his cousin. The two fell to the ground, their daggers flashing. As Arash reached for the soldier, he felt a sharp pain from a knife in his forearm. He caught the man by the neck with both hands and squeezed until the Russian dropped his weapon. Sohrab rolled from beneath his opponent as Arash pinned the stranger down with one knee, a scimitar held to his throat.

"Where is your army?" Arash demanded, noticing that the soldier looked pale. Then he saw that a broken bone protruded from the soldier's pants.

"Nyet," the man said before his eyes rolled back, showing the whites. He was still.

Arash checked his pulse. "I think he's dead. These men must have been quite sick for their regiment to have deserted them like this. They didn't even leave them with guns."

Blood from Arash's wound ran down his arm and made dark

spots where it dripped on the sand. He unraveled his turban to make a bandage, and asked his cousin for a hand. After Sohrab dressed the wound, the two began to climb the gorge to have a quick look around. Gravel slid from beneath their feet and made the ascent twice the work. When they came to the top, they could see for an eternity across the plains. This was their migratory land. On the northeast horizon, a dust cloud billowed.

Arash shaded his eyes with one hand as he studied the cloud. "That could be the Russian regiment."

"They must have come as far as the river and turned back."

"I don't like that they are heading toward our winter village." It frustrated Arash that the shah, his father, was doing little to stop the Russians. He suspected the invaders would not be satisfied with the conquest of the small villages in the north, and would soon set their sights on Marv, the ancient city that he himself would soon govern, and thus chisel out another gem for their czar's crown. It would soon be up to him, as the shah's appointed governor, to organize a defense of the city, but for now he had to make his mother's people safe. The Yomut tribe had traveled this land in peace for hundreds of years; Arash would make sure they did this year as well.

At the bottom of the river gorge Arash and Sohrab found their tribe waiting with the livestock beside the raging water. The animals' cries splintered the air in a thousand excited whinnies, bleats, and bellows. The cousins kissed a dozen of their tribesmen on both cheeks in greeting and gave them the news about the enemy soldiers. All agreed that they must cross the river quickly, putting the water between them and the Russian soldiers. Word passed through the tribe and it was Arash who led the first ox into the swift current. *"Yakh kardam!"* he shouted, I am freezing! Yet the cold water, fed by thousands of rivulets that originated in the glaciers high above, also helped numb his aching wound.

Gripping the beast's horns, he swam the bullock through whirlpools and rapids to the opposite shore. Men followed him on horses, camels, and donkeys. Women, children, and yearlings crossed on rafts held afloat by inflated goatskins. Again and again, Arash and his tribesmen repeated the crossing, wrestling the white water that sucked and tugged at their legs and waists. They did not stop until they had guided every person and animal to the far shore.

At last Arash rested against a poplar tree by the river's edge. His grandfather, the *kadkhuda* of his mother's tribe, approached and laid a hand on his shoulders. "We will be safe here."

Arash couldn't help but look to the opposite heights of the river gorge for men in gray uniforms. His grandfather continued, "We shall miss you when you return to your father's court. It has been seven summers now that you have helped to lead our migrations and never have our river crossings been so successful, with so few losses. The shah was wise in choosing you to be the new governor of Marv."

Arash thanked his grandfather, and saw the sadness in the old man's eyes. *He does not think I will return for the next migration,* Arash thought. Perhaps he would not, now that his father was grooming him for life in his court. He pulled off his drenched, bloodied tunic. Eyeing Arash's arm, his grandfather asked, "Is it giving you much pain?"

The young man tilted his head back—*no*. As he wrung his tunic dry he thought about how much he enjoyed the long summers he spent with his grandfather and mother and their tribe, and how wonderful it felt to escape the shah's harem, where all the women and children vied for the attention of his father—a man who gave more of his time to the officials in the ruling Qajar dynasty than to his many progeny. *I am first a nomad, second a prince*, Arash had told himself ever since he was a boy.

"I will miss my people," Arash said, slipping back into his tunic. "I would rather stay and look after my Yomut family than live in Marv. But I suppose it's a fortune that has been given to me," he said. As a prince born of a northern Yomut mother, he had always known that one day his father would consider him for the governorship of the northern territories.

A young woman approached the two men and offered Arash a skin of water. He poured some into his mouth and spit it out. Then he drank deeply. Giving the skin back, he smiled at her. "Thank you, Jaleh."

The woman winced when she looked at his wound. "You're bloody. Let me get you a clean cloth to wrap your arm."

Watching her walk away, Arash sensed her weariness. Each migration seemed to leave her more drained. Was it the distance? Did she fear the wolves or wild cats or snakes? *She'd as soon settle permanently like those in some of the other tribes in our kingdom*, he thought. "Jaleh will miss you the most, I'm afraid," said Arash's grandfather. "Have you noticed how attentive she is to you? Perhaps, Arash, you will consider her as your wife some day."

"Grandfather, I have no interest in marriage."

"A governor without a wife? Who will be heir to your court?"

Arash thought about how the dynasty's old alliances were changing, how a revolution was at hand. Across Iran, khans, merchants, and clerics were calling for a parliament to rule the land and limit the shah's powers. He said to his grandfather, "The warp and weft of our government bureaucracy is unraveling thread by thread. And I think the Russians know this. That's why they are striking now, when our empire is weak." Arash ran a hand through his hair. "If ever I have a son, I do not know that he would have a province to rule."

"Perhaps. But if you do not have any children, who will continue to walk the migration trail? Surely your sons and daughters will do this just as we Yomuts always have. It is our land that gives us life. It is tradition."

Arash spotted his mother in a nearby group of women; she looked so contented here with her extended family, away from her husband's court. It was no secret that Arash's father chose to marry his mother in hopes of solidifying his domain in northeastern Iran. "I'm afraid there is no time to think about marriage, Grandfather. Not now anyway."

His elder waved a hand as if to dismiss the discussion. Arash said, "You speak to me about serious matters today, as if you will not see me again. I am not going to war, but to Marv. There are no Russians there—as yet."

"It is not your well-being I fear for; I am concerned about my own feeble heart. Allah willing, it will beat for a few more seasons."

Arash gripped the old man's arm in agreement and affection. Then the two joined the others in repairing the rafts, which they would need to recross the Rudkhaneh Bozorg farther south. Rocks had ripped several goatskin pontoons and torn them free of the rafts' log frames. Some men cut new leather straps to refasten the floats. Several women unpacked stashes of goat-hair yarn, the strongest fiber they had, to sew patches. "I worry about leaving our people, Grandfather," Arash said quietly as they worked. "Although we have fine warriors, no one is suited to succeed you."

"What about Sohrab?"

Arash looked about for his eldest cousin, and spoke softly so that he could not hear. "I know he is a well-respected father, and that he can carry a small pony under one arm, but he is prone to jumping to conclusions."

"He will grow into the position. I have faith that our people will choose him." They continued in silence until the rafts were repaired. Then Arash's grandfather rose. As the old man limped to his horse, Arash noticed his unsteady footsteps.

The caravan ascended the riverbank without Arash and Sohrab. They would rejoin their tribe at the next crossing, after setting out to track the Russian regiment.

While Sohrab sharpened his dagger, Arash rested against his stallion and looked to the north, toward Marv, the direction of his future. Black-and-white magpies fluttered in an apple-green sky. A great joy filled him: that his grandfather was still blessed with the pastoral life, which Arash so loved, when so many other tribes had been forced to settle under his father's administration. He wondered how much longer his mother's people could safely travel these high plateaus of Khurasan province and enjoy the advantage of migrating for fresh grass. This life allowed them to keep many animals, which in turn gave them extra meat, milk, wool, and weavings to barter. He knew that if they were forced to settle, they would have to decrease the size of their herds, and spend any profits from growing crops on fodder for their few remaining livestock.

Arash looked now to the west. Earth and sky blended as one in the golden light. The setting sun warmed his face as his eyes swept across the tapestry of barren scarps and plains of his homeland. *If ever I marry,* he thought, *she will be of this land. She will honor our old ways amidst the new.*

His people soon appeared as a thin line traveling south, one caravan among many that would converge upon Mashhad, the great market city along the ancient Silk Road, to trade goods before the summer grazing. Arash adjusted the girth on his saddle. He nodded to Sohrab and the two mounted their horses and plunged back into the Great River in pursuit of the Russians.

A Shepherd, a Gentleman, and a Friend

Dariyoush stood in the doorway of his home, frowning at his parents.

"I am sorry, son. Your mother and I cannot agree with you."

"Men and women bathe in the same rivers on migration. What would it have hurt if the women were permitted to use the men's side of the bathhouse now and then?" Dariyoush said.

His mother looked up from her knitting. "That incident tells me something about Anahita's character. Something which you might find difficult to live with in time."

His father rummaged through his satchel of splints and bone-setting devices. "We need to consider Kadkhuda Farhad's wishes and what is best for the tribe, Dariyoush. He mentioned that the khan has offered to marry Anahita. I won't get in the middle of this. Nor will I allow you."

Swallowing against the knot in his throat, Dariyoush asked, "This is your final word?"

"I am afraid so," his father replied.

Dariyoush turned and ducked under the threshold. *How can they cast off my feelings so easily?* he wondered as he grabbed a few sticks of poplar from the small pile stacked by the door of his mud home. Then he untethered his horse and led the Arabian down the lane to the stream where it could drink. Insects rattled the air as he leaned against a walnut tree, squinting into the sun. He pulled out his pocket knife. For the first time in his life he felt confined in this village. *Maybe I'll ride to Tehran, Tabriz, or better yet, Constantinople! What's the use of staying here if I cannot marry Anahita?*

Looking upstream, he was startled to see her step down the stream bank carrying a pail. Anahita did not see him through the trees, so he said nothing, preferring to watch her as she rinsed out her bucket. *She moves more beautifully than a willow,* he thought.

But now she glanced downstream at him. "Dariyoush," Anahita said with a hint of surprise in her voice. "I did not see you there." She adjusted her scarf.

"Good evening, Anahita," was all he could manage to say, feeling a bit awkward that he hadn't said hello first. He worried that she could see his feelings for her in his face.

"I'm washing this out for my grandmother," she said, walking toward him. "I see you've got sticks and a knife. Are you whittling something?"

"I . . . I'm making a gift for my nephew. Mehdi's boy."

"May I watch?"

"Of course." They sat down and Dariyoush leaned his back against the tree trunk. Running his fingers over the twig, he said, "I usually let the shape of the wood tell me what it wants to be."

Anahita searched the ground beside her and picked up a knotted piece of root. "This reminds me of a camel lying down." She handed it to him. "Can you whittle a camel?"

"Only you could see a camel in this. Here, you give it a try." He handed her his knife.

"Me?"

"Yes, you are good with your hands. You weave a lovely *qali*. Start with little chips. Work the knife away from you so you don't cut yourself."

Dariyoush wished he could enjoy this time alone with Anahita. *It used to be so easy being around her when we were younger.* He wondered if he should tell her that he had asked his parents' permission to court her. But he decided that it would only hurt her feelings if he told her their answer. He also wondered, *Would she even want to marry me?*

Anahita scraped away at her knotted wood but it did not take any recognizable shape. "This looks nothing like the camels we used to leap over." She searched his face, her dark eyes widening. "I think that was my favorite game as a child. Remember how you, Shirin, Mehdi, your other brothers, and I used to run wild, leaping over three, four camels in a row?"

"I remember how much I enjoyed watching you," he said, catching her eye, surprised he had said it.

Anahita looked down at her skirt.

Dariyoush took the wood and knife from her. As he whittled, flakes fell away, and a camel emerged. Within no time he finished the beast and gave it to her.

"It's wonderful. May I keep it?"

"Just a minute." He took it back and reshaped the face.

Anahita laughed. "You made it smile! Dariyoush, you are so talented. You should sell these in Mashhad!"

"Anahita!" Maman Bozorg called from the stream bank, her small arms on her small hips.

Dariyoush and Anahita turned.

"Oh my goodness. I completely forgot I was helping my grandmother. I must go," Anahita said, getting up, brushing off her clothes. "I'll see you tomorrow. We've much packing . . ." Her voice trailed off as she hurried home with her pail.

Listening to the stream rush and splash, Dariyoush began to work on one of his long sticks. Without knowing what it would yet be, he kept cutting until he had the beginnings of a spindle. *For Anahita*, he thought. *To spin the wool for her wedding* qali.

As he whittled he thought about why he worked for Farhad. It wasn't that he hoped to someday succeed the *kadkhuda*, as his parents wished. Farhad would surely hold the position for at least another fifteen or twenty years. It was to be close to Anahita. He sighed. Even if he could convince his parents to allow him to ask for Anahita's hand, they could never match whatever bride price the khan would offer. With this sad thought, Dariyoush finished the spindle. He would sand it until it shone.

The Caravan

"The sky is never filled with enough birds," Anahita said as she packed her sandals and rolled her clothing so it would fit snugly into her satchel. In the coolness of dawn, her tribe prepared its belongings for the long journey to their summer pastures.

Her mother filled *chantehs*, small sacks, with cooking implements, spindles, and goatskins. Her grandmother packed a *Quran*. Anahita slung a saddlebag over the back of her grandmother's donkey. It would hold the fleeces, picked clean and carded for spinning, that would become the yarn for her wedding *qali*.

Anahita then helped her father fold up their black, goat-hair tent, their home in the mountains. As they worked, Anahita worried that Farhad's silence meant the mullah had spoken with him about her wishes to marry the one who solved her riddle.

"Baba, how I long for summer pastures—and for our stop at the bazaar in Mashhad!" she said, hoping to dispel any angry thoughts he might have.

"As someone who refuses to wear the *chador*, I should think you would prefer to skip the market," Farhad teased.

Her father seemed to be in a good mood after all, so Anahita guessed that the mullah had not spoken with him. "And miss all the travelers?" she said, holding the back of her hand to her nose, fingers spread, shading her face as if with a veil. "The sweet smells of spices and soaps? The music, the jewelry, and carpets? I will gladly wear a veil. For one day anyway."

Nearby, Dariyoush tied panniers to the camels' humps: these would carry the lambs that were too small to walk far. The village mothers would soon wrap their own toddlers in soft woven blankets and secure them on the camels, too. Perched in this way, the tribe's most fragile members would survive the two-hundred-mile journey to the mountains.

Almost half of Anahita's tribespeople would migrate this spring. The rest would stay in the village to tend to the fields of barley and watch over their winter homes. For those leaving, the first day's walk would begin after sunset and last only two hours, ending at a village upstream where they would camp. The short distance would allow the animals to adjust to the weight of their loads, and provide the forgetful with one last opportunity to return to Hasanabad to retrieve belongings they had failed to pack.

Anahita's tribe owned thousands of sheep, hundreds of cattle, many donkeys, camels, goats, and horses, and several dogs, which protected them all from wolves, bears, leopards, and wild boars. Because the sheep and goats walked slowly, grazing along the way, the shepherds of the group had set out with their herds before dawn. Anahita had heard the low bongs of the rams' bells when they left the village. Sounds that would help identify the animals, if any were lost.

Anahita finished helping her father tie their tent to the back of a camel and went inside the house to look for things she might have forgotten. Her mother found her there and suggested that they help Anahita's aunts and cousins with their packing. Anahita wondered if it meant seeing Shirin.

As they filled one of Mojdeh's sisters' trunks with bedding, Anahita and her relatives talked about the longer hours of daylight to come, and how nice the walk would be after months of sitting at their looms. An aunt asked, as Shirin walked in the door, "Is it true, Anahita, that you will choose your husband?"

Maman told her! Anahita thought, as she avoided Shirin's eyes. She replied, "I don't know. Baba hasn't given me his word."

"What a wonderful opportunity!" her aunt said.

"Is it?" snapped Shirin.

Anahita looked at her cousin. She knew Shirin would be jealous—even about the *idea* of a wedding riddle—simply because it hadn't happened to her.

"Just think," Anahita said, flinging her cousin a cushion to pack, "if your husband dies, perhaps *you* could choose your next one."

Anahita felt Shirin bristle. "I don't find that amusing."

"Girls," Anahita's aunt said.

Anahita couldn't stop, though. "But remember, you said,

'Better to be widowed than married to someone you don't like,'" she reminded Shirin.

From the flush on her cousin's face, Anahita knew she was thinking about the endless discussions they used to share about not settling for just anyone.

"How about we rest awhile and have tea," Mojdeh said. "Perhaps a little something to eat will revive our spirits." She directed her attention at her daughter. "Anahita, would you please fill the *samovar* with water?"

Anahita gladly went outside to the well. Smelling the wild mint in the air, she found herself thinking about how Shirin had let her marriage ruin everything. She drew enough water for tea, took a deep breath, and before going back inside her aunt's home, released her frustrations on the blowing breeze.

The whole village gathered in the square to await the coolness of the sunset. Small boys collected sticks for toy daggers. Girls drew figures in the dirt with twigs. Some of the mothers rocked their babies to sleep on their legs. The talk among the women moved from the prices they hoped their carpets would bring at the Mashhad bazaar, to the spices, food, and fabrics they might buy there. As she listened, Anahita anticipated the stories the merchants would tell that would come wrapped up with the pepper and parsnip her mother would purchase, and the surprises of her journey that would make it all the more exciting.

Across the square, through the front door of their house,

Anahita saw her grandmother kneeling on her prayer rug. Facing southwest, toward Mecca, Maman Bozorg knelt with her legs folded beneath her, in the same lovely way a camel buckles down. She prayed at dawn, at noon, at dusk, and even now, at a time when the mullah had not called the village to prayer. *Maman Bozorg responds to her own spiritual clock,* Anahita thought.

Dariyoush strode near as Anahita chatted with the women. He rolled a polished spindle between his hands. After the talk lulled he said, "Anahita, I have made this for you. Your other one is worn."

"It's beautiful. I thought you were making your nephew a toy with this wood." Anahita gazed into her friend's face, admiring his elegantly hooked nose, and the spark in his eyes that always seemed to express a sense of purpose.

"I've sanded it so no rough parts will snag your yarn."

"You take such good care of me and my family. We are very lucky. I will spin all the yarn for my wedding *qali* with this."

Dariyoush looked over the women's heads to some spot on the horizon, then back at Anahita. One of her cousins nudged her. Anahita nudged her back, then stroked the smooth cross-slats of the spindle.

"I thought you might like to make use of it on our journey," Dariyoush said, then turned away.

Anahita watched him walk to the men sitting at the low tables in front of Ali and Fatima's teahouse. He would soon ride ahead of the tribe with her father to assess the safety of the road.

"He'd make a wonderful husband, Anahita," one of her cousins said, as she pulled a splinter out of her crying child's finger.

"Dariyoush?" Anahita slipped her new spindle into her waistband as the sun slid toward the distant foothills to cast a saffron hue across the plain. The air cooled suddenly. "If he wished to marry me, wouldn't he have asked Baba by now?"

She thought of the smiling camel Dariyoush had made her, and how his sense of humor came out in unexpected ways. She liked how he seemed content to sit quietly and whittle. To simply be. Much like the mullah. This side of him intrigued her.

Anahita noticed her granduncle in the alley beside her house, carrying a bundle of kindling in his arms. He lay the twigs beside her front door and continued to the village square. As he came toward Anahita, she smiled warmly at the sight of his turban with its multitude of colorful streaks, left when he absentmindedly wiped his indigo- or saffron- or cochineal-stained fingers on its cloth while he was working with his dyes. She knew that his intent for the wood was to light a ritual fire in the hearth of her home. He would repeat this gesture each night after the nomads left the village until he learned that they had arrived safely at their first summer camp. It was an ancient custom that provided protection and preserved the bonds between those who traveled and those who stayed behind.

Standing before Anahita and her cousins, the dyemaster cast a long shadow in the early evening light. "I came to wish you all a safe journey." He opened a cloth sack that he had tied around his waist and handed Anahita a stem from one of his dried plants. "Please collect as much of this *sprak* as you can find in the mountains. Pick it when its petals are plentiful. It gives a pure yellow."

"Certainly," Anahita said. "We've had much rain this winter. These flowers should be abundant this season."

"Inshallah," God willing, her granduncle said. He surveyed his people's activities, before speaking again. "I look forward to dyeing the yarns for your wedding carpet with you when you return."

Anahita wasn't sure she heard him correctly. Did the dyemaster mean to say that he looked forward to dyeing her yarns *for her* or *with her*? She was so excited by the second possibility that she flinched at the sound of her father's loud whistle.

"The sun has set," Farhad announced. "Let's prepare to leave." His order echoed off the lips of all the men. Anahita finished saying good-bye to her granduncle then hurried to Ali and Fatima's teahouse to say that she would miss them. They too were staying in the village this summer, having no sheep to graze. "We'll look forward to hearing *all* your stories," Ali said as his wife grabbed Anahita and kissed her on both cheeks. Lowering her voice, Fatima said, "And good luck with your riddle idea."

Anahita felt a jolt of surprise and a touch of irritation that her story had already traveled to the teahouse. She would have preferred to have had her father's consent before the news spread. Nevertheless, she said graciously, "You'll be the first to know, Fatima. I'll tell you every detail."

The ample woman winked at her, and Anahita smiled a last farewell and ran back to join her family.

Farhad and Dariyoush mounted their horses to lead the caravan out of the village. Women collected the panniers packed with household items and secured them onto donkeys. Men heaped mounds of textiles onto the camels, which the villagers had decorated with woven headbands and tasseled girths. Loading and reloading, they took care that their burdens were balanced just so. Otherwise, the stubborn animals would not budge. At last the humpbacked beasts rose, pitching their heavy wares forward and back. Then the women tied their newborn infants to their own backs, secured their toddlers between camel humps, and gathered beside them the children who were strong enough to walk.

The tribe set out. They took the road toward Mashhad, the ancient city of "holy earth." It would be their second stop on this journey, as they followed the grasses that fed their animals and, in turn, fed themselves. From camp to camp their route would be a trail of sun-blistered soil, rock, and sand into which the traditions and sweat of their people were inscribed. Their caravan would stretch for miles, each family enveloped in its own cloud of dust.

8

The Magic of Mashhad

Human and animal cries filled the air, along with the smell of smoke from the mud houses. Minarets punctured the lion-colored haze. Anahita's tribe had arrived on the outskirts of Mashhad.

She couldn't wait to visit the bazaar, which bustled in the center of the sand-choked city beneath the turquoise and gold domes of the holy Shrine of Imam Reza. She would listen to the pilgrims in the market speak about the marvels of the shrine, which she had seen many times before. Did you see the yellow marble floors in the Chamber of Salutation? The gilt-and-silver doors? Did you touch the Carpet of the Seven Beloved Cities, which took ten thousand weavers fourteen years to make? The one with thirty million knots?

The caravan slowed to a halt. First the sheep and goats. Next, the camels and donkeys, lashed with luggage, women, and children. The tribe set up temporary quarters beside the overcrowded *caravanserai*, a huge shelter in a chain of others that were spaced a day's walk apart along the trade route. Here, travelers could water their animals, cook meals, and rest.

Black tents flapped in the wind. Dust devils appeared and disappeared like magic. Anahita helped her father unload camels and reload others with the goods they would sell in the market: wool and the carpets, salt bags, saddlebags, horse covers, and grain sacks that she, her mother, and grandmother had woven over the winter. The textiles made a mountain of blue, green, and purple on each beast's back.

Anahita and her mother donned their *chadors*, ankle-length black cloaks, and *rusaris*, headpieces that draped halfway down their backs. The *rusaris* fit snugly across their foreheads, barely revealing their eyebrows. Sheer veils stretched across the bridges of their noses, leaving just the tops of their cheeks and eyes exposed. They dressed this way out of respect for the devout Muslim community of the holy city of Mashhad. These cumbersome garments, unsuitable for migrations, usually remained packed away and rarely worn by the women in Anahita's tribe.

And now, Anahita's *rusari* kept slipping off her head.

"You have Maman Bozorg's straight and silky hair, my child," Mojdeh said. "Let me see if I can tie a knot at the base of your neck with braids. Perhaps the *rusari* will hold that way." But it would not, so instead Anahita wore her favorite kerchief with the madder-dyed tassels. Mojdeh pinned a sheer cloth across her daughter's face as a makeshift veil.

"See Maman, I was not born to wear a *chador*."

"And just what were you born for?"

Sometimes Anahita thought that her mother's questions were just as baffling as her father's riddles. Thinking a moment, Rabi'a came to mind. "I was born to show girls how to speak up for themselves."

"And where does this get you, my defiant daughter?" Mojdeh said, shaking her head.

As they dressed, the dust outside their tent thickened in the mounting breeze.

"We won't be so hot in these clothes after all, Maman. Not with this wind."

"Let us hope not."

"Will you come with us, Maman Bozorg?" Anahita asked.

Anahita's grandmother stood quietly in the flapway of their tent, staring out, as if reading something in the millions of sand granules rising and falling like musical notes in the sky. Anahita glanced at the swirling particles, as mesmerizing as a dervish's dance.

"I think not," her grandmother said. "When Farhad is through with his work, he will take me to the shrine."

They left her and hurried along the high walls of the *caravanserai*. The warm wind moved like something ardent against them. Holding her head scarf on with one hand, Anahita pointed to the entrance of the caravan shelter with the other. Its high arch made the full-grown camel tethered beneath it look puny. The shelter's large doors stood wide open.

Mojdeh nodded. "Isn't the woodwork on the doors lovely, Anahita? Let's go inside for a closer look." They walked through the threshold admiring the doors, and into a courtyard the length and width of a small village. In the center of the *caravanserai* stood a modest-sized mosque with a filigreed stone entrance.

"May I go inside, Maman? I've been in so few mosques aside from our own."

"Perhaps on our way back to camp. I'd like to have a look around the bazaar first."

A side door in the *caravanserai* led to the city's marketplace, where the two walked a labyrinth of stalls and workshops. Merchants of every kind had built booths into building alcoves or set up stands on the street. Their cloth canopies helped shelter customers from the desert sun.

Anahita and Mojdeh sniffed spices, tasted sweetmeats, and hurried past the smelly, uncured sheepskins that flapped in the wind. They dodged donkey carts driven by devil-may-care children. They cleansed their hands with perfumed water cut with lemon, and stopped to marvel at thousands of glittering bracelets, necklaces, and other gypsy metalwork.

"Oh, Maman, look at these weaving tools! The combs are carved so beautifully. And look," Anahita exclaimed, as she picked one up and shook it, "this has little charms that jingle! May I buy it to sing to me when I pound the wefts as I weave my *qali*?"

"We must wait until the autumn when we return to Mashhad to sell our sheep and oxen. If we get good prices, you may purchase a comb."

"And the bracelets?" Anahita pleaded, catching a glimpse of golden-brown eyes watching her from beneath a turban.

"I think we both deserve at least one!" her mother said.

When Anahita looked for the pair of eyes again, they were gone.

Anahita and Mojdeh tied jeweled headbands around their foreheads and dangled bangles on each arm, giggling with delight. The merchant frowned at their silliness, so they quickly chose one bracelet each and paid him two *rials*.

Mojdeh walked to a booth selling copper vessels and Anahita stopped at the stall next door where silk carpets hung full length from wooden beams. This merchant had traveled all over the East, from Iran to China and back, peddling rugs one way and silk the other. His skinny body and sunken eyes suggested he had contracted many illnesses along the way.

Gelims, flat woven rugs, hung from all four sides of the stall and lay folded and stacked in piles of reds and golds on the stone floor. Anahita stopped to examine the large carpet with unusual colors that hung in the back. People bustled around her.

"Where was this *gelim* made, if you please?" Anahita asked the merchant, who was shorter than she.

"Here in Mashhad," he said, fingering his curling mustache, the biggest she had ever seen.

"But those colors. Never have I seen such colors. They cannot be from native plants. May I have a closer look?" Anahita wriggled her way through the crowd of shoppers. She ran her fingers over the shimmering rug to convince herself that it truly was made of wool and silk.

"It is a piece commissioned by a noble family." The merchant scratched the dark stubble on his chin. "Our local weaving apprentices used *masnui* dyes, synthetic colors from chemicals which mimic our native flora."

Anahita stood before the carpet until the wave of customers scattered—all the customers but one.

"I do not know whether I like these, how do you say, *mas-noo* dyes . . ."

"*Mass-noo-ee,*" a deep voice politely corrected her in her own Afshari dialect, but with the lilt of a northern accent.

Anahita spun around, startled.

"I'm sorry, miss. I only wished to help you with your pronunciation. I did not mean to frighten you."

"You did not *frighten* me, you merely took me by surprise. There is a difference, you know."

The stranger smiled at her, and his eyes softened as she looked into them. Or was it that his smile relaxed the delicate lines along his brow? She looked away as she had been taught to when around unfamiliar men. But his golden-brown eyes, which shone through the dust in the air, made her look at him again. *He's the one who watched me at the jewelry booth.*

"This *gelim,*" said the stranger to the merchant. "Would you say it speaks the truth of Persian life?"

Such a thoughtful question, Anahita mused. *So much like a riddle.*

"Yes, of course," said the merchant. "It is a beautiful floral pattern. It reflects every Iranian's dream: to have a garden inside his home."

"But there is no *ruh* in this rug; it lacks spirit," Anahita insisted. "The lines are intricate, yes. But they are too perfectly placed. The lower half of the carpet mirrors the upper half."

"Since one side is identical to the other, it can have only half the perspectives of an asymmetrical work," the stranger added.

Anahita liked the sound of his accent: the soft consonants, the slow roll of his r's. "Yes," she continued, looking into the stranger's face this time instead of the merchant's. "Its pattern does not look as if it comes from the weaver's heart. The colors are not real, not of this earth, not of our people."

"Well said." The stranger clapped his hands.

Anahita's face grew warm; she was embarrassed she'd held this man's gaze for so long. Copper pots hanging from a wooden beam in the stall next door clinked and chimed in the wind. She stilled her billowing *chador* with one hand. Quietly, she turned to the merchant. "Will these colors fade in sunlight? And will they not run if this *gelim* is washed in a brook?"

"I assure you! These colors are made from the most extraordinary dyes money can buy. They will hold their own against any plant-dyed carpet," the merchant said, although a shadow of doubt seemed to flicker across his face.

Anahita's and the stranger's eyes met.

"Are you saying that quality is determined by expense?" the stranger asked the merchant.

The merchant fingered his mustache. "Uh, well, you see . . ."

"Surely, you do not—" Anahita blurted.

Between curled lips, the merchant said, "But of course not."

Anahita looked at the stranger again. This time she knew he too felt sad for the merchant who judged worth by money.

The stranger fixed his gaze on the strands of Anahita's long black hair that had slipped free from her tasseled scarf. Aware of this attention, she tucked her hair back beneath her kerchief, and noticed the sheen and texture of *his* hair. Its thick, black curls looked almost blue—the color she could sometimes achieve in her yarns by dyeing a black sheep's wool with indigo. Yet his glimmered much more brilliantly than wool—the way mohair or silk would take up a dye.

Just as if her mother had planned it, Mojdeh appeared beside her with a large copper vessel, interrupting her thoughts. "*Bia,* Anahita, come my dear. We must find the leather shop. Farhad asked me to buy him a satchel."

Anahita turned to the stranger and said, "I . . ." But her mother whispered in her ear, "It is time we go," and took her by the arm.

Mojdeh led her away from the carpet stall. Anahita wished she could have introduced herself to the stranger, asked him his name, talked with him all afternoon . . .

When Anahita left, a shadow fell over the stranger's heart. The faintest smell of a dung fire washed over him, a wisp of air from the folds of Anahita's and her mother's *chadors,* and with it, the scent of jasmine—or rose—and a hint of lanolin. He thought their clothes smelled fresh and earthy like those of his own people. Not like the lung-choking charcoal smoke of this city. *She must be a nomad,* he thought. *Anahita,* the stranger mused. *She is named for a goddess!* Of water, fertility, and war. What a fitting name for a woman whose cheeks had flushed and swelled into the shape and color of pomegranates behind her sheer veil when she smiled. *If only I had learned of her tribe, her home.*

He turned to the merchant, who shook the relentless dust from his carpets and sang to himself, "Ah, the magic of Mashhad—where the air is atoms of gold, celestial perfume, love potion!"

"Excuse me," the stranger said. "If by some miracle this woman, Anahita—who smells of rose water and our beloved land—returns to your shop and asks for my name, please tell her it is Arash of . . ." he hesitated, thinking about where he was headed and could be found this summer, and continued, "of Marv."

Mojdeh led the way back to the mosque inside the *caravanserai.* Before entering the holy space, mother and daughter washed their hands, arms, faces, and feet in a fountain. They then left their sacks and copper pot with the mosque keeper. As she bent over to remove her sandals, Anahita didn't notice that her head scarf had slipped from her hair onto her back. When she stood to follow her mother inside, the wind caught it and the scarf flew away.

"Anahita," Mojdeh whispered, "where is your scarf?"

Anahita reached up to pull it forward but it was gone. She turned around and looked out the doorway but didn't see it. A rush of women pushed her farther inside the shrine. Her mother handed her an extra scarf that she'd pulled from her satchel. "Here, wear this one."

"But that's my favorite scarf, Maman," she whispered.

"Hush for once, my child."

Inside the mosque, large plush carpets glowed in blues and reds. Men knelt on still more rugs, small ones that they had brought with them. Marveling at all the different woven designs, Anahita stopped worrying about her lost scarf. Someone gestured for her and Mojdeh to take the spiral stairs through an onion-shaped arch to the balcony. Here, the women prayed.

From the balcony Anahita could see the tops of the turbans of all the men downstairs. She looked around for the man she had just met, but couldn't see anyone's face. She felt as if her giddiness—her excitement at meeting him—would fill the melon-domed ceiling, and encircle the mosque like the sculpted-marble molding that held the structure together.

Although she thought this building was a perfect theater for Allah's wisdom, she heard little of the prayer leader's sermon, which he recited from the tiled *mihrab*, the niche in the wall pointing toward Mecca. The Traditions of the Prophet Muhammad, the verses of the *Quran*, and the words of the imam melted into one happy song—a melody harmonized by her musings of the man in the marketplace.

After prayers, Mojdeh and Anahita hurried down the stairs again to recover their sandals. The men in the mosque rolled up their rugs and began to file out the door behind the crowd of women. Anahita stooped to shoulder her sacks, stuffing the small ones inside the larger. Remembering her scarf, she looked around for it.

"*Bia*, the sun will set soon," her mother said. "Better to find our way through the tents in daylight." Anahita gave up her search and the two set off for their camp.

The third man to exit the mosque was Arash. As he walked past the mosque keeper, the smell of rose water stopped him midstride. He glanced about. *I must be imagining this.* He shrugged and walked a few more steps. The scent became stronger. Then he saw a cream-colored scarf with tiny madder-colored tassels dangling from a pistachio bush. He grabbed it and looked in every direction for Anahita. Catching the mosque keeper's curious gaze, he slipped the soft item into his sash. *Inshallah, this is an omen that I will find her.*

9

The Migration Trail

A faint breeze played at Anahita's skirt, wrapping it about her legs as she strode. The yellow flowers and blue stripes sewn in her clothing threw splashes of color against the somber plains. Sage and camel thorn pricked her legs as she and her tribe traveled toward a destination not yet in sight.

Anahita walked with her mother and aunt alongside her grandmother's donkey, near the front of the caravan. Her grandmother sat sidesaddle, fingering prayer beads. The slow bong of camel bells and the tinkling of ankle bracelets gave melody to the rhythm of hoof and foot.

Anahita thought, as she often had since, about the man she had met at the bazaar in Mashhad a few days earlier. How did he know of those new dyes? Why did he ask the merchant if the carpet spoke of Persian life? He must be Iranian. Frowning, she remembered that she didn't even know his name. An urge to talk to the mullah about her wedding riddle came on like a sandstorm. Now, more than ever, she had a good reason to choose her own husband. Especially with men like *him* to meet.

She wanted to tell someone about this man. She wished she could trust Shirin with her new secret the way she once could have. For a moment Anahita thought about finding her cousin among the others in the caravan and walking with her. But she never felt comfortable around Shirin's husband, never felt she could gossip with her cousin the way they used to now that he was often there with her. *Shirin's grown tired of me anyway,* she thought. *She prefers the company of the young mothers in the tribe.*

Like water, their caravan flowed along the sand and spilled onto the plains. Anahita watched her father ride his horse from family to family, making sure everyone was comfortable. Her eye fell on her cousin now, walking with her mother-in-law and several other women, laughing and talking. But Anahita found that she wasn't in the mood to talk to anyone after all.

Eyeing the ground, she searched instead for new patterns or colors to weave, a habit on her migrations. As she had predicted to her granduncle, this spring the wildflowers bloomed plentifully due to the great amount of rain and snow over the winter. Whenever she came to a patch of *sprak,* the plant that the dyemaster had showed her, or yarrow and chamomile, plants from which she could make a yellow, green, or golden dye, she cut the most mature ones mid-stem and tied them in a bundle to the pannier of her grandmother's donkey.

As the tribe walked on, land forms sharpened into familiar

shapes for Anahita: the minaret-like rock where her tribe would turn west; the escarpment, dotted with caves, above the village of Abadi-eh-Golab where they would stop for the night.

At last they came to this hidden village, nestled among the hills and alongside a stream thick with mulberry and fig trees. A boy dressed in an embroidered hat ran to greet the tribe. "Are you well?" he asked. He led their camel train, nearly a mile long, to his village. They passed women working with hoes in sugar beet fields, fed by water from distant mountains.

When the last of the tribe had arrived and everyone had settled, Farhad lay on the grass among the children, who played by the stream. "Ah, Abadi-eh-Golab. No other place smells as wonderful as this—like perfume of fruit blossoms."

Anahita, who sat nearby, looked around, taking in the red rock formations that rose hundreds of feet into the air and gave the village its character. While some resembled minarets, others looked as if giant children had made them with dripping sand—the way she and Dariyoush used to make sand palaces with clay after a rain storm.

She studied the caves in the escarpment, where people had lived and worshiped thousands of years before. "Baba, will we have time to explore? I would like to find more figures painted on the cave walls." On a previous summer, Anaita had hiked up to the caves and looked at the ancient paintings of hunters and ibex, shepherds and sheep left by the long-dead inhabitants.

"Time? Plenty. I should like to snooze here a while."

The rest of Abadi-eh-Golab looked much like Anahita's own

village: mud roads, mud houses with thatched roofs, and stone sheds. Every year this small community hosted Anahita's tribe on their way to their mountain pastures. Anahita knew it couldn't be easy to have so many camped along their stream, and she felt grateful each year for their generosity.

"When the men of the village return from the hills, they will be surprised to find us here," Anahita said to her father as she stood up. Farhad crossed his arms behind his head and closed his eyes. "Surprised? Perhaps not. The men of the village are keeping a watchful eye on us at this very moment."

Anahita scanned the hills but saw no one.

A group of children, some from the tribe and some from the village, crowded around Dariyoush and the mullah. Dariyoush spotted Anahita walking nearby and waved for her to join them.

"We're hiking to the caves," he explained, smiling. The children jumped up and down.

"May I come with you?"

"I could use your help." Dariyoush freed himself from the group and whispered to Anahita, "The mullah is coming. He will be the hardest to haul up and down that wall of rock."

With Dariyoush and Anahita walking on either side of the mullah, the group started out. When the children came to the rock wall below the caves they spread out like a family of spiders, scaling it with ease. Anahita, Dariyoush, and the mullah negotiated it more carefully.

"Anahita," Dariyoush said. "I'll hoist you to that ledge, and you can help the mullah from above."

Dariyoush made a stair with his knee. Anahita stepped onto it with both feet. "What if there are snakes or camel spiders up there?"

"Hope for the spiders; they won't kill you."

Anahita rolled her eyes at him. She took off her head scarf and swatted it at the surface above.

"What are you doing?" he said, shaking his head.

"I'm scaring away the vipers."

Dariyoush jiggled his knee; he enjoyed teasing her.

Anahita swayed. "Dariyoush! You'll make me fall."

And wouldn't I love to catch you? he thought.

Pulling herself up with her fingers, she found a toehold and hurled herself on top.

The mullah stood on Dariyoush's knee and then his shoulder. Taking Anahita's hand in one of his own, he pushed off Dariyoush's head with the other and rolled onto the rock ledge. The breeze filled his robes.

"Are you all right, mullah?" Anahita asked, brushing some of the red dirt off him. "Would you like to rest here?" she said, as Dariyoush leapt up to join them.

"I am quite fine," said the mullah, still on his back, his twisted clothing ensnaring him. "I just need to catch my breath. I would not miss having a look at these ancient paintings. At my age I do not take my days for granted."

Anahita smiled at Dariyoush. "Why haven't we come up here more often?"

"Good question. Is it because I scared you the last time?" Dariyoush said, nudging her arm.

"I nearly died of fright," she said, pressing a palm to her breast. "You hid in the cave and growled like a mountain lion. How old were we then?"

"Thirteen, fourteen?"

"I couldn't have been more than ten, the age of some of these children," she said, looking about for them. "Oh, my! They're at the cave already. Dariyoush, you better go with them. There really could be a lion in there. I'll wait with Mullah."

Dariyoush hurried to join the children, not because he was concerned about mountain lions, but because he had an idea for a joke to play on Anahita.

When she and the mullah finally entered the cave, they were engulfed by children, who circled around Anahita, their "captive," and led her to their master.

Dariyoush beat his fists on his chest like a caveman and said, "Ug." In his hand he held a torch and its flickering flames made the ibex painted on the cave walls look as if they were running across the stone.

"I see you have brought the sacrificial maiden," Dariyoush said to the children. Looking toward the mullah, he added, "And her shaman." The children giggled as Dariyoush continued. "All the better, for he can assist in the ceremony."

Dariyoush gave the mullah his torch. Stepping toward Anahita, he said, "Shaman, please allow me . . ." He bowed to the mullah, thinking, *I'm probably in for it now*, and then swept Anahita off of her feet and into his arms. The children roared with laughter, all of them looking at the mullah to see if he would reprimand Dariyoush.

"Oh!" Anahita exclaimed. "Help me, help me," she called, reaching for the little ones. Laughing and charging and shouting, "Get him! Get him!" the children jumped on Dariyoush, pried his arms off Anahita, and wrestled him to the ground. Dariyoush lay there for a while, acting defeated until Anahita gave him a hand up. They stood looking at each other, grinning. Seconds lapsed before either of them let go of the other's hand. Dariyoush almost forgot he was in the cave, or with anyone else but her. He felt a sudden pang in his chest at the thought of Farhad marrying her to the khan. Turning his head, he caught the mullah's eyes. A wave of understanding seemed to steal across the old man's face. Stroking his beard, the mullah turned to the cave wall. Moving from image to image with the torch, he took obvious delight in what he saw.

That evening, Anahita watched the mullah weave through the tribe's cluster of lean-tos, set up as temporary shelter for their overnight stay. The holy man passed mothers playing with their children in the shade and animals drinking from the stream and came to where she and her father snacked on a blanket in the grass. Farhad stood up to greet the mullah and gestured for him to join them in their light meal of cheese, figs, and dates.

Anahita squirmed, suddenly realizing why the mullah had come to speak with Farhad. She had hoped he might have spoken to her first.

Never one for small talk, the mullah started right in. "I've been thinking about Anahita's request," he said as he sat down on the corner of their blanket and crossed his legs.

Anahita felt the heat of her father's gaze, and each muscle in her body tightened. *Please, please, please let him say yes!*

"I have thought about what we discussed some days ago in the village square, Anahita. Something you said struck a note with me. If too many of our women are married out in the interest of making peace with neighboring tribes, children in our village will dry up as quickly as our wells after a snowless winter."

Farhad turned to Anahita. He rubbed his neck. Whatever was in his mind seemed to be causing him pain.

"Yes," Anahita added for her father's benefit. "Choice will allow men and women to marry within their own villages. It's happening everywhere."

"Perhaps not *everywhere*," the mullah continued. "But I know the way the sands blow."

Popping a fig into her mouth, Anahita decided to keep quiet. She thought it was a good sign that the mullah, and not she, had initiated this discussion.

"Choice is an interesting topic," the mullah expounded. "It is paradise for some, hell for others. Choice may lead one to both moral and immoral deeds. But it is my belief that whether or not we argue over who will determine the details of our lives, the important events—births, deaths, or mates—happen in spite of human plans."

Anahita noticed Farhad was still rubbing his neck.

"I'm not sure if I'm softening in my years or if I'm drunk on the scent of all these fruit blossoms, but I don't see what a little wedding riddle would hurt. It will give our people a festivity to look forward to during the long winter to come."

"Oh, Mullah, thank you," Anahita said. She felt like grabbing hold of his shoulders and kissing him on both cheeks, but an unwed female never kissed a man, let alone a mullah. Instead, she held the bowl of dates out to him and said, "Please, help yourself."

Looking from one man to the other, she continued, "Mullah, Baba, I will weave the most beautiful wedding *qali* in all of Iran!"

"Anahita, please compose yourself," Farhad said. "My dear Mullah, I am grateful for your consideration of this, ah, *wedding riddle*. But I must confess that I was not aware that Anahita brought her idea to you." He shot his daughter a stern look. "I'm afraid there is more to consider before this decision is made. It involves the wishes of the khan.

"Perhaps, dear daughter, you would like to explain this small detail to the mullah."

But if the mullah approves of the plan, what do the khan's wishes matter? Anahita wondered. No one was more important than the mullah.

With a slight bow of his head and shoulders, her father excused himself from the holy man. To Anahita he said, "I will speak with you later."

Anahita could not think of what to tell the mullah, who watched her now with such a puzzled expression. Then, just as she gathered the words to explain the khan's wishes, she remembered something the mullah had said to her one morning while they sat on the fountain wall: *Perhaps the khan will be generous again this year and purchase a donkey and cart for the mosque. Oh,* she thought, cupping her mouth with her hand. She realized the mullah truly relied on the khan and that he would not want to go against his wishes by consenting to her idea.

Anahita looked at the holy man. "Um . . ." she began.

"*Dokhtaram,*" he said, raising a hand to silence her. "There is no need for an explanation. I had guessed the khan's intentions toward you."

Anahita dropped her hands to her lap and relaxed a little.

"While I was mulling over your request for a wedding riddle, I was reminded of one of my own sermons in which I had encouraged our tribe to consider new ideas rather than criticize them."

Oh yes, Anahita thought, *the bathhouse sermon.*

"So, I thought that I should set an example and follow my own advice."

"I am grateful, Mullah." She noticed his thoughtful gaze resting on Dariyoush, who led his horse to new shade on the other side of the stream.

"Besides," the mullah said as he got up to leave, "our khan could stand a little competition now and then. Such things keep us humble."

Anahita blinked in amazement. The mullah then smiled and made his way through the lean-tos to another family.

Each fig Anahita ate that evening tasted of hope.

TAUBESTAN
NAKHRISI
VA GUL CHINI
Summer Spinning and
Wildflower Gathering

Princely Days, Duties

Arash and his royal escorts galloped through barren lands to high fertile valleys on their journey to Marv and to Arash's new life as governor of the city. Some of the fields bore wheat, millet, and barley while others flowered with orchards. Inhaling the sweetness of overflowing fruit, he thought, *No wonder the Russians want this territory.*

The journey took many days. In sudden sandstorms the men holed up in the ruins of ancient dwellings. Arash found that he liked these moments huddled in the rubble, watching light and shadow move around the dilapidated shapes of the old buildings. He couldn't help but appreciate how Allah filled the spaces between solid things.

At night they stopped to rest at smoke-filled teahouses. The tiniest village became a new bead on Arash's abacus of knowledge. Yet everything he experienced also seemed familiar—as if it had been locked inside him long before he was born.

In each new village he hoped to find Anahita. But instead, he

found beggars and refugees. They camped in courtyards or loi-
tered about shrines uttering, "Please *agha*, can you spare a *rial*, a
shahi?" Never had he seen so many destitute—their hair crawling
with lice, their scalps marked with ringworm—some clutching
bedrolls, others *samovars* and water pipes. Some told Arash stories of bandits who roamed the northern borders of Iran, raiding their villages, kidnapping women and children and selling
them into slavery in Bukhara. Others described their narrow
escapes on foot from cities farther north that the Russians had
captured. He wondered if his father knew about these unfortu-
nates, and if he was doing anything to help them.

Arash also witnessed women who ran refugee camps and
makeshift clinics in their backyards. Others worked kilns, tended
herds, even dug wells in the absence of their men, who had
either died or gone to fight the Russians. He admired the intelligence they brought to these tasks, which often improved the
existing services. *Imagine what they could do if they received a proper education.* Something he longed for himself.

When he and his men finally arrived outside the palace in
Marv, a swarm of street boys holding birdcages surrounded their
horses. Inside the cages were canaries trained to pick slips of
folded paper from a miniature basket—little parchments bearing portents and poems. The boldest of the boys stepped right
up to Arash's stallion. Raising the cage so Arash could see the
yellow bird inside, the boy said, "Please, *agha*, you *must* want to
know your fortune!" He spoke in Afshari—Anahita's dialect.

"Run along now boys, this is the new governor of Marv, he

can't be bothered . . ." an escort began; however, Arash dismounted his horse. The boy reminded him of one of his young Yomut cousins.

"What is your name?" Arash asked.

"Pirouz."

The other boys backed away from the men, but not far, as if they still hoped to make a sale.

"*You* are the new governor?" Pirouz asked. "You don't look like . . . I mean . . . you are not dressed like one. Governors have never visited with *us*. Do you like Marv?" When he finally seemed to realize to whom he was speaking, he stopped talking. The other boys giggled.

Arash smiled. "I have just arrived and do not know the city yet."

Pirouz straightened up, and tried a different tack. "I can bring you to see the temples, palaces, and mosques. Genghis Khan stayed here, you know."

Now Arash's men laughed, but Arash himself looked thoughtful. "I would appreciate a tour of my new city someday soon," he said, thinking that Pirouz could help him brush up on his Afshari as well as show him the underside of Marv. Things that would be helpful to know as governor.

"You can find me right here, most days," Pirouz said and grinned proudly.

A servant stood among the many palace guards waiting for Arash. After handing his reins to one of his escorts, Arash followed the man, a native of Marv named Ismail, into the palace.

They strolled past an immense pool that was built to reflect the mansion's pink stone, and through a lush *bagh*. "A garden planted one hundred and fifty years ago by the shah's ancestors," Ismail said with a hint of pride.

After allowing Arash time to freshen up, Ismail brought him to his new office. Arash nodded to guards standing on either side of tall, mahogany doors. Their clothes, crafted from the finest silk, shone in stark contrast to the homespun linen in which Arash liked to travel. He looked down at his loose-fitting, nomadic clothing and brushed himself off.

Ismail extended an arm before him. "I hope this meets your approval."

Inside, Arash saw painted, cloth-draped archways and open spaces where three large carpets lay. Each crimson and indigo weaving matched the others in color, but differed slightly in its floral design. Made with mohair and silk, these rugs were more decorative than practical. The one with gazelles and leopards caught his interest. "These are like no other *gelims* I've seen."

"They are eleventh-century rugs from Herat," Ismail said. "The weavers have woven into each the names of the shahs who commissioned them."

Worried about walking on the rugs, Arash looked for an uncarpeted place to tread. But there was none. He thought of the destitute he'd met on his journey and wondered how many tents or wells or medicines could have been purchased for them with the money that was spent on these antique floor coverings.

The two men made their way to an alcove beside a small pool.

Star shapes, cut through the exterior walls, let light into the space, which twinkled like the heavens. "A place for study or repose," Ismail said. Here sat a daybed and low bookcases holding volumes arranged meticulously by height.

Despite the jade-colored drapes in the archways and the carpets covering the cold stone floors, Arash thought his new office lacked the warmth and comfort of the tent-like *yurts* in which his mother's people took shelter. *Maybe this is what nobility is all about—cool, calculated business.*

And business is what Ismail wanted to discuss.

"Ghorban," he began, using the most respectful of words, meaning "one for whom I sacrifice all."

"Please call me Arash," the prince said, his eye caught by a movement just outside the door to his office.

Ismail cleared his throat. *"Agha?"* he asked, settling on a less lofty, but still respectful term.

"If you insist."

Handing Arash a glass of tea, Ismail continued. "Agha, our markets here flourish with fresh goods brought in almost daily by camel train. We are protected by a disciplined regional army, and according to most reports, the shah's administration here in Marv is highly efficient."

Though the sheer draperies hanging from the archways obscured his vision, Arash thought he saw two men in the hallway walking on tiptoe, carrying a rolled-up carpet. "Excuse me, Ismail," he said. "I know I am new here and not aware of the protocol, but I believe two men are taking a very large *gelim* away."

"For cleaning, I gather."

"Yes, of course." Arash said, wondering why he had suspected that the men might be stealing the almost-priceless carpets. After taking a sip of tea, he asked, "Tell me why my father has sent me here to replace the former governor." He knew of his father's penchant for changing governors so that no single prince could gain too much power, but he was curious to hear what he might learn from Ismail.

"I believe the shah felt the former governor did not communicate well with our army, which is largely conscripted from the nomadic tribes of this region. Nor did the former governor manage to stop the local bandits, who steal at will throughout our province." Ismail's hand swept the room. "We have a saying here: 'If you meet a viper and a Marvi, kill the Marvi first,' as he is likely an untrustworthy man. This is not an easy place to govern. But you, we have been told, are armed with a nomad's sensibility, fluency in most Turkman dialects, and plenty of self-confidence. We have great hopes for you."

Arash responded with only a smile that did not part his lips.

Ismail continued. "The less obvious reason is, like a poorly made carpet, the fabric of our *divan* is fraying just below the surface. There are those among the military and civil servants in Marv who are of the mind to run things according to their own wishes." He touched the tips of his fingers together, making a tent of his hands while he spoke. "They wish to pass decrees without first taking their ideas to the shah's Assembly of the House of Consultation in Tehran. They complain it is a world away in distance and . . ."

87

Arash raised a brow, his gaze not wavering from this new adviser's face.

". . . and ideology."

Arash knelt down to look more closely at the lions woven into the border of one of the carpets. Pressing his fingers into its thick pile, he noticed the beasts bore swords.

"Ismail, what do you feel about the manner in which my father rules his kingdom?"

The question hung in the air. Arash examined the *abrash*, the variation of hues within each color in the carpet, thinking that there must be twenty or more shades. "Do you favor a constitutional parliament?"

Except for the sounds of the street coming through the windows—*"Cantaloupe, melons. Cheap! One* shahi *each"*—and the dull creak of wooden cart wheels rolling over stone, the air in Arash's office quivered in silence.

During his first few weeks in Marv, Arash filled his time with work and study, reading long into the night. He found it strange, sitting at his large desk in formal clothing. He preferred cushions on the floor, as he used in his private quarters. He also found that on the days he dressed as himself, and not as a prince, his subjects relaxed and gave him more honest opinions.

Now, a month into his governorship, Arash found himself nodding off as he reclined in his office with a book. He wondered if his fatigue was due to his long journey to Marv, his eagerness to absorb all there was to know about his new principality, or if the feather mattress on the daybed upon which he lay induced sleep. In his drowsiness, he heard utterances coming from the hallway, and saw the tassels from one of the rugs that had adorned his office slip around the corner of the door frame. The rug seemed to vanish as if it were part of one of the street boy Pirouz's magic tricks. "Abracadabra! Now you see it, my prince, and now you do not."

They must be washing the carpets again, Arash thought. He shook himself completely awake and decided he would find the orphan and ask him for another tour of the ancient sites in the area. Arash was amazed how much history the boy knew, and at his gift for unscrambling Marv's two-thousand-year-old puzzle of a past, making a complete picture from the ruins of so many different eras. Arash felt glad that the boy's knowledge earned him a few *tomans.*

When he found Pirouz on the street, the boy's face lit up. "My Governor," the young one said, bowing deeply and nudging his friends to do the same. "Are you well today?"

"Well and willing to follow wherever you lead," Arash replied, bending at the waist. Each of the boys grinned as they watched the prince bow. Arash looked forward to the local lore and gossip that would tumble from Pirouz's mouth; it amused as much as informed him.

After exploring the remains of an ancient Greek plaza, of interest to Arash because of its unusual quadrangular layout, the prince and his young tour guide set out for the mud-brick homes of laborers. Arash made a point of visiting as many people as he could, and Pirouz tagged along, as an ambassador of the streets. They took time to drink tea with several families, and Arash, as he often did on these visits, began to feel the pulse of the city. He asked the laborers how Marv could be improved. When he had asked Pirouz this same question the boy replied, "Guns to fight the Russians."

"Is that all?"

"Well, the warden of my orphanage would say schools. But if you ask me, we need a magicians' guild, for teaching mimes and puppeteers, snake charmers and flame throwers. Have you ever seen the coin-appearing-behind-the-ear trick?"

Arash had invited Pirouz to perform it for him. The boy's hands moved with a flourish, and Arash found him to be slicker than anyone at this illusion.

Now Pirouz led the new governor on what seemed like the long route back to the palace. Arash thought how Marv reminded him of Mashhad, its main features including a mosque, a *madrasa*, and a *caravanserai*. He also realized that he did not see any new construction, as if his father had forgotten about this part of his kingdom. But the old stone buildings, though neglected, held a certain grace and strength, as if they would last forever. He felt a humble fellowship with the place. It possessed the personality of a big gentleman—a grandfather of Persian outposts. Arash resolved to defend it against all enemies.

On the way back to the palace, the prince and boy visited with copper and silver dealers and spice and fruit merchants, switching dialects according to each one's language. While discussing the cost of indigo with a miniaturist who was painting a picture of the legendary Shahrazad, Arash caught a glimpse of a carpet in a nearby stall that looked very familiar. It depicted a lion and sword and had tassels just like the *gelim* that had disappeared from his office that morning. He decided to stay with the artist as the man mixed his pigments so he could watch the comings and goings of the carpet stall. Arash thought that the bearded man, who was now leaving the shop, resembled a servant from the palace. Walking briskly, the man glanced over his shoulder as if he hoped not to be seen.

"Pirouz," Arash whispered. "What do you know about the merchant who runs that carpet stall?"

"He runs a shady business. But please don't say I told you so."

Arash reached in his pocket and gave Pirouz several *tomans.* Many more than he usually gave him for his services. Pirouz's eyes grew round and a huge smile revealed two or three bad teeth. "Please follow that man," Arash said, pointing at the bearded fellow who had left the stall. "I want to know where he lives and works."

Pirouz drew his eyebrows together. "You want me to . . . I've always wanted to be a spy!" He turned to run, but Arash caught him by the sleeve.

"He's not to know he's being followed. Snoop without being seen. When you have news, come to the palace and give the guards your name."

"You mean I will be permitted to enter the royal palace?"

"If you serve me well."

"Trust me," Pirouz said, straightening his shoulders, then slipping into the shadows.

That evening in the palace garden Arash met with his advisers and visiting emissaries and learned about schools throughout the kingdom. They discussed the theological school in Qom, and the *madrasas* that the clerics had begun to organize in the farthest-flung villages, in tents if need be. The wife of a civil servant seated beside him spoke up. "There are women in Tabriz and Tehran who wish to open private schools for girls. The key to strengthening Iran lies with literacy and learning, for women, too."

He thought about the women and girls in his father's harem; the women he saw on his journey to Marv; Jaleh from his Yomut tribe; and Anahita—wherever she was—all of whom he felt would be glad to go to school. "I will look into this," Arash promised, a bit embarrassed by his delayed response.

He stayed in the garden long after his guests left, enjoying the sound of the running water in the gullies that had been carved alongside pathways and steps. He wondered if a school for girls in Marv would be well attended, and whether it would be accepted by the clerics and community.

As a younger son of the shah, he had not been considered important enough for a thorough education. His studies, supervised by a court tutor, had been limited to the classical texts of Persian literature, Arabic syntax, calligraphy, and the rudiments of Islam. Had he been given the opportunity to attend the Dar al Fonun school in Tehran like his older brothers, he would have learned more about economics, mathematics, world history, and current affairs, all subjects that would help him in his new post. Arash vowed to educate himself, to learn from as many sources as possible so that he could become an informed governor. The words of a former tutor and dervish friend came to mind: *Practice humility, Arash. Any being in the world can teach us what we ignore.* He wished he could bring education to all of those whom he had met on his journey to Marv, even to the beggars and street children like Pirouz. And no sooner had he thought of the boy than a guard announced his arrival.

When Pirouz was brought into the garden, he exclaimed, "Wow! Is this what is called a jungle? It is so leafy in here! The breeze feels as juicy as figs." The boy's unrehearsed conversation was a welcome contrast to the dull and guarded speech of the palace advisers and servants, who all seemed to have perpetual headaches.

"So what news do you have for me, young spy?"

Pirouz looked to both sides and over his shoulder, then lowered his voice. "The man I followed, his name is Khosro. He is a servant in this *very* palace."

"And, for whom does he work?"

Pirouz put on an innocent but unconvincing face. "Was I supposed to find that out, too?" The boy palmed his forehead in a self-reprimanding gesture. "I'm so sorry, I must have forgotten." Looking sideways at Arash, he continued, "But a few more *tomans* might help me to remember."

Arash simply tilted his head back, no, and waited for Pirouz to continue.

The boy snapped his fingers. "Come to think of it, I recall that the title of the person your carpet thief reported to has something to do with money."

"The vizier, who oversees the management of the whole palace?" Arash offered.

"No."

"The royal treasurer?"

"No . . . doesn't sound right."

Arash narrowed his eyes at Pirouz, beginning to tire of the boy's antics. "The palace accountant?"

"Yes, that's it."

Arash leaned forward. "Did you hear anything they said to each other?"

"Now that, I'm afraid, will require additional pay, my prince." Pirouz extended an open hand.

Arash tried to conceal his smile, knowing the little fellow had gotten the better of him. He reached into his pocket and gave him one glinting coin.

"I heard the accountant say something about 'com-pen-sation for civil servants.' What does *com-pen-sation* mean?"

"*Compensation* usually means pay for work completed." Arash laid a hand on the boy's shoulder and turned him toward the nearest way out of the garden. "Thank you, Pirouz. Now you may take your leave."

Pirouz plucked a date from a palm tree before joining the guard who would see him back to the street.

Amidst the moist greenery, Arash pondered what this all meant.

Carpets disappearing and apparently being pawned, but why? And why hadn't anyone in the palace seemed to notice? Or brought it to his attention?

Later, while sitting on cushions in his quarters, with his legs stretched out in front of him, Arash felt a twinge of homesickness for his relatives and old friends. He looked at the tiled wall where he had hung an eggplant-colored carpet that the women of his mother's tribe had woven and given him the day he had bid his family farewell. He read the calligraphy running around the perimeter, taking to heart the words of the ancient Sufi, Sa'adi: *A ruler given to tyranny undermines his own sovereignty.*

Then he lifted his gaze to the tasseled scarf he'd fastened to the rug's upper left corner. It rustled in the breeze coming through the window. Little bursts of scent, messages of smoke and rose, reminded him of Anahita.

A memory of his grandfather's words consumed him. *"Who will be heir to your court?"* *Why is it I pine for this woman I hardly know? A woman I may never meet again. How am I ever to rule, if I'm daydreaming like this?* When these moods took hold, as they did some evenings, Arash tried to read or do some kind of work. But tonight, by the light of three feeble-flamed oil lamps, he could not break the flow of his thoughts. Getting up, he walked over to the niche in the stone wall above his bookshelf. The small space kept cool whatever refreshments servants placed there. Before pouring himself a glass of pomegranate juice, he fingered the poem carved into stone around its opening: *Delight in good, for surely it is Allah who assists.* Then he reached for a book of Jalaluddin Rumi's poems given to him by his dervish friend. Opening it, he came to his favorite poem, "A Great Wagon." He read:

When I see your face, the stones start spinning!
You appear; all studying wanders.
I lose my place.

Water turns pearly.
Fire dies down and doesn't destroy.

In your presence I don't want what I thought
I wanted, those little hanging lamps.

Inside your face the ancient manuscripts
seem like rusty mirrors.
You breathe; new shapes appear,

and the music of desire as widespread
as Spring begins to move
like a great wagon.
                    Drive slowly.
Some of us walking alongside
are lame!

A Khan, a Gentleman, and a Diplomat

The khan slid off his Arabian and landed heavily on his feet, then handed the reins to his servant. "Take care of him for me. I don't dare ride him any farther into this . . . this *slum*." The khan lifted his calico kitten off the saddle and cradled it in the crook of his arm as a mother would her infant. "And meet me back here with the horse before sunset."

"As you wish," his servant said, bowing slightly and looking around. "Do you really think someone would try and steal . . . ?"

The khan glared back at him, silencing the man's doubt with his gaze. Straightening his turban, he felt for the peacock feather to make sure it was still intact. His fingers caressed the gemmed broach holding the plume in place. "By the way, did you manage to buy something for Kadkhuda Farhad's daughter?"

"Young Anahita?"

"Yes, her," the khan said, stroking his kitten.

97

A trace of guilt crept into the servant's bony features. "Sir, I thought since I don't know her very well, and since it is a gift from you to your . . . your . . ."

"Bride-to-be?" the khan offered, clearing his throat and raising his chin.

"Yes," the servant said, "your bride-to-be, that perhaps it would be more fitting if you picked out the gift yourself."

"I don't have time for such nonsense," the khan snapped. "Get her silk or something. Don't all women like silk?" He started toward the one-storied mud homes in southern Mashhad and then stopped and looked back at his servant. "I almost forgot. Purchase some fine carpets for the landowners—the ones in the west near Mount Binalud. The Afshars will be migrating back through their land this autumn. I can't have any clashes between them and Kadkhuda Farhad's tribe."

Not this coming autumn anyway, he thought. *I've got to keep my Afshars happy with me. At least until Anahita is mine.* He thought wistfully about the visit he had made to Hasanabad a few years back when he began to look at Anahita as a woman. He could still picture her slender fingers wrapped around the pitcher of water from which she had served him, how her hands had lost their baby fat. And how she peeked at him from the weaving alcove with her liquid eyes, black as obsidian, alluring as his first—and favorite—wife, peace be upon her.

On his way here, the khan had ridden through the finer neighborhoods of Mashhad with their courtyards, brick homes, and balconies, waving or nodding to men as he went, and allowing the children he passed to pet his little cat. But here, among the one-storied tenement *manzels,* with the salt plains just beyond, he walked quickly without stopping.

"The world could be a beautiful place if it weren't for all these untidy neighborhoods, Kitty. I'll bet you ran away from a place like this. Wasn't your fluffy red hair all covered with thorns and thistles when fortune brought you to the foot of my camel?" Chatting with his kitten like this, the khan hurried between the small houses, and only once did he pause to ask for directions to the home of Master Reza, the schoolteacher.

The khan knocked on what he hoped was the right door and was greeted by a buxom woman in her middle years with full lips. She looked to be about his age. The khan glanced around for a man of the house, but saw no one. He smiled graciously. "I am sorry to intrude on you and your family, but I am looking for a Master . . ."

"Master Reza?" Her face brightened. "Such a wonderful young man. What brings a distinguished gentleman such as yourself to call on dear Reza?"

"You flatter me," the khan said, certain the smile behind her sheer veil was meant for him. *Perhaps I should court this woman for my wife as well. She clearly likes me. Though whatever is she doing living here among the riffraff?* He felt he could make her much happier in a home on the other side of Mashhad.

"Look at that adorable kitten you have. Just one minute," the woman said, disappearing into another room. She came back carrying a bowl, which the khan thought was for his pet until she said, "Please follow me." Turning sideways, she squeezed by him through the door. Her touch gave him a thrill. His eyes fell to her hips as she walked.

They walked to a neighboring *manzel*. The door was open and a cockatiel in a tall cage near the entrance squawked at them, its voice carrying into the courtyard.

"Master Reza," the woman called inside. "Someone is here to see you."

A young man looked up from where he sat reading on the floor. He smiled at the woman and got up to greet them.

"Here, my growing young man," the woman said, pressing the bowl into his hands with her slightly wrinkled ones. "*Mast-o khiyar.* Just the way you like it—with two dashes of mint and one of garlic."

"You spoil me," Reza said to his neighbor, who pinched his cheek and left without returning the khan's gaze.

The khan cleared his throat, hoping she might turn around, but she didn't. He touched his peacock feather and smiled at Reza, who looked at it and then at the kitten in his arms. Raising an eyebrow, Reza asked, "Have we met before?"

"I don't believe so. I am the khan of the local Afshar tribe from Hasanabad. My quarters are here in Mashhad. You teach my colleague's son. I wish to speak to you on a matter of business."

Preoccupied with his mission, the khan entered Reza's home without invitation. He took inventory of the furnishings: three plush pile carpets, a bundle of clothes in one corner, and a few pillows. *A pauper's belongings,* the khan thought, until he turned to see a stack of linen- and leather-bound books that reached nearly to the ceiling. Other books—as large as a doormat or tiny as a wafer—lay open on the floor, showing words, pictures, and blank pages.

"I hope to have shelves made for the books," Reza said as he picked up a few to clear a space for his guest. "If I'm ever paid my wages for my teaching."

"I see I have come at the right time in your life." The khan plopped himself on the floor, round and bottom-heavy as an olive oil urn. "I know about the shah's financial woes and his inability to contribute generously to our *madrasas*. It is a disgrace and this matter should be discussed at the Assembly of the House of Consultations, among other issues. I, for one, am working toward better days to come."

"For all?" Reza said, pouring water into his *samovar* to make tea.

"But of course," the khan said, nodding slightly. "This is why I am here this evening. I would like to make you an offer. One you will find difficult to refuse."

Reza leaned back into his pillow and squinted, though the khan knew the sun was not in the schoolteacher's eyes. The khan then noticed the schoolmaster following the roll of his kitty's red head across his own forearm to settle facing the cockatiel. The bird ran back and forth on its perch.

"She's a stray," the khan said. "In some ways I was one myself, orphaned at a young age." He stroked his pet. "This kitten won't let me leave her. She runs up my garb if I put her down. It's easier just to take her with me." Crossing his legs in a different position, the khan said, "Don't worry. I won't let her eat your bird."

"Cockatiel. His name is Genghis."

"Yes," the khan said. "Cockatiel. Funny, birds never interested me. Now where were we?"

"Your offer?" Reza said, his tone of voice impatient.

"I plan to marry this autumn and would like to hire a tutor for my bride-to-be. I'll not have an illiterate for a wife. I understand that you attended the esteemed Dar al Fonun school in Tehran. I will pay you twice whatever it is you are paid now. You come highly recommended to me."

Reza took the teapot from the *samovar* and poured the steaming liquid into two small glasses.

"I would miss my students."

He's playing with me, the khan thought, *but every man has his price.* Twisting the gold ring on his smallest finger with his thumb, he said, "I will make it worth your while."

"I don't know. I enjoy a full classroom. The energy among the students, all their questions."

"It will be a new experience for you. I'm sure a man like you would not shrink from such a challenge."

"I've never taught a girl."

"She is quite beautiful. She would be a pleasure to teach."

Reza traced a finger around the lip of his tea cup.

"So it's settled? The khan does not like to take no for an answer."

Reza's cockatiel squawked. The kitten lurched from the khan's arms but he held it back.

"I'll have to think it over," Reza said.

"Good." With his free hand, the khan lifted his glass to Reza's. "You'll have her molded into a stately woman in no time." He slurped his tea. "I will call on you before the wedding to help polish her. You do know how to ride a horse, don't you? As this job requires that you travel to a nomad camp . . ."

High Pastures

Anahita's first glimpse of their summer pastures—jagged snowy peaks and a valley vibrant with color—cheered her. She picked a purple lupine and two red poppies, sniffing each. Pulling the scarf from her head and thinking of the favorite one she had lost outside the mosque at Mashhad, she loosened her long hair and placed the flowers in it—her summer ritual, a little indiscretion no one seemed to mind here in the mountain wilderness. She loved the feeling of nothing between her and the clouds billowing by.

Wind swept cool air from snow fields high above as she helped Farhad, Dariyoush, and his brother Mehdi assemble their family tent in the center of the camp, at the same fire pit and collection of hearth stones they had used the year before. Mojdeh and Maman Bozorg unpacked their camels and donkeys. Together Anahita and the men stacked rocks into a rectangular tent foundation, erected willow branches for poles, and stretched and pulled a large black cloth—woven from goat hair—over it all.

Each family in Anahita's tribe pitched their tents in the same manner about twenty paces from one another for privacy. They would camp here for many weeks before moving to greener pastures.

While they worked, Anahita said, "Baba, I have a riddle for you."

"Not now," he said, shaking the tent frame to test it.

She looked to her mother but Mojdeh's expression offered no sympathy. Anahita knew she was the cause of her parents' bad humor of late. Ever since the mullah had given his consent to her wedding riddle, her father had said little. Even Dariyoush seemed quieter than usual. *Maybe they are worried about the Russian cavalry,* she tried to convince herself. Local villagers had warned the tribe that the Russians might be nearby.

When they had finished assembling the tent, Anahita decided to collect the wildflowers she had seen near the foothills on their way into camp: the tall mullein with yellow flower tops that were ripe for dye. She grabbed a handful of raw wool and her new spindle and set off following a stream. Placing her spindle against her thigh, Anahita gave it a quick flick. As she walked, it turned round and round while swaying back and forth like a pendulum, in rhythm with her stride. She fed it wool from the combed strands she had wound around her wrist, and made an even yarn with no lumps. Anahita spun her wool counterclockwise in the opposite direction of the sun's path. She believed this would bring good luck to her and her partner in life. Should someone study a weaver's unfinished work, her grandmother said, they would discover all her methods and intentions.

Anahita found the repetitive task of spinning comforting. It could calm her when she was anxious and clear her mind when she was upset. By the time she had reached the place where she had seen the dye flowers, she had half a whorl full of wool and a pleasant state of mind.

She tucked her spindle into her waistband, pulled out a knife, and began to cut the mullein. She could use both the blooms and stems for a golden dye. *I must bring our camels here to eat what I don't collect,* she thought, knowing the plants were too tall and tough for sheep to graze on.

She gathered an armful of flowers and headed back to camp. The stalks were the height of her, the tips of them dotted with tiny yellow petals. She looked as if she carried brightly lit torches. She would hang this bunch in the tent to dry, and when summer was over, she would bring it and the other blossoms she'd collected back to her granduncle and use the yarn he dyed with the flowers in her wedding *qali*. In this way, her *qali* would always remind her of summer migrations—the fields full of wildflowers and the snow-capped peaks.

Near camp, Anahita came upon Shirin washing clothes in the stream. No one else was around, and Anahita knew she would have to speak to her cousin. But before she could say a word, Shirin spoke. "Not that you're interested in my advice anymore, but I think you're a fool not to marry the khan." It was clear she had been hoping to say this for some time.

"Good afternoon to you, too," Anahita quipped.

Shirin cradled her clothes basket with both arms. "Most

women would jump at the chance—bolts of cloth, jewelry, silver mirrors and candelabras . . ."

"I won't marry for silver, Shirin."

"Do you expect some *jinn* to appear with the man of your dreams? Nobody marries for love in our tribe. What makes you think you can?" Shirin placed a hand on one hip.

"What makes me think I can is because I've dared to ask for this. I'm willing to fight for the privilege." Anahita fumed, thinking how Shirin only took the given route, voiced the safe opinion.

"Even if your father does agree to a contest, the khan might win," her cousin said. "If you don't accept his offer now, and he's forced to win you through your silly game, he might make your life miserable . . . if you know what I mean."

Anahita crossed her arms. "No, Shirin. I don't know what you mean," she lied, not wanting to acknowledge that anything of what her cousin said might be true. "Perhaps only a 'married woman might understand,'" Anahita added, mockingly. More than once her cousin had said these words to her, implying she knew all there was to know about "grown-up" life because she was now a wife.

Shirin's eyes narrowed. "You are so naive, Anahita."

Anahita didn't respond. Once Shirin would have taken her side in any dispute. She wondered how could she win her cousin over because she really needed an ally now. Maybe the mullah would have some advice about this, as he was one for turning people's attitudes around: *"Be kind and honest, and harmful poisons will turn sweet inside you."*

Shirin gathered her laundry and turned to walk away. Over her shoulder she said, "On the other hand, marrying the khan is quite the bittersweet opportunity . . . kind of like a kiss of death, wouldn't you say? I always thought you looked good in white . . ." Shirin didn't elaborate, she was laughing so hard.

She didn't need to say more. Anahita knew that her cousin meant her white death shroud. *Ooh!* Anahita felt the pulse in her neck quicken. She dropped her bunch of flowers on the ground and dove onto her cousin, tackling her. The clean clothes in Shirin's basket flew in every direction. "Ahh!" her cousin yelled.

Anahita pinned Shirin on her stomach, twisting her arm behind her back—a move Dariyoush had taught her when she was eight and he was twelve. Pulling it off so easily now, after so little practice, brought a surge of pleasure.

Shirin spat dirt from her mouth. "Let me go!" she screamed, loudly enough so that anyone within a half-day's walk from camp could hear.

Anahita got up, but not because Shirin commanded her to. She had nothing more to say to her cousin and this small humiliation would last longer than any verbal retort. Brushing herself off, Anahita picked up her flowers and walked away.

Anahita returned to her family's tent. Inside, she found her mother stacking their extra bedding on a platform of rocks at the back of the tent. The rocks would keep the textiles clean and dry. Maman Bozorg sat on the carpet rubbing her feet and calves with a salve as her legs had stiffened from the day's journey. Anahita, who was feeling almost lighthearted after her fight with Shirin, tickled the side of her grandmother's face with the fuzzy leaves of her yellow dye plants. *Maman Bozorg is like a dye wildflower,* Anahita thought. *Her skin is as rough as a weed's, but inside she blooms with color.*

"Aren't those lovely!" her grandmother said. Then noticing Anahita's clothing, she said, "You look a little rough-and-tumble."

"I . . . I tripped," Anahita said, brushing the dirt off her skirt.

Her grandmother looked at her quizzically but said nothing more. Anahita hung the bunch of mullein from one of the rafters and went outside to help her father, who was building a pen for their livestock beside their tent. He looked up. His slight smile seemed to signal he might be in the mood for talking. "Baba, have you ever had a fight with someone and felt good about it afterward?"

Farhad glanced at her dirt-streaked skirt and raised an eyebrow. "Well . . ." he said, continuing to weave reeds into a sturdy fence, "this may not be what the mullah would like me to tell you, but yes." He grinned at her.

Anahita laughed as she picked up a few reeds to help him. His smile was the first he'd given her since the mullah agreed to her wedding riddle idea. Seeing him so cheerful, she decided to take a risk. "Baba, since the mullah says it is all right, will you tell the khan about my wishes for a wedding riddle when he comes this summer?" Anahita bit her lip when she saw her father's expression sour.

"Anahita, we've been through this before."

"But Baba, the mullah . . ."

"You consulted him without my knowing."

"Are you angry that I did not ask your permission?"

"The issue with the mullah is not one of *permission*. I've always encouraged you to speak with him about whatever might be on your mind. The issue is one of respect for that holy man. You led him to believe I approved of this wedding riddle. You failed to tell him that the khan, a well-received man in this province, a devout Muslim who gives generously of his money to the mosque, *and a person whom the mullah respects*, had made his intentions known to me of his wishes to marry you."

Anahita lowered her eyes, her head hanging. "But the mullah guessed . . ."

"That does not matter. *You* did not tell him. You were deceitful and impatient and thought only of yourself."

His words stung. *All I want is a choice*, Anahita thought.

"Baba, surely you can understand my despair?"

Anahita stared at nearby goats chewing on the ropes that held them fast and a lump swelled in her throat. She drew on an inner strength, on Sufi Rabi'a's strength, and she spoke again with words barely audible. "Surely you have met someone in your life who repulsed you. Would you want to spend every day of your years with that person?"

Her father looked up from his work and stared off into the distance.

"You wish to tether me to the khan like a goat. I am not refusing to marry, but I want to have some say in the matter. That is all. At least with a riddle, I'll know that whoever solves it will share my deepest sentiments."

Farhad said nothing. But it seemed to Anahita as she wiped her face with her sleeve and turned again to her fence building, that he had heard her at last.

In the days that followed, Anahita tried not to dwell on her wedding riddle nor think about the khan's pending visit. She helped her mother and grandmother build a coop near their tent for their small collection of chickens, which she fed each morning. Each afternoon she toggled the goats' necks together so they wouldn't run away as she collected their sweet, white milk. It was a treat each spring and summer for Anahita to make butter, something she missed in the fall and winter when their does rarely nursed.

In quiet moments, she set off on her own through the grassland to collect more mullein, chamomile, or *sprak* for her dyes. She thought about how these fields and flowers flourished in silence. "Let your tongue become the petal," her grandmother had often said to her. "In your stillness the music of the mountains will feed you."

Most evenings she gathered with the other women of her tribe to sew, knit, lace, and embroider. Shirin and Anahita's aunt often joined them. Ever since their fight, her cousin rarely spoke to Anahita, except to answer a direct question. On these evenings Anahita found herself remembering a discussion she'd had with her grandmother two months ago: "Perhaps Shirin would have liked more of your company during her courtship, Anahita. Your preoccupation with the dyemaster and the clothing cart has

robbed her of your friendship. Maybe she's sought compan-
ionship with the others because you have left little time for
her."

The sound of Shirin's knitting needles clicked in Anahita's
ears. *But why would I want to spend time with her now? She's so ornery.*

One day Farhad invited Anahita to ride into the mountains
with him to meet up with the tribe's scouts.

Seated on the horse behind her father, Anahita could see snow-
capped ridges filling the northen horizon—*Mountains with white kerchiefs,* she thought. Far in the distance glistened a lake.

"Oh, Baba. I could live in the mountains the year round. I
would not mind the snow. And that lake! Look at its blues."

"It is rightly named Sapphire Lake, is it not?"

"It is how I imagine the Caspian Sea. I am going to dye yarn
for my wedding *qali* indigo. Each time I look at it, it will remind
me of the sea, of my dream to go there."

"You are full of dreams. I suppose this is good. My father used
to tell me one day they might keep me alive."

Farhad took up the reins, signaling the horse to stop. He let
them fall slack, easing the strain on the bit in the horse's mouth.
"We've ridden up here not only to meet our scouts, but so that I
can explain something to you."

Anahita bit her lip and fidgeted with her head scarf.

"Look across the plain below us." Farhad's arm swept over the
expanse of high desert.

Her eyes followed his hand.

"Do you see where the two branches of the river flowing from the lake meet?"

"*Baleh*," Anahita nodded. It was so far, she could barely see the spot on the horizon.

"Just below that," Farhad said, "is Hasanabad."

Anahita imagined the mud homes, slanted minaret, and barley fields of their distant village.

"There are many, many tracts of land between where we stand on this mountain and Hasanabad. The tracts belong to different khans and landowners. The stretches of river within each tract of land are theirs as well. The *qanat*, the underground irrigation ditch that follows the river, is owned by the shah and regulated by his administration."

"Yes, I know this," Anahita said.

"What you do not realize is we live downstream and if any of these landowners become greedy with their water, it will not reach Hasanabad. Anytime they wish, they could divert the flow of the river with irrigation channels onto their own land. The *qanat* only supplies a third of our water. For the rest we rely on the good graces of the landowners upstream." Then turning to look at his daughter, he said, "It is our khan who sees that we don't dry up."

Anahita felt sick. *He hasn't even considered consenting to my wedding riddle*, she thought.

Farhad continued, "I hoped that by bringing you here, you would better understand my need to maintain his friendship."

Anahita gave him a halfhearted nod. She rubbed her fists

against her legs. *What I understand is that as the* kadkhuda's *daughter, my wishes are always second to the tribe's welfare.*

Farhad nudged their horse and headed for the ridgeline. They rode in silence. Anahita thought about dreams—dashed ones. Then she said, "Do you have a dream, Baba?"

Instead of responding, he jerked back on the reins to stop the horse. Anahita saw him anxiously studying the ground.

"What is it?"

Farhad swung his leg over the horse's neck and jumped down. Squatting, he poked at what looked to Anahita to be a small pile of fresh dung. Her father looked up at once, scanned the scrub oak, the outcroppings, and the valley below them.

Two men galloped toward them. They appeared to come from the eastern ridgeline of this chain of mountains, which ran from Tehran in the west toward Herat in the east. Scouts from her tribe.

"We've found further evidence of skirmishes with the Russians to the north. A calvary is heading this way," a scout called out, his horse tossing its head, prancing sideways before settling. "But there is no sign of anyone moving into the drainage where we are camped."

Farhad frowned. "We'd better pack up and move to the south of this range for the rest of the summer. Please ride on and tell our shepherds. Tell them also to be on the watch for a snow leopard. I'm afraid this dung belongs to no other."

The scouts nodded to Farhad then spun around and rode off. Pebbles flew beneath the hooves of their horses.

Anahita jumped from the horse and knelt next to the small pile of excrement—so fresh it steamed. It was strung together with what looked like the course white hair of an ibex or sheep, and the leaves of the thorny, pink-flowered plant that grew at that altitude. A small black hoof, like that of a lamb, protruded from it.

Even though she'd slaughtered animals for her own food, something about the undigested hoof made her grimace. "Baba, you've chased away a leopard before."

"It was long ago. *Bia*, let's be on our way."

As Farhad helped her mount the horse again, she said, "I want to learn how to chase one in case I must defend our flocks."

Farhad looked at her. "Someday you plan to fight off leopards? There will be no men in your life to do this for you?"

Anahita rolled her eyes and adjusted her head scarf. She held up her chin. "Please, Baba. Tell me how you did it."

Farhad mounted the steed, coaxed it to walk, and began the tale. "Early one morning when I was nearly eighteen years old, while everyone in our summer camp slept, I woke to an unusual kind of yowl. Three in a row. I knew they were not those of a wolf, nor any of our livestock. I sensed unrest among our herd and slipped out of the tent to look around, but saw nothing. Yet the horses, camels, sheep, and donkeys had drawn close together and moved in a loose circle, young ones in the middle.

"Taking my father's rifle, I walked the perimeter of the camp. Beyond the last tent, several strides away, I saw a large lump, lying still on the horizon, and a long golden tail moving back and forth. The snow leopard had taken down a filly and dragged it onto the plain."

Anahita fixed her eyes on the side of her father's face.

"I will never forget it—the sound or sight of it: the blood and bones and hooves and horse head, nearly ripped apart. But in a strange way I thought it beautiful—the leopard with its white underbelly and golden-spotted fur. The steam coming from its jaw in the early morning chill. How it looked up from its prey and watched me, its head lit by the first ray of sun over the peaks."

"You didn't shoot it, Baba," she said.

"No. I didn't feel threatened. It seemed the leopard didn't feel threatened by me either. She stood her ground and ate for what seemed like a long while, me leaning on my rifle like a staff. Then she dragged the carcass farther away, into the rocks, until I could no longer see it. For days we could hear her calling out to protect her stash of meat—a tremendous hissing."

"The poor filly!" Anahita said, seeing an image of a small horse hoof in place of the lamb's hoof sticking out of the fresh dung.

"Rather, the poor family who lost that filly," Farhad said. "They relied on alms from the rest of our tribe until their mare gave birth to another. That dead filly was a year's wages. So you see, Anahita," Farhad continued, "there is no secret to facing the snow leopard. I have only learned to keep my face turned to the invisible. There, something always awaits."

The snow leopard, too, reveals itself like a riddle—leaving behind clues of scat or carcasses. Anahita shuddered. *Just like the little creatures of the night whose tracks I discover in the morning sand.*

Nudging the horse to a trot, Farhad said, "The scouts have brought sad news—some of the best grazing is on the northern drainage of these mountains. For generations our people have camped here." He fell silent as they descended the summit. Both of them leaning back to keep their balance on the horse as it dropped forward beneath them, the stallion slipping every so often on loose stones. Anahita scanned the horizon for leopards.

"You asked me if I have dreams," Farhad said. "I have three: that there will be peace in this land, that the people I love will keep their health for the length of their lives, and that you, my sweet daughter, will marry someone who will care for you as deeply as I."

Mating Calls

Anahita's tribe packed its belongings and crossed over a high pass in the mountains to a plateau where the animals found fresh grass to eat. Here they might be safe from the Russians. Days flew by like the birds—geese, herons, and curlews—making their way south from the Caspian Sea to Arabia and Africa. Nights frosted. Mating calls of oxen and sheep echoed in the valley. A bull and his harem frolicked near a shepherd's tent.

On a cool evening at their new campsite, still safely inside the Afshars' traditional grazing lands, several men, women, and children gathered in clusters around a fire as Dariyoush, his brother Mehdi, and others made music with *santurs* and lutes. Anahita noticed how attractive Dariyoush looked leaning against the saddle he had tossed on the ground. On this night, when the moon cast a clean line between the plains and the shadow of the mountains, he seemed more than his everyday self. She admired the fine beard he wore now, and the angles of his face, chiseled like the rocks on the moraine field above them.

A chilly wind hummed. Anahita pulled her cloak about her and watched Dariyoush's fingers strum the strings of his instrument. These fingers that healed lambs this summer, would mend threadbare carpets this winter, matching new threads to old, preserving the legacy of their people as he worked.

She admired his skills, how he could pick an injured lamb out of a flock of hundreds or tend to any animal's problem: a thorn embedded in a hoof, sores caused by rubbing panniers, or less noticeable problems such as the wheeze in the breath of her favorite ewe, Tayebeh, who had followed her home as a lamb from her cousin Shirin's flock. Dariyoush knew exactly how much grain to feed her so that she did not gasp for air.

The notes he played now seemed to Anahita to have a hint of love, a hint of longing. As if the melody asked a question of her. For a minute she was in the painted cave again, swept up in his arms.

When Shirin left the circle by the fire, Anahita watched her walking two steps behind her husband. He faced ahead, as if he didn't know she followed. *I can't imagine going to live with my husband's family*, Anahita thought. *I love my own too much.*

She thought of the playful glances her parents often exchanged, and of the whispers and the rustle of bedding on nights they did not fall right to sleep. She wondered if it was like that for Shirin and her husband. Anahita felt a pang of jealousy. Shirin did in fact know what it meant to be a grown-up woman, what it was like to be intimate with a man. *I am not ready for this*, Anahita thought. *It all seems so frightening.* Whether or not she would be allowed to have this riddle contest, at least with everyone's deliberation she had bought herself time. Time to belong only to herself.

Anahita got up to turn in for the night. Looking once more at Dariyoush, she caught his eye. *Did he wink or was it a flicker of firelight across his face?* Confused and yet elated, she hurried away.

The next morning, not long after the mullah chanted the *azan*, Anahita stood outside feeding the hens, scattering as many thoughts of Dariyoush's wink, and the man from Mashhad's smile, as she did handfuls of grain. She said to her grandmother, who kneaded the day's bread nearby, "Do you think it would be wise for me to marry someone from outside of our tribe? Someone whose family we do not know?"

Maman Bozorg paused to wipe her doughy fingers on her tunic, then took hold of Anahita's hands. "This idea of marriage for love is no better or no worse than the customary one. Both may bring happiness and sadness. The choice, it seems, is between the familiar and the unknown. And my dear, ever since you could toddle, you have seemed happiest when pushing your boundaries."

"So you do not think my riddle idea is a bad one?"

Before her grandmother could answer, they noticed Dariyoush's father approaching with a stranger, who led a horse bearing a large sack. "This is a courier of the khan, here to speak with Kadkhuda Farhad," he said to Maman Bozorg as he tied the man's horse to the fence of the goat pen, and the messenger lifted down the sack.

"Please come this way," Anahita's grandmother said, showing the men into the family tent.

Anahita wondered if she should follow them. Instead she walked quietly over to the side of the tent and listened. The man and her father exchanged pleasantries, and then the messenger said, "The khan asks in particular after your daughter, Anahita. He has sent a gift for her."

Anahita could hear the sound of rustling and then her mother's gasp of delight.

Gift? Anahita shuddered. *If Baba accepts this gift, will my fate be settled? Will I have to marry the khan?*

The man continued, "Also, the khan asks me to tell you that he will arrive tomorrow with an esteemed guest. He hopes that you will welcome him."

"Of course," Farhad replied.

Mojdeh emerged from the tent with bedding and *gelims* for airing. When she saw that Anahita had been listening in, she said, "Come away with me, daughter. We will leave your father with his guest."

Glancing back at the tent, Anahita reluctantly followed her mother to the goat pen, where they could drape the rugs over the reed fence to beat them.

"Why does the khan send us a messenger, Maman, to tell us he is coming? Does he want a carpet rolled out? And what does the messenger mean about his 'esteemed guest'? Who is he bringing with him?"

"The courier brought you a very nice gift from the khan," Mojdeh said. "A bolt of purple silk."

"Purple silk! What am I to make from that? A skirt that saddles will chafe? That will be pummeled by sand or splattered with dung? It's bad enough we have to help put up that huge tent of his every summer that he hardly uses, then lug it to each new camp just so he can make his grand appearances." Anahita took hold of two corners of the large blanket that Mojdeh held. They each took a step backward as the fabric unfolded, and shook the sand from it high into the air.

"And what about the summer we had to wash the gigantic carpet he brought for his tent? It alone weighed down one camel. It took eight men to haul the wet rug from the stream. All because of a little spill."

"Anahita, you know how horrible fermented mare's milk smells when it soaks into wool," Mojdeh said. "The khan deserves respect. Did he not stop another khan upriver from diverting the water from our stream to his own estate? He works hard so that we may pass through private lands with our animals to reach these mountains."

"That's what he might have us believe. He's not loyal to our ways. I can see it in his eyes, hear it in his voice."

Mojdeh folded the blanket and reached for another.

"The khan knows Baba is the most respected in our tribe," Anahita continued. "He needs him to help keep peace between our people and the landowners. We Afshars are all bandits in the city people's eyes, aren't we?"

"I'm not so sure everyone believes we are bandits," Mojdeh said. "I'll agree there is something about the khan that is troubling. He's more likely to think with his fists than his head. But perhaps I mistake one thread for the whole carpet."

"There. You see, Maman. I'm not crazy. You don't trust him either."

"I did not say I didn't trust him," her mother corrected.

Beating one of the *gelims* with a stick, Anahita said, "Don't you think the khan looks much like a bullock?"

"Anahita," her mother said, sternly.

"Surely he does—his big frame, his large nostrils, his sagging jowls."

Her mother frowned at her.

"And what about the peacock feather he wears?"

Mojdeh turned her head. "I will listen to no more. Surely the Compassionate and Merciful will come to your aid. You are quick to judge and are harsh on the khan."

The two finished their chore in silence.

That evening, eavesdropping once more through the tent's weave, but this time from inside, Anahita heard the last part of a discussion outside between her parents and grandmother.

"Rumors of this wedding riddle have already traveled from caravan to caravan, teahouse to teahouse. Why would any man seek for a wife a young woman bold enough to hold a . . . a wedding riddle contest? If it weren't for the khan, she might have no suitors," Farhad said.

Anahita felt as if she might explode. In her foul mood, she reached for and unwound the bolt of silk from the khan. The fabric slipped between her fingers. *Just like the khan,* she thought, *slippery.* She picked up a pair of scissors.

Farhad continued, "And then, there's the chance the khan will take back his offer if he hears of this riddle idea. In that case, a contest *may be* the only answer. We will have to hunt up a husband for her."

"It's unthinkable," Mojdeh said. "And it's impious to change tradition."

"Maybe so, but how does this 'riddle contest' fly in the face of tradition?" Maman Bozorg asked. She moved in front of the tent door, into Anahita's view. Winding yarn onto her spindle, she continued speaking. "Anahita is not doing anything against anyone or any custom. Just as every other woman in this tribe has done after reaching puberty, she will weave a dowry and marry a man with the mullah's blessing."

"But to marry a man we haven't chosen and know nothing about?" Mojdeh said. "This is not traditional."

"The two of you are allowing your fears to muddle your seeing." Maman Bozorg spoke loudly above the noise of the hens squawking and clucking. Anahita grinned at what her grandmother said. She covered her mouth with one hand and opened her ears wide.

"Mojdeh, you have convinced yourself Anahita will marry a distant stranger and you'll never see her again." Giving her spindle a swift spin, her grandmother said, "And Farhad, you are focused solely on your responsibility to marry her to the right man. Neither of you can see this game for what it is."

Maman Bozorg pulled a sliver of grass from her thread. "Understand that Anahita is not asking you to relinquish the selection of the suitors, but merely to widen the pool. I think the mullah recognizes this, too."

Finally, someone sees it my way, Anahita thought. *Now's the time to fight for what I want.*

Mojdeh appeared at the tent door, kicked off her sandals, and stepped inside. Her face first showed a look of surprise, then her eyebrows knit together when she noticed Anahita slicing into the silk. "What are you doing with that lovely fabric?"

"Sharing it." Anahita had decided to make each woman in her family, first and second cousins included, a kerchief from the khan's gift. *Maybe Shirin will think it's a gift of reconciliation after our scuffle,* she thought. From the glint in her mother's eye, she knew Mojdeh understood that her intentions to share the wealth weren't entirely pure. Anahita could not wait to see the look on the khan's face when he saw that she had cut his expensive bolt of silk into one hundred head-sized swatches.

The next morning the khan arrived. With him was a bespectacled man in good shoes. The tribe had erected a tent for the khan the day before, and Farhad was there now, meeting with the leader and his "esteemed guest."

Leading two goats to water, Anahita made a point of walking by the khan's tent, where she saw the three men sitting under the shade of an awning. The khan's small cat, which he kept on a leash, was curled up at his feet. The men spoke over cups of tea. Anahita noticed Farhad watching her. The young man sneaked a glance at her, also, without her father or the khan noticing.

She wore one of the purple kerchiefs she'd made the night before, which she knew stood out boldly against the dull sky. The khan stared in her direction longer than he should have by any standard of discretion. His hair had turned mostly gray since she'd last seen him. Every now and then he would feed his cat a few morsels of mutton, letting it lick the grease from his fingers.

Anahita heard the words: tutor, Mashhad, marriage.

Tutor! she thought. *School? The khan is proposing to marry me and hire me a tutor . . . That young man must be a teacher.* How she wanted to learn to read and write! But not to please the khan.

Pretending to fix a goat's harness, she heard the khan say something to her father that she understood well, "You stroke my back, I'll stroke yours." Coming from him, she didn't like the sound of it.

Anahita spent the rest of the day spinning wool, an activity she could do anywhere and that thus lent itself to eavesdropping on the visitors. Unfortunately, she gleaned no more information about the khan and his guest, not even from her mother. However, that evening, before the khan retired to his tent, Mojdeh insisted that Anahita go with her to thank him for the silk.

"The silk?" the khan said, a blank look on his face.

Hadn't he noticed half the tribe wearing it? Anahita wondered.

Looking at her scarf the khan said, "Oh, yes. The silk. You are most welcome to it, my little *dokhtar*." He reached out as if to finger the side of her face, the tufts of gray hair on his knuckles still streaked with brown. Anahita turned her cheek. She hated how he had called her "my little girl," as if she were his pet. Tightening her lips, she fought back the words *I'm not your anything*.

The khan looked at her head scarf again, and then from one purple-scarved woman in the camp to the next, before settling his eyes on Mojdeh's black kerchief. A wave of realization seemed to ripple across his large features. Anahita wrinkled her nose, understanding that he had not known what gift his messengers had sent on his behalf.

She thought she noticed the khan's jaw tighten. "I see you have already put my gift to good use," he said, his leer fading. She had to admit, he really wasn't quite as ugly as a bullock. Except for the puffy circles around his eyes, he was somewhat distinguished looking, as her grandmother had once said.

"Good evening," the khan said to Anahita and her mother before stepping back into his tent.

As the tent flap opened Anahita's eyes met the teacher's. *They're so blue!* No one in her tribe had blue eyes. She noticed he was about her height and his hair held an unusual red hue. *Though maybe it is just the lighting inside the tent*, she thought, *with the red carpet and all*. The tutor pressed his palm to his breast and bowed. His humble gesture of submission to her made Anahita feel special. He then leaned sideways to peer out at her as the tent cloth began to close.

A sheep bellowed as she and her mother walked back to their tent. Anahita whispered, "The khan could have at least introduced us to his guest, Maman. Do you think Baba will agree to let him tutor me?"

"Wouldn't that mean marrying the khan?" Mojdeh asked.

As if on cue, a camel moaned. The animal held the tinny-sounding hum for so long, it seemed as though it was incredulous at the mere thought of such a possibility. Anahita and her mother laughed.

The Ultimatum

That evening Anahita's family drank tea inside their tent, the flame of a butter lamp swaying right and left. A soft pile of purple scarves—leftovers Anahita would save for the clothing cart—shimmered in the dim light. Shirin had just left, after having stopped in to thank Anahita for her scarf. "It was good of you to think of me," she had said. "I needed a new scarf." Shirin declined an invitation to tea, mumbling some excuse that involved her husband, which Anahita didn't listen to because she was still getting over the shock that her cousin had come in the first place.

With his eyes mostly on Anahita, Farhad said to the three of them, "The khan has offered to hire Anahita a tutor, should I give him her hand."

"The blue-eyed . . . I mean, the young man who came with the khan?" Anahita asked. "Why did the khan bring him here?"

"I believe he brought him up here to convince me I'd be a fool not to take him up on his offer. The tutor is a polite and intelligent fellow. He is willing to instruct you even though you do not know your basics in language or mathematics."

Anahita felt a rush of blood to her ears and a stab of pain in her chest brought on by a mix of longing, sadness, and frustration. Physical signs of her biggest wish in life: to learn. She also felt insulted. *How could I weave, if I couldn't count? And my carpets are full of a language of their own. Full of stories—full of me. Surely my wedding qali will convince Baba of this. One day I will meet someone who sees that my rugs are more than the sum of their knots! A kindred spirit who will understand that the riddle I weave does not require words, but that every aspect of my carpet has meaning, clues.*

In a soft voice, her father continued, "Anahita, this is more than many suitors would offer."

"In other words you ask me to accept the khan's offer—this 'slap in the face'—rather than wait for a 'hoped-for sweet'?"

Her father looked away. "If I refuse the khan, he will no longer work on our tribe's behalf. As I've said before, our water and migratory privileges are at stake." Farhad took off his turban, ran his hand through his hair, and put it back on. "He is building the framework for a parliament. Our people would be lost without him. None of us could find our way around the halls of the provincial *divan* in Mashhad. Few of us read."

"He has offered you no camels but given you an ultimatum?" Mojdeh asked. "What kind of bride price is that?"

"I told you he is not loyal to us, Maman." Anahita spit the sentence out with more venom than she intended. She didn't think the khan had the strength to threaten her father. She drew her legs closer to her body and moved another cushion behind her back.

"My daughter is worth one thousand camels!" Mojdeh said. "I have never seen this stingy side of the khan before."

"Nor this impatient side of him," Farhad said.

"Perhaps because until now he's never wanted anything of yours so badly," Maman Bozorg said, squeezing Anahita's shoulders. Her words seemed lost on Farhad.

Could I live with those jowls? The sickening thought settled into Anahita's mind and stomach at the same time. *Baba could keep his position . . . I'd be educated.* For a minute she pictured herself sitting next to the tutor as he pointed to an exotic city on a map. But her daydream, and this burst of compassion for her father, dissipated as quickly as they arose. She would sooner die than marry the khan. The only alternative was her riddle idea. And she knew her grandmother would stand by her.

Anahita looked at her elders. Her mother held her gaze. Her father looked into his tea as he stirred it. Her grandmother was expressionless, as she formed lace with a needle and thread.

"Baba, did you mention the wedding contest?"

"It would have fallen on deaf ears. The man knows what he wants and will stop at nothing to get it. His target this year is you, my daughter."

And perhaps if Farhad hadn't said these two small words, *my daughter*, maybe the sweet angels' voices inside Maman Bozorg's head would not have tingled, she later told Anahita. Now her grandmother rested her hands in her lap. "You would

trade your daughter for water rights? Allow a self-satisfying, bul-
lying man *who has lost three wives,*" she added for emphasis, which
nearly made Anahita giggle aloud, "to take from you what you
hold dearest?"

Mojdeh looked at Maman Bozorg, at Anahita, and then at
Farhad. To Anahita's delight her mother reached for one of the
silk scarves from the pile. Mojdeh slipped off the black one she
wore, and pulled on the purple one.

For the rest of the summer the days grew shorter and the
evening air brisker. Anahita spun while her father and Dariyoush
tended to the affairs of their camp. The spindle Dariyoush gave
her grew smooth and tawny from her touch and from the natural oils of the wool. Thinking of him, she wondered, *Are his parents keeping him from me?* He seemed busier than usual with work for
his own family.

In spite of the khan's threat, she felt that her father's mood had
lifted, and the riddles flowed between them like a mountain
stream. She began to believe he would agree to her riddle contest.

Before falling asleep one night, Anahita gazed at the thin,
tilted moon that shone through the tent's windscreen. Her grandmother snored softly beside her in the space they shared—cur-
tained for privacy—across the tent from her parents. In her mind
Anahita heard the snippets of conversation she had had with the
friendly man in Mashhad, and which she'd long braided together
into a favorite memory. *Forgive me if I've startled you. Merchant, do you
feel this* gelim *speaks of Persian life? This carpet can have only half the per-*

spective of an asymmetrical work . . . Thinking of him, everything inside her tent seemed to glow in the light of his smile: the copper pots dangling from the rafters, the dried flowers hanging upside down beside them, the back of Maman Bozorg's head. *Will I find him in Mashhad when we return to our village?* That a man like him would solve the riddle she would weave in her *qali* . . . She would keep praying—and pleading—for such a chance.

Weeks after the khan and his guest left, by the first autumn snow, Anahita had one hundred skeins of undyed yarn prepared for her wedding rug. No sooner had she finished her spinning than Farhad announced to his family and those who had gathered round their fire pit that a few of the scouts' horses were lame and the migration back to their winter village would be postponed by at least a week.

"Does this mean we will skip going to Mashhad?" Anahita asked.

"I know you look forward to Mashhad. We shall see. The winds have been blustery. It could mean storms at this elevation. Sand or snow, or even worse, a mix of both. Either can be disorienting."

Anahita looked north, east, and west. She could barely see the mountains through the sandy haze.

"It may make better sense for us to head south to lower pastures, and then directly to our village, rather than south and east to Mashhad. We will save three days' journey. The men can travel to Mashhad later with the goods we have to sell," Farhad said.

I must visit Mashhad, Anahita thought. *I've got to speak with the carpet merchant—to ask him if he knows anything about my new friend . . . my ashena.*

"Baba, can we not at least try to travel to Mashhad when the horses are well? A little dirt in the air is nothing."

"You forget that among the tribe are many who are less sturdy than you. And what of our livestock? Animals are just as fond of a comfortable path as are we." Farhad tore an old piece of clothing into strips for horse bandages as he talked. "Of all people, you should understand this. Your favorite sheep wheezes from the debris in the grain she eats. The scouts will borrow other stallions and we will ride ahead this afternoon to check that the route is safe. I will reconsider in a few days, when I return."

Anahita felt her hope snatched from beneath her like a carpet, its dust billowing in her face. Frustrated, she decided to wash clothes, and went inside her tent to collect the soiled items into an animal pannier. After she gathered the laundry, she went back outside and untethered her donkey, pausing to watch Dariyoush, Mehdi, and their father, the bonesetter, working nearby. The men were wrapping the strips of cloth from Farhad's old tunic around the legs of the scouts' lame stallions. Then they walked the animals in long, wide circles. Each lap of the horses seemed to take an eternity. Would they never gallop again?

Blinking against flying particles in the air, Anahita set off for the stream. She watched the parched soil from the gullies swell in waves of yellow and gold against the mountains. Sand collected in her nose, ears, and under the rim of her head scarf. She was sick of the wind, sick of the summer camp, sick of everything.

"Time crawls like a scorpion across the desert," she said to her donkey. At the stream the animal slurped long and loud. Anahita sat on the gravelly bank out of the wind, deciding not to wash her clothes. If she hung them to dry back at camp, they'd only collect sand. She tossed rocks into the water, one after another after another.

Her donkey roamed nearly to the other side of the stream before she noticed. Wading into the gently running water, she took a step, slipped on a slimy stone, and tumbled backward onto the streambank, where she hit her head on a rock. Her vision went dark.

She opened her eyes to Dariyoush kneeling beside her, his head resting ever so close to her face and chest as he listened and felt for her faint puffs of breath.

"You gave us a fright," he said, as he glanced over at Shirin and Mojdeh crouched beside him.

"Are you all right, Anahita?" her mother asked, cupping her daughter's cheek in her hand. Feeling her forehead for fever, she said, "Let's try and sit you up." Mojdeh and Dariyoush lifted Anahita, supporting her back.

Anahita moaned. "My head hurts."

Her mother motioned to Dariyoush to lay her back down.

"What happened?" Shirin asked. "Your donkey wandered back to camp without you."

"I don't know." Anahita struggled to remember. Shirin soaked a scarf in the cold stream and placed it on her cousin's forehead. "Thanks, Shirin. It feels good." Then feeling a pain shooting up from her foot, Anahita said, "I think I've hurt my left leg."

"May I?" Dariyoush asked, looking at Mojdeh for permission to examine her daughter. Mojdeh nodded. Dariyoush felt along the back of Anahita's head, neck, and spine for broken bones. Then he knelt at her feet. With both hands he pressed his fingers along the outer edge of her injured foot. "Does this hurt?"

"Not really," she said as he palpated the bones and slid his fingers below her ankle.

She flinched. "That hurts."

"I think it's sprained. Allow me to check a few more things." He held her heel in his hand and moved the ball of her foot forward and back, side to side. Then he gently pulled and pushed her foot to and away from her knee, as if trying to loosen it from her leg. "Everything seems intact."

Anahita winced. "Aren't you supposed to be healing the horses?"

"They can wait," he said looking into her eyes for the first time.

Does he really mean that? she thought.

He examined her shin. "It seems nothing is broken. But your ankle is the size of a melon," he said, running his fingers over the bruised and swollen skin.

His calloused hands felt soothing and comforting. *Do the sheep and horses feel this from his touch?* she wondered.

"Let's try and sit up again, Anahita. We should get that ankle into the cold water. It will help the swelling go down."

Anahita held the bump on the back of her head as she sat up and scooted on her bottom to the edge of the stream.

"I'll go and prepare your bed," Mojdeh said. "I think rest will help. It's a good thing our caravan has been delayed. You're not fit to travel."

Shirin and Dariyoush sat with Anahita as she soaked her ankle in the stream. It was the first pleasant moment—without any bickering—that she had spent with her cousin for some time. Anahita listened quietly while Shirin and Dariyoush talked about healing lame legs. She knew her cousin would enjoy a chance to learn these skills and felt bad that Shirin's marriage put an end to these dreams. *My marriage will not end my dream of becoming the dyemaster's apprentice,* Anahita vowed to herself.

When Anahita's ankle had numbed from the cold water, Dariyoush lifted her into his arms.

Shirin collected the clothing Anahita had brought for scrubbing. "You were planning to wash on a day like this?"

Anahita hadn't the strength to answer.

"Sometimes chores can be as good an excuse as any to collect your thoughts, or toss a few good stones into the stream," Dariyoush said.

Anahita looked at Dariyoush. *Had he been watching her?*

He carried Anahita to her tent and kicked off his sandals to join the sloppy row beside the door. He stood in the flapway while Anahita removed her sand-filled scarf and shook it. Mojdeh came to help Dariyoush lay her daughter on her bed. They made Anahita as comfortable as they could.

Turning to leave, Dariyoush said, "I'll be back with a splint for you."

"Thank you," Anahita said. "Won't you have something to eat with us first?" she pointed to the collection of fruit, nuts, and bread on the nearby plate.

"A date is all I need right now." Reaching for one, he winked at her—*For real this time,* she thought. "Keep your leg elevated," he said, then left.

For the next two days, grains of sand blew into Anahita's tent with every blast of wind. Hours filled her teacup. Were it not for Dariyoush's visits, she thought she would die of boredom.

"Maman, when will Baba return?" she said, as she picked up her embroidery and stabbed the needle into her handiwork.

"Gently, Anahita. No need to get exasperated. Your ankle will heal soon."

"I just wish I hadn't hurt myself, and I wish that this sand-storm would pass." She left out that she also wished to be on the road to Mashhad.

"There will be other visits to the bazaar," Mojdeh said, as if reading her mind. Some of Anahita's cousins and aunts, who had gathered in their tent that morning to darn socks and embroider, assured Anahita of this as well.

"But I'll be married by then." Anahita's words snapped like the wind-blown tent, flapping with the angry gusts.

Mojdeh raised an eyebrow at her daughter as she threaded a needle.

Anahita pretended not to notice. She couldn't sort out her feelings. In an odd way, she liked that she was injured—Dariyoush had never been more attentive.

"Anahita's mad because for once something's working against her," Shirin said.

"And you have no wish to visit the market this autumn, Shirin?" Anahita said, but thought, *She knows there's something I'm not telling her. If I confided, would she use it against me?*

Anahita's aunt looked at Shirin, and began to collect her things. "Perhaps it's time we go."

When Anahita's relatives left the tent, Dariyoush announced himself and stepped inside. He held a newly carved cane in his hand. Kneeling next to Anahita, he lay the knotted stick on the carpet beside her and adjusted the cushion beneath her leg.

"You must not let this splint work itself loose. Here, I will fix it for you."

Dariyoush wound a clean rag around the piece of sapling he had cut to fit under her heel and run up either side of her ankle. Anahita noticed her mother watching Dariyoush over her shoulder as she selected herbs from the bunches that hung in the rafters.

"There," he said. "The bruises are lightening up; they're nearly yellow now."

He seems to have forgotten the cane, Anahita thought.

"Dariyoush," Mojdeh said, "I don't know what we would do without you. We appreciate that you are treating Anahita so carefully. Especially when you are busy with the horses."

"We can't have anyone lame when we set out for Mashhad."

He looked at Anahita. "I should probably take you to the stream to ice your foot again today. One last time, for good measure." Her face lit up. *Anything to get out of the tent, or to be with him.*

"Did you say Mashhad?" Anahita asked. "Is Baba back? Did he say we will go?"

"No, but I know how much you enjoy going there. The sooner you and the horses are healed, the better the chances."

Picking up the cane he said, "Maybe this will help."

"Dariyoush," Anahita said, taking it from his hands. "Look at all the birds and flowers you've carved on it! Maman, Maman Bozorg, come see. I will try it out right now." She started to push herself up.

"Just a minute," Dariyoush said. "You better wait a day or two. Your foot is not ready to support your weight. The cane will bear some of it, when the time comes."

"You will see, Dariyoush. My recovery will be swift! Your work will not be wasted on me."

Squatting beside her, he rested an elbow on one knee. Then he ran a finger up the sole of her bandaged foot and across the smooth skin on the tips of her toes. He said, "I don't consider helping you as work."

Anahita's foot tingled. Her heart soared.

The sun never seemed to set that day, or if it did, no one could tell through the dust. Just before falling asleep Anahita said to her grandmother, "I have been feeling happy one minute, sad the next, and at other times hopeful for something I can't seem to grasp hold of."

In a tone that meant more than the words, her grandmother said, "I think the tempest outside tells all." Anahita's eyes had been closed, so it seemed as if her grandmother's voice came from out of the squall.

The sandstorm went about its business, erasing traces of Anahita's tribe: swallowing broken scrub the goats had chewed, tiny grains of feed the chickens had missed, and the hoofprints the sheep had left. Soon the whole face of the land would be changed and cleansed, every line.

Autumn Market News

"Baba, what are you doing with that parchment?"

"Announcing your wedding riddle contest!" He grinned as he hammered a thin nail into the message board at the entrance to the *caravanserai*.

"Here?" Anahita's eyes darted in all directions. "You are announcing this to the entire city of Mashhad? It seems so impersonal, so . . . public!" Gripping her mother's arm she asked, "Why didn't you warn me? I thought we'd handle this privately—from home." A wave of nausea filled her stomach.

"Warn you? Isn't this what you've been waiting for? We wanted the announcement to be a surprise. We've made smaller parchments to post about the market as well. Look, aren't they lovely? Maman Bozorg and I pressed wildflowers into them, and the mullah's calligraphy is written with walnut-brown ink."

"You've made *others*? How many?"

"Dozens."

"Dozens?"

"Anahita," Farhad said, "I'm afraid that the men I had hoped might ask for your hand wouldn't dream of a woman daring enough to test her wit against theirs. Not even Dariyoush's parents have approached me. Opening a contest up to the whole province of Khurasan will surely draw a few good candidates."

"I see," Anahita whispered. *That's why Dariyoush has never asked me about my wedding riddle.* She cinched her new *rusari* more snugly about her face and lowered her gaze from the onlookers—all of them men. Even though she wore an all-concealing *chador*, nothing could have prepared her for how naked she felt.

"This is unheard of!" the khan said, tearing the oversized piece of parchment off the message board and holding it in Farhad's face. He read it aloud as a small crowd gathered:

> The Kadkhuda Farhad of the Province Khurasan
> cordially invites suitable suitors
> to participate in a Test of Wit
> for the hand of his daughter
>
> The Seventeenth Night after Nooruz
>
> Selection of suitors to be held the day before,
> reliable references requested

"Have you lost your mind? You *know* of my wishes to have

Anahita for my wife, and that I will provide for her. I do not understand why an arrangement wasn't settled months ago."

"This contest is Anahita's wish. I gave her my word," Farhad said.

"Have you forgotten what we discussed?" The khan struck the parchment with the backs of his fingers. "Your decision to hold this 'test of wit' shows you are not thinking clearly. Perhaps it is time for me to look for your replacement."

Farhad squared his body with the khan's.

"You are a fool, Farhad. This contest will bring to your doorstep all the riffraff coming through these parts." The khan forced out a laugh. He tossed the announcement on the ground and stomped on it.

"With due respect, dear Khan," Farhad said, picking up the parchment and brushing it off. "Most men in this land need merely to bargain for wives and could arrange a marriage in their sleep. Half the time their relatives do it for them. Only the strongest will rise to this occasion."

A faint, smug smile spread across the Khan's face. "Do you have the consent of the civil court for this?" Farhad looked at him blankly. The khan sneered and thought, *I'll see to it that he never gets it.*

The khan stared long and hard at Farhad, realizing that the *kad-khuda* hadn't taken his ultimatum seriously. He looked at each and every young tribesman standing behind Farhad, who suddenly busied themselves swatting unseen flies, kicking pebbles, and adjusting saddlebags that did not need to be adjusted.

Farhad spoke. "In six months Anahita's *qali* will be complete.

At that time you may line up with all the rest of her suitors and test your wit against theirs." Pausing slightly, as if to give the rest of what he had to say more emphasis, he continued, "And hers."

The khan's face reddened. "Suitors? What other suitors?"

Farhad tilted his head toward the group of young men. "And more will come from Abadi-eh-Golab village. The odds are quite high."

Disgusted, the khan waved a dismissive hand. He brushed past Farhad and plunged into Mashhad's maze of streets toward the office of the *mujtahad*, the jurists of the civil court.

News of Anahita's wedding riddle spread through the Mashhad bazaar like a brushfire—glowing even in the most pious of enclaves. "She will marry *only* the man who can solve the riddle she weaves into her carpet," clerics and merchants whispered alike.

When the gossip had reached the carpet merchant whom Anahita visited before her summer migration, a wistful gleam filled his eyes. "Ah, yes. The pretty one from Hasanabad—the village of my best carpet repairers—who comes each spring and autumn and asks so many questions. She would be quite the catch!"

The carpet merchant's stall looked different to Anahita. *But this must be the right one,* she thought as she limped near, knowing it was just past the copper-pot booth and beside the one selling sticky, fly-ridden candy.

Leaning on her cane, she said to the merchant whose back was to her, "Excuse me, sir."

When he turned around, Anahita recognized him at once: his large curling mustache and devious-looking grin, probably formed from years of cheating his customers. She thought he would recognized her, too—after all she'd been stopping by his booth for the past few years—but he only seemed to stare at her cane.

"Is there anything I may show you, miss?" he finally said with his broadest smile.

"No, thank you, but I am curious about someone," she said, silently thanking Allah for settling the dust storm and allowing her this visit to Mashhad. Then she lost her courage to ask. *Maybe I shouldn't do this,* she thought, knowing she risked publicly shaming herself and her parents.

"I'm sorry?" the merchant asked, apparently not hearing her.

"Yes," she decided to say. "I'd like to see your carpets made with synthetic dyes."

"For you, anything." The merchant turned his back and sorted through a stack of *gabbehs,* loosely woven rugs.

Anahita bit her lower lip and closed her eyes. *I've got to ask him. We leave tomorrow. It's my last chance.*

The merchant held up a small rug, his knobby elbows sticking out behind it on both sides. "Here is a splendid *qaliche.* It would be most lovely for your dowry."

"My dowry? How do you know about this?"

"Forgive me. It was merely a fantasy, I mean, a slip of the tongue, I mean . . . uh . . . a coincidence . . ."

Just then, a man wearing a turban and several women and girls enveloped in black *chadors* came to the stall carrying a large pile carpet. The merchant excused himself from Anahita to help the family. Anahita overheard the wife complain. "We wish to exchange this carpet. Its colors have faded in the sun. We would like a carpet made with natural dyes." Even though the merchant ushered the group to the side of his shop, she could still hear him say, "I'll make you a deal."

While he spoke with his dissatisfied customers, Anahita once again mustered the courage to ask her question. She knew her mother would soon finish at the metalsmith's booth next door. As the family searched through the carpets for a different rug, Anahita said softly to the merchant, "Last spring I came to your booth and a man—taller and older than I—inquired about your carpets. He asked you if you believed one of your rugs made with synthetic dyes spoke of Persian life. Do you remember him?" She examined the merchant's face with hopeful eyes.

The skinny man stroked his chin. "So many people travel the Silk Road, *dokhtar*. You ask me to remember just one?"

Anahita looked at the ground. She had been afraid he would answer her as he did.

"But I seem to remember one gentlemen. Yes, yes," he said, holding one finger in the air. "The man said his name was . . . hmm. A strong name it was. Ar . . . er, uh . . ." A sly smile came across merchant's stubbled face, and he stopped himself mid-sentence. "I cannot seem to recall his name. But I believe he said he was from Marv. Or perhaps it was Bukhara . . . or maybe it was Samarkand."

Marv? Samarkand? So far away! Anahita thought. She uttered her thanks and turned from the stall.

Caught in the wave of shoppers that seemed to carry them along, Mojdeh, Maman Bozorg, and Dariyoush approached Anahita. Her mother jingled a weft comb high above her head, so Anahita would recognize them among all the black *chadors*. Anahita squeezed through the crowd and hugged her mother. "Oh, you bought me one! Thank you, Maman." Taking it and jingling it herself, she turned to her grandmother. "Have you ever seen such a comb?"

Her grandmother smiled and tilted her head back, no.

The four made their way to the spice market with Anahita leaning on her cane now and again for relief. Entering the spice merchant's dim alcove, she was overcome by a strong waft of cardamom. Shelves filled with glass jars lined both sides of this shop from floor to ceiling, some collecting more dust than others and together emitting every scent imaginable.

Here Anahita would find the other dyestuffs her granduncle would need, those unobtainable on their migration route. She knew he would want her to buy indigo because it didn't grow near Hasanabad. He would also be low on madder and cochineal, roots and insects that gave red dyes. At one time he had grown his own madder, but harvesting and pulverizing its roots became too strenuous for his ailing back.

Another customer asked the shopkeeper, "Do you have any willow sticks and sour cherry tea?"

The merchant, Anahita, her mother, grandmother, and

Dariyoush all took a step back from the woman. Everyone recognized the cure for malaria and diarrhea! After helping the poor woman, the spice merchant turned to Anahita.

"Two sacks of madder root, please," she said. "But not these two sacks here on display. They aren't ground well enough and will not yield a strong dye. Have you any other?" Anahita's request brought a grimace to the merchant's face, who she knew wished to sell the sacks on display. But soon he smiled, as Anahita knew he would, when he considered the quantity she ordered and the price it would fetch.

She noticed Dariyoush watching her as she moved through the spice shelves: shaking jars, smelling herbs, fingering acorns. It made her uneasy. Since when did she feel self-conscious around him? She felt a phantom tingle, the touch of his finger running up her foot.

"A dozen stones, please, of your bluest indigo, twelve dozen walnuts, and let's see—" her eyes met Dariyoush's—"five scoops of cochineal." As the spice merchant repeated aloud what he had scribbled on a sign over the bin of insects, SPECIAL: 3 RIALS A SCOOP, Anahita's eyes stayed with Dariyoush's.

When she looked away, she noticed a vase of fall-blooming, purple crocuses that the merchant had placed on a shelf beside bowls of crocus petals and saffron powder. Twirling a finger among the flower tops, she looked for the ones with the most red stigmas among yellow stamens. Then she held the bowl of crocuses to her nose, knowing the coloring strength of the flowers was related to their aroma.

"I offer the best of prices, madam. My crocuses are grown locally," the merchant said, addressing Anahita as though she were a married woman. Anahita exchanged smiles with Dariyoush, both knowing that the shopkeeper had assumed they were husband and wife.

"What do you think?" she held the bowl of petals out for Dariyoush to smell.

"Perfect," he said.

Anahita handed it to the merchant. "I'll take these," she said. Turning to her mother and grandmother, who were busy counting the money they had between them, she said, "All of this will make luscious dyes, especially as blends with the *sprak* and mullein I picked at summer camp."

Anahita paid the merchant twenty *rials* and ten *shahis*. Dariyoush offered to get their donkey from the *caravanserai* to haul the sacks of madder.

"That's kind of you, Dariyoush. We'll go on to the cotton market," Mojdeh said. But Anahita begged to skip that stall. She wanted to be alone for a moment, the conversation with the rug merchant now creeping to the forefront of her thoughts.

"Maman, I'll go with Dariyoush." She saw a faint smile come over her friend's face. "I wish to see the dervishes perform. I hear they will dance the *sama* in the plaza. Could we all meet there?"

"As you like."

Anahita admired how the brotherhood of dervishes traveled about working for alms to feed the poor. They had visited Hasanabad not long ago. She thought about the impression they had made on her and how, shortly after they left, she had started the clothing cart.

She also loved how agreeable her mother was whenever she came to the bazaar. Maman had just as much fun here as she did herself.

A large crowd had gathered in circles, seven rows deep around the thirteen Sufi dervishes who stood in formation in the middle of the square. Their black cloaks swept the flagstone floor upon which they moved, leaving wide sweeps of sand-free stone. They wore tall, black felted hats, symbols of tombstones, that looked so different from the turbans worn by most men in Mashhad.

Dariyoush stood close to Anahita. "Maybe it's time you sit," he said. "You've put miles on that healing foot."

"I'm all right," Anahita said, straining on tiptoe to see the dervishes dance.

Dariyoush thought about how he had enjoyed watching her in the market today, selecting her dyestuffs with such assurance.

Every time someone in the crowd squeezed by them, Anahita leaned into Dariyoush. He liked her softness against him. He wished he could pick her up in his arms as he had by the stream and whirl with her here like the dervishes. Though he was caught up in the excitement of the crowd, he wasn't much interested in the devishes' dance, and didn't understand their Sufi world.

He wanted to talk to Anahita about her wedding contest, about the near-irreconcilable rift between him and his parents over his desire to marry her, and about his and Mehdi's recent plans to join the fight against the Russians on the borderlands. On this visit to Mashhad he had learned that the shah was organizing an army and needed young men. He'd pondered what to say to Anahita, but it was difficult for him to express his thoughts. Because anything private in their tribe often became public knowledge, he had long learned to keep things to himself.

"Anahita, I've been thinking . . ." he said, at the same time Anahita said to him, "Dariyoush, I'll wait for you . . ."

She'll wait for me? She'll marry me after I return from war? How could she possibly have known this is what I wanted to ask her? So taken aback, if only by his own wishful thinking, he said, "I'm sorry, Anahita, you first."

"I just wanted to say that I'll wait for you here while you go and get the donkey. I want to watch the dervishes dance."

Dariyoush's spirits slumped, and so did his shoulders. *Maybe this isn't the right time,* he thought. He said quietly, "Your father wouldn't like it."

"Remember when we climbed to the painted caves? We didn't ask my father first. Go on. What could possibly happen to me among this pious gathering?"

Dariyoush thought, *What I remember about the cave is the feel of my hands on your waist helping you down off the rock ledge.* But he said, "The mullah was with us. What better chaperone could your father have hoped for?"

"Chaperone? It was only you who I was going with," she said, only half-looking at Dariyoush as she watched the performance.

Only me. What does she mean by that?

Then Anahita asked, "What was it you wanted to say to me a minute ago?"

"It is not important." Turning toward the *caravanserai*, he half-walked, half-ran for the donkey, thinking, *No, this isn't the right time and place to talk with her.* While Dariyoush had enjoyed the afternoon with Anahita at the spice market, her behavior also gave him pause. He didn't know if he felt embarrassed by her forwardness with the merchant or simply unneeded. *I should have handled such business for her.* Picking up his pace, his mother's words came to mind: "That incident tells me something about Anahita's character. Something that you might find difficult to live with in time."

Would she ever consider calling off her contest just for me? Would I truly want her to?

Anahita watched Dariyoush go, then turned back to the Sufis. She could hear the repetitive clang of a hammer and anvil ring from a blacksmith's stall somewhere in the distance. Its rhythm harmonized with the beat of the dervishes' drum and soothed her. Her disappointment over the carpet merchant's poor memory slipped away like the sand beneath the dancers' feet.

Anahita knew every element of the *sama*, the dervishes' whirling dance, was symbolic, celebrating both joy and pain. The dervishes believed their ritual was one of the paths leading to Allah. She wondered about the secret hidden within the rhythm of their music, and considered how their dance was like a riddle turning both inward and outward, an attempt to understand the mystery of all things. Anahita, too, believed that beneath her own appearance, behind her words and thoughts, another world awaited within—one so vast it must be the source of all.

When these bearded dancers let their black cloaks fall to reveal the white robes beneath, Anahita knew this signified rebirth and a new understanding of life. She imagined a woman spinning among them: Rabi'a. Herself.

Clustered on the ground sat the dervishes' bowls—symbols of receptivity. She put a coin into each.

Just as the Sufis spread their arms like wings, one palm up to gather divine grace, the other down to give it to the earth, Anahita heard the high-pitched hum of excited camels behind her. She turned to see one of a pair break loose from a little boy's grip. It took off running in the hitch-along way camels move, while the other folded its legs under itself and sat down. The boy tugged and tugged on the halter but the beast would not get up.

Someone from the crowd ran after the other camel. Shoppers leapt out of the way. The dervishes danced on, splitting into two semicircles, their whirling becoming more fervent. Much of the audience turned and watched the little boy, who began to kick the remaining camel.

His chest heaving slightly from the chase, the man who had captured the runaway led it back toward the boy. The closer the man came, the more Anahita thought she'd seen him somewhere before. *Abadi-eh-Golab?* The crowd moved out of the way of the man and camel, and so did Anahita, caught in the shuffle of people. The man knelt on one knee so that he could speak to the boy eye-to-eye. He whispered something to him and the child smiled.

Then the man crept next to the double-humped animal and held tasty pellets to its lips. When the man stood up, so did the beast. Rubbing the boy on the head, the man flipped him a coin. "Buy yourself a sweet and one for your camel."

The boy's eyes lit up. Thanking the stranger, he led his camels onward through the maze of shops, his small shoulders thrown back as if he had gained a new confidence in the goodness of this world.

The stranger's tenderness with the child and the camel impressed Anahita. At that moment an image came to her: She was a little girl and a camel had nipped at her. The khan had come to her aid, slapping the animal on the side of its head. Anahita shuddered and drew a deep breath against the memory.

The dervishes circled, their bodies' trajectories like the orbits of planets in the cosmos. The audience squeezed together as they moved from the dancers' paths, spitting Anahita out of the crowd. Just then, the man who had helped the boy with the camels took a step back and bumped into her.

"Oh!" she gasped at the jolt.

The man spun around. "I didn't mean to frighten you, miss. I was not aware that you were behind me."

"You didn't frighten me, you merely startled me."

In a rush it all came back to Anahita, his accent, the delicate lines on his brow.

The man broke the silence. "There is a difference, you know," he teased, finishing Anahita's sentence. His voice sounding a bit raspy, as if he were thirsty.

They both laughed nervously. "You remembered," she said. "I feel silly." She noticed again how his eyes were the color of wet sand in a gulch after rain—both golden and brown, depending on the light.

"That memory has been my companion," he said. His voice reflected a certainty he must have felt inside, which took Anahita by surprise and made her feel uncomfortable.

"Do you always carry camel treats in your pocket?" she asked, not knowing what else to say.

"Not always." He smiled. The smile she had seen all summer in her memory, a smile that cheered her just as rabbit prints did when she found them fresh in the snow.

Casting her eyes to the ground, Anahita noticed a book at the man's feet. Bending on one knee to pick it up she asked, "Is this yours?" As she offered it to him, she noticed a scar on the side of his face, near his ear. She hadn't remembered this from before.

"Oh. Yes. It must have dropped from my pocket when I knelt down to speak to the child. It's a gift from one of the dervishes performing here."

Anahita looked at the dervishes with awe.

Her new acquaintance glanced at the cane she had tucked under one arm. He seemed to take in the shape of her forearms—her sleeves pushed back from her wrists in the heat.

"Are you injured?" he asked.

"This?" she said, touching her cane. "I'm recovering from a sprain."

"May the Merciful One come to your aid."

Anahita looked toward the men entertaining the crowd. She still held the book, and now she studied its title even though she couldn't read it. *He is educated,* she thought, feeling weak-kneed beneath her *chador.* For the first time ever, she felt tongue-tied. In a strange way, she felt frightened, as if she'd stumbled into unreadable sands. She stepped between the walls of two shops for privacy, because chatting with a strange man was socially unacceptable, if not forbidden. She was glad when the man followed her.

"What is your book about?" she ventured.

"Rumi."

Anahita nodded, this time noticing the glint of the dagger resting on his hip, the scar on his arm, his unkempt appearance. He looked like someone capable of the noblest or the most atrocious of acts. *For all I know, this man's a bandit of some kind,* she thought. *Yet his smile, his soft-spokenness . . .*

"Rumi was a Sufi poet. He was born in Persia many centuries ago but moved to the city of Konya, in central Anatolia," he said.

. . . his poetry . . . she thought, too. *Surely he's a good person.*

Her new friend glanced behind her as if he expected to find someone. "In Rumi's day the city of Mashhad belonged to the empire which ruled our homeland from Konya—before the Mongols invaded. It is said that Rumi awoke in the people there a devotion to his spiritual ideals. His personal example inspired the founding of an order of dervishes. The very same from which these dancers come."

"Was he Muslim?" Anahita looked into the man's face. Her legs shook even more.

"He practiced Islam and believed in the communal nature of worship, yet some say his poems and stories begin where religion leaves off. He seemed to relate to Allah in a personal way."

Like Rabi'a, Anahita thought.

"I like reading Rumi's work. He had a special vision and talent that broadens my mind, my ways of seeing in this world and into the other."

A boy passing through the crowd with a water cart forced Anahita aside. Her friend reached out, held her long enough to steady her, then drew back.

He's a gentleman, Anahita thought, keenly aware of the shiver, the message his fingers sent up her arm. "And what do you mean that Rumi helps your way of seeing into some *other* world?"

He seemed to search for the right words. "For me this is difficult to explain. But I believe that when Rumi says, 'Be melting snow. Wash yourself of yourself,' he is really suggesting that to reach this other world, this inner reality in which material things have no place, we must forget our wants, and let go of our self-centeredness."

"He speaks in riddles."

"Yes. There are always stories within his stories."

Anahita flipped the cloth of her *rusari* over her shoulder. "Just as there are stories within the warp and weft of the carpets I weave, which are every bit as real as the stories I tell with the patterns and designs on the surface."

"Yours is an interesting interpretation. It reminds me of something else Rumi said. 'Wool, through the presence of a person of knowledge, becomes a carpet. Earth becomes a palace. A spiritual man creates a similar transformation.' People claimed that when near Rumi, they could think more clearly—gain special insight— even without having spoken to him."

Anahita's eyes widened. "And what is there for the living in this world without material things?"

"Pure love."

Am I really standing here talking with a strange man about love? "The same love as between a man and a woman?" she asked.

He eyed the dervishes as he spoke, and then Anahita. "I cannot say from experience, but this is something I seek. Others claim it is a love more sweet than that of a man and woman, if you can imagine, a love that is not fleeting."

Anahita looked down. *This man touches a place somewhere inside me, yet outside the world of reason.*

"My grandmother is much like this man, Rumi," Anahita said. "She often reminds me that a flower grows in silence and that I should let my tongue become its petal."

"I would like to meet your grandmother," he said and smiled. "And by the way, we haven't introduced . . ." he began, but let his voice trail off as he looked over Anahita's shoulder. Dariyoush drew up behind her with the donkey, two sacks of madder root draped across its back.

"Anahita. I'm sorry, I didn't mean to be so long. I went to the spice shop before coming for you." Stopping beside her, he looked in the direction of her gentleman friend, who had moved away to blend in with the crowd. "Was there a man here bothering you?"

The donkey twitched its ears at the flies.

Anahita looked past the people whom her new friend had let come between them, knowing he had done this for her sake, so it would not look as if they had been talking. Shaken, she said, "Of course not. We, ah, he . . ."

"Anahita, Dariyoush," Mojdeh and Maman Bozorg called out. "We thought we'd never find you. *Bia.* It's getting late." Mojdeh threaded her arm through her daughter's and pulled her along with her. "We must make one more stop on the way."

As Anahita sought the nice man's eyes, she saw her grand-mother take stock of him in one swift glance, which included the gilded *jambiyah*, the dagger he wore on his hip.

His book! Anahita thought, *I still have his book.*

"Anahita, why do you hesitate?" her mother asked.

Slipping the collection of Rumi's poems within the folds of her clothing, she fell in step with her mother. *If I never see this man again, at least I'll have this keepsake.*

16

Leaving Mashhad

"Hmm," replied the merchant. "Many women, every day I see. You expect me to remember just one? They all look the same in their *chadors*."

Arash stared at him, his jaw tightening with impatience as he waited for the merchant to mumble through excuses.

"I vaguely remember such a woman."

If Arash hadn't just come from the public bath, where he had freshened his royal clothes and soothed his hot head in a delightful pool, he might have pinned the merchant against the wooden frame of the stall and shaken the truth from him. "I just spoke with Anahita this afternoon. From what I know about her fondness of carpet weaving, it seems likely you would know her, or have done business with her before."

The merchant crossed his arms. "I have worked with the carpet repairers in her village—that is, if we are speaking of the same woman, of course."

"And would you by chance recall the conversation she and I had with you this past spring? Just after *Nooruz?* Might you also remember that I asked you to give her my name and tell her she could find me in Marv?"

The merchant stroked his chin. "Yes, yes, come to think of it, she was here." His smile a thin line.

Locking eyes with the shopkeeper's in what could have been a hand about the skinny fellow's throat, Arash said, "I do not enjoy games when my concerns are at stake." This conversation seemed as fruitless as the one he had earlier that day with a gathering of landowners, khans, and members of the local *divan*.

The merchant glanced at Arash's official-looking clothes. He swallowed hard.

"Have you any news of which village this woman Anahita winters in? To what tribe she belongs? I also wish to know if she asked about me."

"I am not certain," said the merchant, "but she might be an Afshar from the village of Deh-eh Hasan." He scratched his chin. "Or, perhaps it was Hasanabad. Somewhere near Nishapur."

"And did she ask for me?"

The merchant hesitated, and said, "No."

Irritated with the shopkeeper, troubled by his words, Arash decided he might as well be on his way to Marv. He had searched the *caravanserai* for Anahita and, when he could not find her, suspected that her tribe had left Mashhad for home. If only he could discover where she lived.

He thought about what a blessing the terrible sandstorm was— how it had kept him here an extra two days, giving him a chance to see Anahita. He smiled as he remembered how her rose scent had tickled his nose just before he had bumped into her today. How lucky, after all these months of thinking of her, to have been near enough that he could have taken her into his arms and held her.

Then, recalling Dariyoush, Arash's mood fell toward despair. *She's married,* he thought. He had studied Dariyoush for some resemblance to Anahita, some feature that might have suggested he was her brother or cousin, such as a smooth-tipped nose or rounded cheeks, but he had found none.

Perturbed by this thought and by the merchant's tight lips, Arash stepped away from the carpet stall and into the throng of people moving through the market. "Deh-eh Hasan? Hasanabad?" he said aloud. *There must be a thousand villages in Iran with "Hasan" in their names!*

A puff of wind blew a small parchment decorated with flowers off a beam on which it had been posted. The parchment flew up into the air, twirling above people's heads before it descended to cling to Arash's leg. He peeled it from his pants and skimmed the information written on it: "A Test of Wit." *For a hand in marriage?!* Arash thought. *These reformists aren't the only signs of change in this kingdom.* Without giving it a second thought, he tossed the sheet back into the air.

On his way out of the city, Arash promised himself he would search every black nomad tent for Anahita. *If I am separated from her, I will turn entirely to thorn.*

✳ ✳ ✳

Before leaving Mashhad, Mojdeh, Maman Bozorg, Anahita, and Dariyoush made one last stop at the bazaar. With the money Farhad paid him for his help over the summer, Dariyoush purchased three different-sized knives and selected a fine dagger for himself

"A dagger, Dariyoush? Why do you need that?" Anahita asked.

"The new decree. Able men over sixteen are needed to serve in the shah's army. I may have to use this sometime . . ." he said, leaving out the word *soon*.

"I've heard about the skirmishes, but will a *real* army be formed?"

"From what I have gathered, our minister of war has ordered all eligible men to report to their provincial headquarters for duty. The term is for one year."

"Who is this minster of war?"

"I suspect one of the shah's relatives. But what difference does it make who made the law? It's not as if you or I can do anything to change it. When would we ever meet anyone from the Qajar court?"

She didn't know if she liked the tone of Dariyoush's voice. *Is he mad at me?* "I don't feel well, Dariyoush. I'd like to go back to our camp," she said, wanting to be alone.

Dariyoush gave her a tender look, as though he thought her sudden sickness arose from her worries over his enlisting.

When the four passed a two-storied schoolhouse, Anahita inspected it. She thought about the khan's promise to hire her a tutor. A pair of blue eyes came to mind. *What was his name?* she tried to remember.

Several schoolboys ran across their path, chasing and calling insults, "Melon rind! Camel spit! Nose hair!" They ran between crates of books and parchments. Some leaflets rose up in the breeze and rained down on fruit and bread stands. Others stuck to the wheels of carts as they rolled by. It looked to Anahita as if the students had been packing up their classroom, but decided that playing was much more fun. She smiled at them and walked on in the direction of the *caravanserai*. Beneath her *chador* she clutched her book of Rumi.

Anahita tried to distance herself from the others in her caravan. She rode her mule, laden with dyestuffs, and kept her veil on, though they had left Mashhad, with its pious Muslims, days ago.

It had been a long night and Anahita's eyes stung from lack of sleep. In the morning's mounting heat, her tribesmates argued among themselves while their livestock withered from a dearth of water. On a forced march back to Hasanabad, the Afshars suffered from the khan's revenge—his refusal to negotiate their usual right of passage across the two estates just east of their village. Each was so great in size that a horse would take a full day to gallop across it. With no permission granted to camp for the customary one day and one night, Anahita's tribe had to walk continuously so that their livestock would not deplete the landowners' crops along the way. There would be no lingering at any of the wells.

Tempers, like the brittle heat in the air, ran high.

"We've crossed this land without opposition for as long as anyone can remember, Farhad," Dariyoush's father said. "If my yearlings perish before we reach home, I am sorry, but I will demand that you replenish my stock."

"I understand," Farhad replied as he nudged his stallion up the line of people.

Hearing this, Anahita winced. As she watched her father attend to the tribe, she ruminated until she could stand it no longer. *It's all my fault—I never should have asked for a wedding riddle contest.* The sun bore down. Beads of salty sweat formed above her lip. She licked it for the moisture; she wanted to spare the water that was left in her goatskin.

Anahita's father kept himself aloof from his people, too, speaking only when spoken to, and he left it to her mother to smooth things over with the women of the tribe. Everyone was angry about their predicament. No one held back their frustrations.

"Anahita," said a dark-lipped woman with her infant hitched on her hip, "our children need rest . . ."

"We have no well water for diaper washing," said another.

Shirin rolled her eyes at Anahita as she passed. "You're so spoiled. Now look what you've done."

Anahita ignored her cousin but squirmed when Dariyoush rode up to her on his Arabian. He looked at her with what seemed like a discerning gaze, the usual playful spark in his eyes gone.

"How are you faring in the heat?" he asked her, holding his reins in one hand and popping a date in his mouth with the other, fruit she had seen him get from Maman Bozorg, who pampered him at every opportunity. He'd always had a big appetite. For a moment Anahita smiled to herself as she remembered how, when they were young, the smell of cardamom wafting from her mother's cooking pots had always produced Dariyoush, as if by magic.

"Oh, I'm not finding it too bad," she lied. She was so thirsty, she could have drunk an ox's share.

"May I ask why you are wearing that veil?"

Anahita hadn't felt silly in her veil until that moment. She wore it because it helped make her feel as if the world were far away.

"It keeps the sand out of my nose." Anahita adjusted the fabric over her face and held her head up. She knew from Dariyoush's raised eyebrow that he didn't believe her. The air couldn't have been more still or stifling that day. "My mule kicks up dust." Pulling its halter rope to the right, she kept the animal from rubbing up against Dariyoush's horse. She wanted to keep the pannier, which was full of fragile dried flowers, from getting crushed.

"How is your ankle managing with this constant traveling?" he asked.

Did he have to mention this . . . this march? Allah spare me from this embarrassment.

When she didn't speak, he continued, "Even though it's nearly healed, you are best to stay off it until we're home."

"Thanks, I will." She watched him ride away toward Mehdi.

What hurt Anahita the most was her father's silence. She

thought this rift was much wider than the one they had hurdled earlier in the summer, when the riddles between them had dried up. *He's definitely angry with me, and maybe with himself for consenting to my wishes.*

She didn't like to see her otherwise gregarious father so grave. She didn't like her mother's hushed, serious tone of late, as if she wished not to worsen her husband's mood. The only person with whom Anahita felt comfortable talking, and who received her with pleasure, was her grandmother. When the caravan rolled to a stop for a brief rest at a cluster of date palms, Anahita clicked her tongue, signaling her mule to trot on. She found her grandmother removing her head scarf.

"What am I to do, Maman Bozorg?" Anahita said, jumping off her animal. She stood beside her grandmother as the old woman dampened the scarf with water from her goatskin and dabbed the back of her neck.

Without having to ask her granddaughter what she meant, Maman Bozorg said, "Anahita, I do not recall that you ever thanked your father for this contest."

A sharp pain clawed deep inside Anahita's chest. She fussed with the long stems of mullein she had tied on her donkey. "Of course I have . . . I—" she fiddled with the heavy sack of madder root. Then she recalled what she'd said when her father had nailed the parchment announcing the wedding contest on the *caravanserai* wall: *"You are announcing this to the entire city of Mashhad? It seems so impersonal, so . . . public! I thought we'd handle this privately."*

Anahita's hands dropped from the saddlebags. She stared

across the plains, a rising wind whipping her veil. She yanked it off and tears began to fall. *How could I have been so ungrateful that I did not thank Baba?* With her tears, all of her regrets streamed into her mind: how she had manipulated the mullah—not telling him the whole truth about the khan, how she pestered her father about the contest, how she had neglected her cousin then argued with her—even tackled her!—when Shirin's nastiness obviously came from hurt. Her father had been right to call her selfish. She truly only thought of herself.

Drying her tears with her veil, Anahita turned to Maman Bozorg and said, "I owe Baba an apology." *I owe one to Shirin, too.* But her cousin's would come later, sometime when Anahita could stomach the bad medicine that had soured Shirin's words of late. For now, exhausted as she was, speaking to her angry father was about as much as she could handle.

Anahita walked to where her father was mounting his horse. She felt as though something inside her was racing, yet her spirit plodded. More than anything, she wanted his forgiveness. When she caught up with Farhad, he gave her a hand up onto his stallion. A line of sweat, the length of his spine, darkened his garb. He smelled of desert. As the two strode, the rest of the caravan began to follow. Anahita shaded her eyes with one hand and looked behind her. She saw that Maman Bozorg led her mule beside her own. The tribe reached far, far into the distance, the last ones in line looking like nothing more than dark specks on the horizon.

Wiping her sweaty palms on her thighs, she said to her father's back, "Baba, I want to thank you for consenting to my wedding riddle contest. It is a privilege I do not deserve."

Farhad said nothing.

The horse whinnied as if it could smell home.

Still hoping for her father's blessing, she continued, "I understand that this contest is not to everyone's liking." Her hands trembled. She hesitated before she could speak her next words, for in saying them she would cast away any possibility of courting the man in Mashhad. "If you decide to call it off, I am willing to marry Dariyoush."

Anahita rocked with her father in rhythm with the horse.

"Dariyoush's father has still not sought your hand for his son. After this inconvenience, I do not expect that he will be rushing to our tent to offer me a bride price." Farhad removed his turban, looked inside it, scratched his head, and put it back on. "Your wedding contest will go on, Anahita. This incident—the khan's behavior—convinces me that he is not to be trusted with the livelihood of our people. He would risk our welfare for his own ends, and his self-serving behavior is not what any of us need during these unstable times. I do not believe our khan should represent this tribe. I am no longer concerned about pleasing him."

Anahita wasn't sure that she heard her father correctly. *Does he mean that he no longer has any misgivings about not marrying me to the khan?! Delight in good, for surely it is Allah who assists.* Her spirits began to rekindle.

"But Baba, what might the others think?"

"Time will tell. I believe they will see things from my perspective. I do not feel I am being rash when I say that I do not intend to bend to the khan's will and give in to this act of aggression."

Later, around the family's dinner campfire, Farhad seemed almost relaxed. Anahita listened as her parents talked.

"But the khan has threatened to depose you. And who will represent us with the government? As you've said, none of us can read or write."

"Have you not heard about the Rural Madrasa Servanthood? I learned in Mashhad that we will benefit from the latest program instituted by the clerics. A teacher will be quartered in our village. I plan to enroll in the new school myself." Farhad patted his wife on the knee. "Perhaps it will be your own husband who will grace the corridors of those fancy offices in Mashhad."

"Baba," Anahita ventured, not sure any of her comments would be well-received. "Won't you be the oldest student in the class?"

"I may be old," Farhad said, "but I'm still sharp enough to stump you with a riddle, now and again."

PAIZ
RANG
RAZI
Autumn Dyeing

Earthen Pigments

It was midmorning, and Anahita walked briskly from the mosque with an empty basket, thinking about how nice it felt to be in Hasanabad, even though many women of her tribe still snubbed her. As she passed Shirin, who sat with a friend on the fountain wall in the village square, her cousin looked the other way.

"Hello, Shirin," Anahita said anyway, tired of this silliness. But Shirin threw her head back and laughed as if whatever the woman sitting next to her had just said was the funniest thing on earth. *Who needs fake camaraderie like that?* Anahita thought. *I have the dyemaster's company to look forward to this afternoon.*

Anahita arrived home and set her basket by the back door. Before she could go inside, her father called to her from the shed, asking for her assistance. She had tried to help her father as much as she could ever since the migration. She felt it was the least she could do, and that perhaps she'd eventually gain his full forgiveness. When she made her way through the skittering sheep to where her father stood, he handed her a sharp knife.

"I'll throw them on their sides for you, Anahita, so that you may help me trim their hooves. The flock will be contained within a very small space this winter. We must take care to prevent foot rot should the ground in the pen become too soiled with dung."

Farhad held a ewe down with his knee as Anahita reached for one of its kicking legs. Carefully she cut the tough, overgrown skin that curled under the hoof. The animal bellowed. Anahita finished, then reached for the next foot, thinking how glad she was that her own had healed.

Ever since her father had mentioned the new school, Anhita had thought about how much she wanted to attend. The school was nearly built now, and she had yet to bring the topic up with Farhad. Thinking that perhaps now was a good time, she backed her way into the conversation by talking about "change."

"I've been thinking, Baba, that life really is like a garden. Even our barns burst with new life each year, with all the lambs."

Farhad flipped another sheep on its side. He cocked his head toward his daughter, and gave her a look which meant, What are you buttering me up for?

Anahita glanced at her favorite ewe, Tayebeh, as it bullied another sheep for grain. She'd never seen a sheep more conscious of its head—butting it against others, rubbing it on posts and her own leg.

"Baba, I've been wondering. Might news of my betrothal travel as far as Marv?"

Farhad smiled at his daughter, who talked more than she listened, whose community projects she carried out as skillfully as any man, gifts that had brought her the bad with the good. "Such an abrupt change of thought," he said, selecting another sheep for trimming.

"Do you think the news will reach Bukhara?"

"Bukhara! Where do you hear of such places?"

"In the market, Baba. People come to Mashhad from everywhere."

"I *suspect* that news of your wedding riddle might spread to Bukhara or Marv, if it had a little *help*." Farhad cocked his head toward her again. But Anahita did not return his gaze. She grabbed the next hoof. The autumn breeze carried away the flies.

"Anahita, be sure to trim off the little flaps of skin at the heel so nothing collects beneath it. I leave them intact only in the spring and the autumn for the migrations. The extra padding helps soften stony paths."

"Like this?" Anahita sliced.

"Wonderful! Perhaps I will retire and let you take over the herd."

Anahita rolled her eyes and said, "Baba, the men are making nice progress with the school. They have laid the foundation stones already. When do you think they will finish?"

"Perhaps a month or more."

"A month or more!" Anahita groaned as she reached for another hoof.

"Why does this cause you distress?"

"Baba, I . . . I wish to attend with you."

A lamb baaed. Then another one. Standing beside her father,

she could smell his scent above the sheep odors. Strong and sweet, it was like no one else's in world.

"My dear daughter, you have a rug to weave and the dyemaster to assist. Not to mention helping your mother and myself. As you know, Dariyoush is soon to leave. And by the way, have you thought of a riddle for your wedding *qali*?"

Just the mention of her wedding riddle sent a shiver through her. *Nooruz* was months away. She still had plenty of time to think of one, and face up to her wedding. "No, Baba, I have not. But I will get my wedding *qali* woven and all my other work done, I promise. Besides, even the khan wishes for me to be educated. Didn't he fund all the costs for the school?"

"That tactic won't work with me, Anahita. Haven't we learned that the khan does not hold your welfare to heart? He is trying to win over the tribe after causing us to make that potentially perilous march."

Anahita ignored her father's comment. "If we both went to school, we could help each other with the lessons. I want to learn to read and write. If I learn to read riddles for myself, when you are away I can still enjoy them."

Her father shook his head, and Anahita persisted. "The only words I recognize are the Arabic words in the *Quran*. I want to become fluent in a language other than Afshari. I want to read and write in Farsi, the language spoken at all the bazaars and in all the cities. Whatever I am taught will make me even more helpful to the dyemaster."

"Young lady, your perseverance normally serves you well, but lately it has taken on an ugly shape of relentless wanting. It's unbecoming." He looked at her directly. "I must ponder this idea of schooling. I'm not promising anything."

His words hurt. *I only want to learn!* she thought. The knife she held became a ruler. She imagined herself there in the classroom, measuring lines, forming letters with chalk and slate, listening to stories the schoolmaster would read aloud, adding sum after sum.

For the rest of that morning the sheep Anahita tended looked blue-eyed. She wondered what had become of the tutor who had visited her summer camp.

Anahita gathered the *sprak*, mullein, and chamomile she had picked over the summer, and the indigo, saffron, and cochineal she had purchased at the Mashhad bazaar. She stuffed them into her *chantehs* and went outside to ask Farhad to strap the two fifty-pound sacks of madder onto her donkey. This afternoon she would visit her granduncle, the village dyer, whose only dream in life was to create unforgettable, unmatchable, unsurpassable hues. Since their tribe's return to Hasanabad, she'd been too busy helping her parents to visit him and bring him all the dyestuffs she had collected. Today she was looking forward to a few hours of his company, learning his secrets.

Anahita could hear her granduncle before she could see him. A low monotone hum escaped from the door of one of his dye sheds.

"Ahhh, yummm, ahhh, naa, yaa, yaa, hummm."

If she hadn't been surrounded by his colorful skeins of silk and wool, hanging from leafless tree branches, and by the piles of shriveled acorns, limp chamomile stalks, and used madder root— she might have thought she'd entered the mosque. The dyemaster's hum sounded much like the mullah's *azan*.

"Oh master?" Anahita called, not wanting to enter unexpectedly for fear she'd disturb his work.

"Ahhh, yummm, ahhh, naa, yaa, yaa, hummm," her granduncle sang.

"Master?" Anahita repeated. She decided to enter his shed anyway. To make sure she looked presentable for the elderly man, she pulled her head scarf completely over her ears and tied it under her chin. Then she stepped inside, thinking that he was not only forgetful, he was becoming hard of hearing. *Perhaps I should ask him today if he'll take me on as his apprentice. After all, what shape might he be in next week?*

Turning to Anahita with a smile, and taking the dye flowers from her, the bald and bearded master said, "Ah, such beautiful *guls*. These will make very nice dyes. They will be fast—they will keep their color in the hottest desert sun! So good of you to think of me when you were in the hills, Anahita." His hands quivered, and his fingernails looked more purple than usual today.

Knowing her flair for riddles, the dyemaster said, "What, besides a flower that has gone to seed, is prime for the harvest of life?"

Anahita bit her lip. She must have look perplexed because the old man immediately gave her the answer.

"Why, the dyemaster in his old age, of course!"

"If you weren't my granduncle," Anahita teased, "I'd encourage you to enter my wedding riddle contest."

This brought a smile to his face, rounding out his hollow cheeks. Together they walked out of the shed and lifted the sacks of madder from Anahita's donkey, carrying them into the work shed and depositing them onto the floor. Dust rose and mixed with the musky smell of the dried flowers and herbs dangling from rafters above their heads. The two sorted the indigo, saffron, and cochineal. They placed each dyestuff in its respective wooden box on shelves above the chest-high counter, which the master had built to accommodate his back. The counter, Anahita noticed, suited her height perfectly.

She watched the village dyer as he went about his work. He weighed a handful of chamomile petals on a small brass scale. Next, he selected a jar of white powder from the row of colorful ones containing alum, tin, chrome, and lead. She wondered just how many years he had studied his craft and what secrets he had learned from dyemasters before him.

The sun and light breeze inspired the dyer to move his work outside. He chopped up the yellow rosettes of yarrow and button-topped tansy, and spindles of mullein, and threw them all into the same pot along with bits of their stems. They would simmer in the cauldron over an open fire.

"Mind the flames, Anahita. You do not want the water to boil. That will cause the golds to turn brown." Anahita inhaled the fragrant liquid wafting from the dyepot as it warmed. *No wonder every* insect but flies sips the nectar of these flowers. Together they smell a little like licorice.

Her granduncle dumped one scoop of dried cochineal insects into a different vat and set it over a flame. When the water heated, it began to turn a purple-red.

In another vessel, the dyemaster sprinkled a palm-pinch of saffron florets, letting them brew and turn the water a bright pink-orange. "Saffron is much like indigo, Anahita. A little goes a long way. And it is messy. If you are not careful, it will get all over everything." He wiped his fingers onto his turban. Orange-yellow streaks joined the kaleidoscope of colors already there.

Then the dyemaster walked to a mud-and-thatch shed, which stood apart from the others. Anahita followed, watching closely. He dropped two blue stones—the fermented, compacted sludge of indigo plants—into a vat filled with a clear greenish-yellow liquid that he said had been simmering for weeks. The solution smelled so bad it made Anahita gag. She covered her nose and mouth with both hands.

The dye did not turn blue as Anahita had expected. She was particularly interested in the blue as she planned to weave the color of the sea into her wedding qali. She asked the dyemaster about this.

"It is not the simmering that turns the indigo blue, but the air that causes the dye to color. Hand me a skein of your wool. We shall see." He dipped her yarn into the vat of indigo and stoked the flame beneath. After some time he removed the skein from the warm solution. When it met the air, the skein turned a light shade of yellow-green.

Anahita's eyes widened. Still, this wasn't the shade of blue she had in mind for her rug. "But . . ." she began.

The master dyer raised his finger, signaling her to be patient. Anahita watched him dip the skein back into the dyebath a second time. Then he shook a special powder into his pot. "This removes the air from the solution," he said. "It's my secret." He winked. Beneath thick hooded lids, his eyes seemed to glimmer. This time, when he raised the yarn from the dyepot, it turned green-blue.

Anahita smiled. She watched him dip and redip the skein of yarn until it turned blue, then a darker blue, and then its deepest blue. "The color of the Caspian Sea!" she exclaimed.

Exhilarated by this seemingly magical process, Anahita said, "Dyemaster, I desperately wish to learn your craft. Would you consider taking me on as your apprentice?"

He looked at Anahita, drawing together his bushy eyebrows before raising one. "Do you think I would allow just anyone to nose around my stock room and shop for me at the market?"

She wasn't sure what he meant, and lost her nerve to press him. Instead she said, "I see many dull blues on the carpets in Mashhad. Our tribe's carpets always exceed the others in shade and hue."

"In many ways my colors depend on what the villagers have to eat."

What? she wondered. *Surely he is going senile.*

"You see, my dear, indigo is not soluble in water, though urine will dissolve the blue stone. Whenever men from the village visit my dye house, I ask them to relieve themselves of the tea they've drunk that day into this jar!" With a childlike smile he held up a liter-sized vessel.

Anahita wrinkled her nose. "No wonder the dye smells so awful." For a moment, she thought maybe she'd forget about being the dyemaster's apprentice. But the allure of learning his special methods outweighed the bad smells and blue fingernails that went along with the position. Her granduncle threw a handful of skeins into the indigo vat.

"Dyemaster, I must tell you about the dyes I saw at the market in Mashhad." Pronouncing each syllable she said, "They are called 'mass-noo-ee.' Have you seen these colors?"

Her granduncle folded his arms and looked somewhere past her. "I am not certain. Dariyoush brought a carpet to me a while ago. He had been repairing it for a merchant in Mashhad. The rug's hues looked solid, equally saturated throughout, but with no variation to please the eye. Do you know how they are made, Anahita?"

"I believe they are made without plants."

"No plants?"

Anahita tilted her head back. *"Na."*

"And what is your opinion of these dyes, Anahita?"

"Well, they don't have what I call earth-beauty. They are not of our people."

"Ah yes. Not to look at and use nature in one's own work is wrong to me. Nature has been inspiration enough for millions of years, how could it ever be exhausted?"

As usual, when the dyemaster finished all of what he wanted to say or all of what he wished to teach her, he fell back into the silence of his own thoughts. Anahita understood this as her cue to leave.

She piled her one hundred shimmering skeins of newly spun yarn on his counter like catches of fresh fish. She untethered her donkey and left the cluster of little sheds where she would come to spend more and more of her time this winter.

"Ahhh, yummm, ahhh, naa, yaa, yaa, hummm," she heard as she walked away, beginning to hum the tune herself.

18

Fatima's Fire

A ribbon of smoke rising in the sky over the village square caught Anahita's attention. She stood watching over her flock, which grazed on the stubble of harvested barley beside the stream.

"Fire!" Anahita heard Dariyoush shout. "Fatima and Ali's place is on fire!"

Anahita ran. Black smoke rose as flames licked the teahouse and bakery's thatched roof.

"Fire! Fire!" The alarm spread from person to person until the whole village arrived in the town square. With pails in hand they formed four human chains: two from the stream to the teahouse, and two from the bathhouse.

Anahita and Dariyoush squatted next to the deep pool in the men's side of the bathhouse. The thick mist in the subterranean room filled the domed ceiling and made it hard to breathe. Scooping buckets of water, they passed them from hand to hand, between women and children, out the door and up a flight of stairs. Aboveground they reached men who threw water on the burning bakery and the roofs of the nearby homes.

With each scoop, Anahita accidentally splashed herself. The curtains that sectioned off the women's side of the bathhouse billowed in the commotion. After a while, Anahita straightened and rubbed the back of her neck.

"You are holding up well," Dariyoush said to her and smiled.

He seems himself again, she thought. *Less guarded with me than he was on our long walk home from Mashhad.*

Crack! They heard a loud noise from the village square. Anahita stared wide-eyed. Dariyoush ran up the stairs to the bathhouse door and looked out.

"A beam exploded. The men have taken cover. Faster with the buckets!" Dariyoush ordered.

They worked without speaking, even the little ones in the line whose arms sagged under the weight of the water.

By the time the villagers squelched the fire, only one blackened beam remained of Fatima and Ali's roof. Flakes of ash circled the air. Anahita could read only the date, "SINCE 1257," on the burned bakery sign.

As women and children left the bathhouse, Dariyoush and Anahita went back inside to collect empty pails and pick up lost belongings. Anahita's clothes dripped.

"Thank goodness no one was hurt," Anahita said as she reached for a soggy slipper.

Pulling a wet head scarf out of the pool, Dariyoush said, "We'll have a new roof on before long. Let's hope their ovens were spared."

Anahita nodded. "I don't see how Ali and Fatima could replace them before going to the spring market." Looking around, then pointing to the rim of the pool, she said, "I hardly noticed these blue floral tiles." Her eyes fell on the water next. "Oh, look, Dariyoush, a pail has sunk to the bottom."

"An invitation to dive in," he said, then grinned.

Neither of them moved.

Finally Anahita said, "Are you going to get it?"

"I meant for you," he said, crossing his arms. "You are the one who is curious about what it is like to float."

"Dariyoush!" Anahita said. "This is the men's bathhouse. I . . . what, what will people think? Remember the stir I caused last year by *simply asking* to bathe in this pool? Some are still mad at me for . . ."

"There's no one here, Anahita. They'll never know."

"But I'd get all wet."

"You are all wet."

Anahita looked down at herself. Her skirt clung to her thighs.

She nodded, eyed the pool and then Dariyoush. "It really is fun to bathe—I mean swim—isn't it?"

"It is luxurious. Go on. You may never get this chance again. I'll watch the door."

Anahita sat on the edge of the pool. "Is it deep?"

"About shoulder height. Just right."

Giving herself a push from the lip of the pool, she slipped into the water. The wetness seeped through her clothing and warmed her skin. "Look," she exclaimed, bouncing off the tips of her toes.

"The water holds me up!"

Dariyoush smiled. He peered out the door and back at Anahita where his eyes lingered.

Anahita lay back on the water and tried to float. But she began to sink. Kicking, she said, "Oh no," as she caught herself with one foot. She spit out a mouthful of water.

"I can't float."

"You must relax," Dariyoush said. "Lie back, take a lungful of air, and wave your arms slightly to your sides."

She tried again and sank.

"Your clothes are weighing you down." Dariyoush glanced out the door again. "Level your body in the water, and hold your feet slightly beneath the surface."

"I am floating!" she exclaimed. "I'm floating!"

"You are what?" Farhad said, tearing open the curtains from the women's side of the bathhouse, his face and clothes covered in soot.

Dariyoush turned pale. Anahita gulped. She splashed to her feet. "I . . . we . . . we were collecting sunken pails." Anahita looked furiously about for the bucket.

Closing the curtains behind him, Farhad said, "Anahita, get out of this pool and go home."

Her arms shook as she pulled herself out of the water, her dripping clothes hugging her body. Leaving a trail of wet footprints, Anahita stopped to pick up the two buckets she had brought to the fire, then began to climb the bathhouse stairs.

* * *

"Please forgive me, Kadkhuda Farhad," Dariyoush said. He lowered himself into the pool to retrieve the pail. "We were getting the buckets . . . we got carried away."

Farhad crossed his arms. "Dariyoush, I think of you much like the son I never had. But the fact is, you are not. And what I have witnessed here is my daughter bathing with a man who is not related to her. What could this suggest of my daughter's character to anyone who might not understand that you and she have basically grown up as brother and sister?"

Dariyoush climbed out of the pool. He wrung out one sleeve, then the other.

"This is not how I would like things to be between us when you leave for the border brigade tomorrow."

"Nor I," Dariyoush said. He looked at his hands.

"Then let us keep this incident between the two of us. Mojdeh would be horrified to learn that her daughter bathed with you. And Allah knows she has been through enough lately. She's still mending friendships after our journey home from Mashhad."

Farhad brushed some ashes off the hair on his arms. "Dariyoush, you are a fine young man, and I look forward to working with you when you return. Please keep in mind that Anahita is a wedding candidate. She is in the public eye more than ever with this wedding riddle contest."

"Yes, Kadkhuda. I understand. My own parents have warned me as such."

Farhad raised an eyebrow.

Dariyoush ran a hand through his wet hair and looked at the

cone of light cutting the mist from a window in the dome ceiling. "They have asked me not to get involved with this, with Anahita's wedding plans. They are aware of the khan's wishes and, sir, they haven't been happy with Anahita—the fact that our migratory rights are suspended."

Farhad laid a hand on Dariyoush's shoulder. "Someone will win Anahita's hand, my friend. I would be most pleased if it were you. Then, should I catch the two of you bathing, I shall say nothing."

Dariyoush cracked a smile.

"If you do not enter Anahita's contest, will you ever find peace with yourself?"

19

Weaving a Plan

Arash, his advisers, and young Pirouz, who had charmed the prince into allowing him to come along, sat inside a lavishly carpeted tent at the horse race in Bagh-e Shah. This was a seasonal event of great importance on the royal calendar, and the shah had requested that Arash attend. The race attracted the nobility and the nomadic horse breeders of northeastern Iran. For this reason alone, to meet with *kadkhudas* from the region, Arash agreed to go. Horse racing itself did not interest him, especially now that news had reached him of a skirmish between his Yomut tribe and the Russians. Now his main concern was to help his people secure a place to spend the winter. *None of them may dare lay their heads to rest.*

Arash gave the speech at the grand opening of the race, which seemed superficial to him—like adorning a dead camel. Written by the shah, it glossed over the recent royal orders that required nomads living on the borderlands to acquire migration permits to travel through lands they had walked for centuries—a measure that would lead to their forced settlement. Arash wished the shah had come to deliver it. Then it dawned on him that the shah had sent him here to smooth the court's relationship with the nomads. *I am his pawn.* The shah hoped to benefit by his nomadic blood, shared with these Turkman, Tajik, and Yomut tribes. He knew his father feared a nomadic rebellion more than the talk of the constitutional reformists or the greed of the landowners and merchants; the latter were too comfortable to risk losing their possessions by undermining a king.

Arash knew that if the nomads united, they would make a formidable force. They would ignite with an energy so great, they could overcome the shah's military or the Russians' guns without firepower. He wondered what the nomads really stood to gain from an allegiance to the shah.

He noticed that the palace stables had sent three hundred fine horses to this race, yet the troops in the frontier garrisons traveled by foot. Perhaps he'd discuss this horse problem with his men. But first, he wanted to relay to them what he had learned while meeting with the local assembly in Mashhad. As Pirouz served tea, Arash began. "I found that the reformists in Mashhad suffer from a local khan—an odd fellow who travels with a cat and uses his fists against tables and walls." Whose eyes, Arash remembered, were that of a tiger's—two slits, blade-like, capable of cutting deep furrows. "If this man could flip his self-interests to serve the locals' wishes, their small but strongly voiced call for a constitution would strengthen. But for now, I feel no pressing need to address their demands. I will meet with similar groups in other cities before considering taking their requests to Tehran—to the Consultative Council."

Arash's subjects spoke among themselves. A few nods. The tinkling of spoons.

"I also discovered in Mashhad the waning coffers of the royal treasury. Much like in our own palace at Marv, carpets and other finery have disappeared from the offices of city officials—pawned for cash to pay civil servants. Carpenters, street builders, and gardeners have been denied months of wages and are offered instead bricks and brass fixtures pilfered from crumbling government buildings—"

"*Ahem*," one of Arash's subjects cleared his throat loudly. Catching Arash's eye, the man tilted his head toward Pirouz, who distributed damp hand cloths and slices of lemon to the men for freshening up.

Knowing the man was concerned that Arash was addressing matters of state in front of a civilian—a street boy—he nodded back at him, indicating that he appreciated the man's concerns. Arash continued, "This is something I would like each of you to address at once. I need the records, receipts, and expense sheets of those who work in the various departments of the *divan*. Decide among yourselves which cities and villages you will visit. I will bring this to the attention of the shah at once. It is our people who make a nation strong," Arash insisted. "We must provide for our workers."

"Please, may I go, too?" Pirouz piped in. "I could cook for any of you on the road. I have a knack with fire!"

Ismail, Arash's chief adviser, curled an arm around the boy and said to the prince, "We will do whatever it takes to straighten things out, *agha*." Then he looked at Pirouz. "Perhaps you can ride with me."

"Thank you," Arash said, his mind beginning to wander. More than ever, since Mashhad, Anahita crept into his thoughts. He wanted to ask his subjects a favor in regard to her.

"While you are traveling about, I must ask all of you for help. I wish to find a weaver named Anahita. I am told she winters in a village called Hasanabad, or perhaps, Deh-eh Hasan. It may be near Nishapur. Though, unfortunately, I cannot trust my source."

"You wish for us to help you find a woman?" one of his men said, surprised.

"Pardon me *agha*, did you say Nishapur? Is that not the birth-place of our beloved Attar, mentor of the poet Rumi?" Ismail said.

"I believe so. I wish for you to search all the villages in this land whose names include 'Hasan.' Anahita is an Afshar," Arash contin-ued. "This should be of some assistance in finding her—there is only a small band of them in Khurasan. Most of them live near Kerman and Isfahan. She is a weaver of great skill. I hear every loom she warps blossoms beneath her fingers. She can match her wit with educated men. And I believe she knows much of animal husbandry. But more importantly," he drifted, "she seems to lack interest in things that can be bought or sold . . ." *"Surely you do not judge worth by money . . ."* Arash heard Anahita's voice as if she stood there with his men. He gathered his thoughts. "To the first of you who finds this woman, I shall give a stallion."

"Forgive me, my Prince, but how are we to be certain we have found the right woman? There are many, many weavers through-out the land. Could you give us some physical description of her?" one of Arash's subjects asked.

Arash looked into the faces of each of his men. The question caught him off guard. "Hmm," he began, "she looks . . . she has black hair."

Black hair the men scribbled on scraps of parchment, then looked up at Arash for further details. But Arash was lost in thought. He gazed outside the tent at a young filly racing across the plain.

"Excuse me, *agha*," another said. "Might you have something else to tell us about her? Something which might make her, well, sir, something which might distinguish her from the others?"

Arash still gazed out the tent. Some of the men smiled at one another.

"Oh, yes. I'm sorry. This woman, her . . . her cheeks," Arash said, "are the shape and color of pomegranates."

Two of Arash's men stole glances at each other and covered their mouths to hide their grins. But when they could no longer contain their mirth, one, then the other, broke into a chuckle until there was no holding back. The tent filled with laughter.

"Pomegranates?" Ismail said.

Arash looked at his men and laughed himself. He knew them well enough to know they meant no ill will. He shook his head. He was half amused, half frustrated at his circumstances—that he was in love with a woman who was most likely married, and who had managed to appear and disappear from his life twice. Arash said, "Yes, I'm smitten with this woman. But my affection for her is something I wish for you to keep to yourselves. There could be more than one weaver out there with the name of Anahita. No sense having them all think a prince wants to wed them. As far as anyone needs to know, this mission is strictly business. If anyone asks, tell them I am seeking a dyer for the royal textile workshop."

"*Agha,*" a subject said. "Not all weavers are dyers. Perhaps this woman will not respond to your subjects' inquiries."

"Most weavers do some dyeing," Ismail offered.

"My Prince," Pirouz stood up. "I may be the youngest one here, but I am no stranger to romance." A few of Arash's subjects chuckled and Pirouz looked down. "May I suggest something?"

"Of course."

The boy stepped beside Arash and raised himself on his toes to whisper in the prince's ear.

Arash nodded as Pirouz talked. The prince's face broke into a smile, thinking this was a brilliant plan, but how did Pirouz know that Anahita did not care for synthetic dyes? Arash glanced at Ismail, with whom he recalled sharing this information. His adviser was obviously a bit of a gossip.

"You are truly a wizard, young man," Arash said, holding Pirouz by the shoulders. Facing his men, Arash announced, "This is my plan: Each of you shall carry bottles of synthetic dyes—I will give you money to purchase them. They are the most expensive and lavish colors available anywhere. Offer them to the weaver you meet who calls herself Anahita. If she does not accept the dyes, I am certain this must be the woman I seek."

The men exchanged puzzled glances. Then Ismail said to the

rest, "Come, gather around this map. The going will be danger-
ous, the weather on the mountain passes this time of year
unpredictable."

"And love will fill the air!" Pirouz cried and the laughter
erupted again.

"Please, men," Ismail continued. "Compose yourselves. We'll
start with all the villages surrounding Nishapur and those with
the name 'Hasan' . . ."

Before the races concluded, Arash's men mounted their
Arabians. He watched his subjects as they rode away from the
cheering crowds into the silence of the desert. He wished to be
with them but his tribe depended on him now. After the races he
would return to his mother's people, where his allegiance, in spite
of his absence, had always been.

He consoled himself with the thought that his men would find
Anahita. Then he would go to her. Thinking of Anahita now
brought to mind words from his favorite poem, which he one day
wished to share with her,

> You appear; all studying wanders.
> I lose my place . . .

Knowing she had kept his book of poems quickened his
blood—as if by fingering each page she'd be touched by a memory of him. He hoped that perhaps she'd find a quiet moment to
read this very same poem—its sounds resting in her ears, its words
settling in her soul.

A Lesson of Her Own

A huge husky chained to a stake beside Hasanabad's new school snarled as it chewed the fleshy hindquarters of a sheep carcass. Reza gave the dog a wide birth, eyeing its spiked collar and the mud house beyond to which it belonged. The teacher took down the sign from the school's entrance, which had announced: REGISTRATION TODAY.

But it had been word of mouth, rather than his sign, which brought potential students to his door, and the day's results pleased him. Men, women, and children visited the school in ones, twos, and threes to enroll. Some came simply to have a look inside. "My Karim," one said, "he built these walls." "My Akbar," another said, "he built the window frames." Fatima and Ali's girls arrived with tea and bread for the grand opening. For this, Reza felt grateful and welcomed.

So far, several students had signed up, including a few parents. Reza was surprised and pleased when Kadkhuda Farhad added his name to the list of enrollees. He wondered—no, hoped—that he would bring his daughter as well.

From where he stood, Reza could see from one end of the village to the other. He figured he could spit across the length of Hasanabad. Loved ones here were never really out of earshot, let alone out of sight of a relative. Perhaps this is why it seemed that the women and children of this village enjoyed freedom—visiting wherever they liked by themselves. It wouldn't happen in Mashhad.

This town held a certain charm for Reza. He liked how old most everything felt. The small plaza in the center where the people gathered for important and not-so-important events. The mosque with its minaret, forever slanting toward sunrise. The mud homes that baked continually in the sun. And his very own schoolhouse conveniently located only a hazelnut's throw from the center of things. Yet he missed his home in Mashhad and his cockatiel in its too-cumbersome-to-carry cage. Reza was thankful that the widow had offered to keep the bird, and that his lovebirds had traveled well with him on the journey to Hasanabad.

The dog's bark pulled Reza out of his thoughts. Expecting no one else to register at this late hour, he stepped back inside the school and out of the chilly wind. He sat cross-legged beside a dung-fired stove on one of several small carpets. Leaning against a cushion, he opened a book and began to read when Anahita appeared at the door.

Closing the book with his fingers still inside it, Reza stood up. His lovebirds chirped in the corner of the room. He liked the pattern on Anahita's skirt, as busy as it was with birds.

"May I come in?" she asked.

"Please," he said. "May I fix you a cup of tea?"

She nodded. "I stopped to welcome you to our village. I am Anahita, daughter of Farhad and Mojdeh. We met in . . . well, we nearly met at my summer camp."

"How could I forget?" he smiled.

"I was just on my way to the dyemaster's. He lives three houses up," she pointed over her shoulder.

This amused Reza. Who could mistake the dye house? Its tree branches were the most colorful around—strewn with dyed yarn set out to dry.

"I've watched this building go up brick by brick," Anahita said. "It's so exciting to see it completed and to have you here with us."

"It is my pleasure." His voice wavered a little as he wasn't yet convinced he'd done the right thing—volunteering for the Rural Madrasa Servanthood and moving here in hopes of getting to know Anahita—with the chance of crossing paths with the khan. The peacock-feather-flying man irritated him. Reza recalled the diplomat's vague excuse for withdrawing his offer to pay him to tutor Anahita: *Something has come up and I won't be needing your services right now, Master Reza.* The khan failed to tell Reza the truth, that Kadkhuda Farhad had refused to give the khan his daughter's hand. Reza learned this news soon after moving to the village. Surely the khan would not be pleased should he ever find Reza near Anahita.

Anahita set her empty satchel next to the stove and knelt in front of it to warm her hands. "I believe it will snow tonight."

"And why is this?"

"The air feels wet this afternoon." Anahita rubbed her fingers against her thumb. "People say I've inherited my mother's thin skin."

Reza glanced at her face and hands. "Your skin looks anything but thin. Sun-tinted and healthy maybe . . ."

Anahita smiled. "You see, my mother is attuned to the weather. She celebrates rain and snow. She insists we weave cloud bands into all of our rugs. It is mostly the winter snow which feeds the groundwater for our wells in Hasanabad."

She slid her legs beneath her and stirred her tea. "Mount Binalud, just north of here, steals the clouds from us. We get very little rain to fill our roof catches. My mother can feel any trace of liquid in the air—sometimes a day before the blessing comes. The smell of rain is her favorite, next to certain spices."

Reza took off his spectacles. "In Mashhad, I never gave this much thought. Water is something a boy sells to me from his cart each morning."

Anahita turned her head toward the lovebirds, which seemed to twitter and chitter their sweetest song for her. "What beautifully colored birds!"

Placing his book on the carpet, Reza opened the door to the cage. He moved his hand inside with his index finger extended, and brushed the peach-colored one on its belly. The lovebird stepped one foot, then the other, onto his finger. Anahita smiled as he backed his hand out of the cage.

"It's so tame. How did you do that so easily?"

"Nothing comes easy. It took me months to train these two. Would you like to try with the other?"

"May I?"

"Surely. Just stroke the belly downward. Your finger will trip the bird off of its perch."

Anahita did as Reza said, and the other lovebird hopped onto her finger. "Its little claws feel so delicate, they tickle my skin. Aren't birds the most beautiful creatures on earth?"

Next to you, Reza wanted to say. *Perhaps my year in Hasanabad won't seem so long after all,* he thought.

"What are their names?" Anahita asked.

"Lemon and Acrobat."

The names brought a smile to Anahita's face. "Will they not fly away?"

"They used to, but now they heed me. I taught them to come to the sound of the bell on their mirror. They have been my most faithful companions of late."

Anahita wiggled her finger so the lovebird would jump back onto its perch. "I must confess. I came here not only to welcome you, but also to ask a favor," she said, pulling her hand out of the cage.

Reza raised an eyebrow as Anahita pulled a book from her satchel. Looking at it he said, "So you like Rumi? His spiritual mentor, Fariduddin Attar, hailed from Nishapur—very near to here."

He noticed her hand shook slightly as she gave the book to him. "Do you have a favorite poem of Jalaluddin Rumi?" Reza asked, holding the book in one hand and putting his lovebird back with the other. He closed the little reed gate on the cage.

"No. I mean, yes." She looked down as if she felt uncomfortable.

"This is your book, is it not?" he asked, thinking perhaps it wasn't.

"It was given to me by someone, though." She hesitated. "I cannot read it."

"I see. Well, you've come to the right place now, haven't you? Here, give me this book. I shall treat you to one of the most beloved Persian authors. Please sit and have your tea."

The book fell open in Reza's hands to a page that had been dog-eared. He pulled on his glasses and read the title, "A Great Wagon."

Anahita brushed lint from her skirt and stirred the tea in her tiny glass cup. The spoon made a tinkling sound that the lovebirds returned with notes of their own.

Reza read:

When I see your face, the stones start spinning!
You appear; all studying wanders.
I lose my place.

Anahita looked up, surprised.

Water turns pearly.
Fire dies down and doesn't destroy.
In your presence I don't want what I thought
I wanted, those little hanging lamps.

Inside your face the ancient manuscripts
seem like rusty mirrors.

Reza paused, thinking how well this stanza applied to his guest.
When he looked at Anahita, she turned her face from his to the birds.
He read on:

You breathe; new shapes appear,

and the music of desire as widespread
as Spring begins to move
like a great wagon.
                    Drive slowly.
Some of us walking alongside
are lame!

The two sat quietly for a minute before Reza said, "Your friend
who has given you this book selects a good poem."
"Selects? Why do you say this?"
"This person, is it . . . ?" Reza flipped to the inside cover of the
book and read the inscription. "This person, Arash, has dog-eared
this page."

"Arash?" she half asked, half exclaimed.

Reza studied Anahita's expression. *Had she not known that the letters on the inside cover spelled a name, Arash's name? She must learn to read,* he thought. *I will teach her.*

"Is this not who gave you this book?" Reza's interest piqued by Anahita's obvious uncertainty.

"Oh, yes. Arash," she said, eyeing the book. "He will remain a mystery to me, I'm afraid."

Anahita looked as if she wanted her book back, so Reza gave it to her. She nearly grabbed it from his hands, as if she couldn't wait to inspect every page. *This person, Arash, must be someone special to her,* he thought. *Perhaps they are studying Rumi's work together. Maybe Arash is a dervish.*

"Mystery can often be explained." Reza gestured to books of all sizes around his classroom. "People spend lifetimes at it."

"What about those mysteries that are part of life that we cannot understand with our minds, such as why only a mountain can turn minerals into rubies, or why many things contain their opposites, like goodness and evil." Anahita clasped her hands together. She looked up. "And what about love? Are there books that can explain this?"

My goodness, Reza thought, *she is one to contemplate things.* "The mullah would be more qualified than I to delve into such questions."

Anahita touched her head scarf. "Thank you for reading the poem to me. I really must be on my way. My granduncle will wonder what has happened. I was only to deliver a few skeins to my aunt—yellow yarn she had asked him to make green. I forgot myself here."

As Rumi loses his place? Reza thought, but said, "Will you attend my classes with your father?"

"I hope to. The decision is his. I'm afraid he worries I take too many liberties—and I'm not exactly on his best side right now." Anahita's voice softened as she looked at the carpet. Her next words came out like a sigh. "He may be right. As my cousin Shirin says, 'A woman doesn't do what she wants, only what she has to, except for that Anahita . . .' School may be where my father draws the line."

Reza knew all about "the march," as the villagers called it. It was the current favorite topic at Fatima and Ali's. The stories amused Reza. Each person inflated the time, length, struggle, and lack of water on their journey back to Hasanabad from Mashhad. It was like a game he sometimes played with his students where they would whisper a story from ear to ear, a method of his in teaching them good listening skills.

It was in the teahouse that Reza had also learned of Anahita's wedding riddle contest, now deemed by some "the cursed contest." And it was there that he heard mention of some incident that happened a year or so ago involving Anahita, which they referred to as "the bathhouse petition." But he never fully understood the details of this, nor did he feel it was his place to ask, though her antics intrigued him.

Reza looked at her intently. "But surely your father will come to see things as our clerics, who have called for rural *madrasas*, do—that education is good for girls. Remind your father of this. Perhaps it will help persuade him."

"I will," Anahita said, as she and Reza stood up. "I must be going." She slipped Arash's book in her satchel and pulled on a large woolen scarf. Wrapping it about her head, shoulders, and waist, she waved good-bye and slipped out into the village under a veil of snowflakes.

Perhaps he could be of some help in convincing her father. *She seems so eager to learn,* Reza thought. *And how she would brighten my class with her smile . . . and energy.*

After watching her walk down the road and disappear around a corner, he turned his face to his classroom. *She'd soften the edges of these books . . . and these slates on which we write.*

The dog tied to its chain barked again, making Reza's heart trip. Eyeing the canine, he thought about how interesting it was that even though Anahita could not read, she was articulate. And supposedly quick with riddles. Surely he should enter the challenge for her hand. *I'm good at tests, and perhaps even cursed contests,* he thought, smiling. *Who would have better insight than her own teacher?*

Bride Price

More than a week after registration day and the grand opening of Hasanabad's new school, the khan rode into town with his retinue: horses and camels piled high with goods, fellow politicians, scouts, bodyguards, and his personal scribe.

He dismounted and, carrying his cat, went directly to the school, while his men struggled behind him with an extraordinarily heavy carpet that bore a larger-than-life image of the khan himself. As he approached the school, he caught a glimpse of the back of a woman as she left the classroom and disappeared around the corner. A man, presumably the new teacher, followed her as far as the threshold. The teacher's face came into focus, and the khan thought, *This comes as no surprise. After meeting Anahita, that bird-loving opportunist wasted no time in having himself transferred to this village.* "Good day, Master Reza. What a coincidence to find you here. Or is it?" he sneered.

Reza said nothing and looked at the carpet.

"Mouse got your tongue?" the khan said, his cat curling her tail around his arm. "I suppose the clerics in Mashhad at the Rural

208

Madrasa Servanthood simply pulled Hasanabad out of their administrative hats when they assigned you here."

"Surprising how the universe works." Reza leaned on the door-jamb and crossed his feet at the ankles.

The khan held the teacher's gaze. "Puzzling, isn't it?" He looked around for anyone who might hear him. "I have come to donate this *qali* to the students of Hasanabad. It's the least I could do for my dear, dear tribesmen." Snapping his fingers at his men, he said, "Let's try it on for size, gentlemen. Haul her in."

Two of the four people holding the rolled-up carpet pushed past Master Reza, carrying it to the wall opposite the door of the classroom. But the carpet was so wide, the other two rug-bearers were left outside with the excess rug. Reza's birds chirped and fluttered at the intrusion.

"I appreciate your thinking of my school," Reza said, "but I don't think this *qali* will fit."

"Perhaps we just need to turn it sideways," the khan said, stepping inside with his cat. "I commissioned it from weavers in Mashhad. It is made with the newest dyes on the market."

Reza squinted at the colors on the underside of the carpet. "They must be quite dazzling right side up," he said, eyeing the cat. Then he said, "Please sir, your pet will upset my lovebirds."

"Your birds will live," the khan retorted. "And yes, this *qali* will be a dazzler—splendid for the grand opening." The diplomat felt a twinge of excitement for the ceremony.

Reza looked from one grinning dignitary to the next, those inside and outside. "Our grand opening was last week."

The khan's face fell. "Well, this simply cannot be. I have been misinformed. We shall hold a second grand opening tomorrow. Scribe, please post this announcement about town. It was I who financed this school. I deserve some recog—I mean, I deserve to enjoy my constituency enjoying their new school."

"Your constituency?" Reza pressed. "Have we achieved a constitutional monarchy already?"

"Er, uh, did I say 'constituency'? I meant, my people," the khan said, sweeping an arm around the room. His gesture allowed his cat just enough leeway to leap from his hold toward the lovebirds.

Feathers flew. Screeches reached ear-piercing levels as the khan's cat slunk around the cage. Reza dove for the prowler, grabbed it by the scruff of its neck, and threw it out the window. The feline hissed as it sailed.

"How dare you treat my cat in that way!" the khan yelled. He ordered one of his men, "Go and get her." Then he stepped up to Reza and poked a finger at the schoolmaster's chest. "I'll see that you find no work once you return to Mashhad. And if you go near Farhad's daughter, I will see to it that no one in the whole of Khurasan province will ever hire you."

Reza squared his shoulders. "Only months ago you were keen that I teach Anahita. Are you afraid, now, that if I do, I will learn something about her for which you have never taken the time?"

It incensed the khan to hear Reza call Anahita by name, the schoolmaster's informality suggesting a shared intimacy with her. The khan drew back a fist and threw a punch. Reza ducked and scrambled out the door.

* * *

Calling for her father, Anahita sprinted into her house.

"Baba, the khan is here and he's planning a second grand opening."

"For what?" Farhad said, rummaging in the back room for a knife.

"The school. And he's brought all sorts of goods with him, camels and horses and . . ." Anahita stopped when she heard someone at the front door.

Maman Bozorg opened it. There stood the khan with two of his men, carrying some sort of daybed piled high with embroidered cushions, bolts of cloth, copper cookware, and silver serving bowls.

Anahita brushed past her father and out the back door. She had to get out of there. She knew what the khan was up to and could not bear to listen to him bid for her like chattel. Tears of frustration smarted her eyes. *How dare he come here, after interfering with our migratory rights?*

She wandered toward the mosque thinking she might visit with the mullah, but what she really needed was to talk with a woman. Preferably, someone unrelated to her. *Fatima*, Anahita thought, and headed to the square. As she came to the plaza, she heard a tumult of whinnies and moans, and the clapping of hooves on cobblestones. The village square looked and smelled like the market in Mashhad. Sweaty, travel-wearied animals stood everywhere. Good ones. Arabian horses and Khurasan camels, a crossbreed between the Arabian single hump and the Bactrian two humped—Farhad's favorites because they were stronger than other camels and fared better in cold winters. *I'll bet the khan thinks he can win back friends with these,* Anahita thought. Their raw scents tormented her, reminders of the diplomat's unsavory intentions.

She wove through the smelly four-legged omens into the tea-house. Parting the new embroidered curtains in the doorway, she found Fatima with her feet up, cracking pistachio shells with her teeth.

"Anahita," the woman said, wiping her hands on her tunic. "What a pleasant surprise."

Anahita responded with a flood of tears.

"Now, I'll have none of that. Our teahouse isn't a place for crying but for laughing. Come sit with me and tell me what is the matter."

"Oh, Fatima, those animals are the matter. The khan is the matter! I just want to run away, leave this riddle contest behind . . ."

Fatima reached for Anahita's hand and pulled her onto the bench beside her. "Back when I was a ripe young thing, when I lived in Bukhara . . ."

Anahita nodded, wiping a tear from her face.

"I once hid in an old minaret—the tallest in Asia at the time of Genghis Khan—in fact, emirs used to throw people off of it."

"They didn't!" Anahita said, feeling the knots in her stomach loosen.

"Anyway, this minaret was built over the grave of a holy man who requested of his murderer: 'Lay my head on a spot where nobody can tread,' or so the legend goes. Some people used to say they heard voices inside the tower."

"And you *hid* there? Why?"

"The idea of ghosts never scared me, dear girl. Why, they tell the best stories!" Fatima slapped her knee as she laughed. Anahita shook her head. One by one, her tears of frustration became beads of mirth. "What on earth were you doing in a haunted minaret?"

"Well, I figured no one would ever follow me there. I had been betrothed to the youngest grandson of the infamous Nasrullah Khan—otherwise known as 'The Butcher,' but only called that behind his back, of course. He ascended the throne by killing his brothers and relatives, twenty-eight of them, I believe."

Anahita gasped and covered her mouth with her hand.

"*Oh, yes*—gasp away, my child. Imagine how I felt. I wasn't going to have that sort of blood mixing with my own. 'But he's *nothing like* his grandfather,' my father used to say to me on my suitor's behalf. Bah! I thought. Youngest grandson or no, up that minaret I went with my skin of water, cheese, and sack of *naan*—even then I made the best flat bread around."

"What happened?"

"No one would ever climb that minaret unless they were hauled up against their will. I was gone long enough that people worried I had been sold into slavery, or possibly had perished in the desert. When I came home my parents were so happy to have me back, they heeded my wishes not to marry the man."

Fatima's bosom heaved as she took a deep breath. She smiled then cracked a pistachio between her teeth, chewed, and swallowed.

"But I am not suggesting that you run away, Anahita. Just

that I understand your feelings. Remember, our khan is not a murderer. Only a bit conceited."

"But he's lost three wives!" Anahita's statement gave Fatima pause. The woman sucked in her breath, emitting a hiss of concern.

"A shadow *does* seem to enshroud the man," Fatima said, crossing her arms. "Yet he carries on in wholehearted oblivion, as if he doesn't notice that the people in his wake are dropping like flies! Peace be upon them all, of course."

Anahita giggled at Fatima's audacity.

Looking out the teahouse door, the woman continued, "And my, oh my is the khan impaired when it comes to social graces! Does he really think his horses and whatnot out there in the square—belching and farting and crapping on my doorstep—will mend friendships?" She sighed and got up, saying, "I've got to tend to my girls. Don't become disheartened. You are too strong for that."

Anahita wandered back home and spotted the daybed, too large to fit through the front door, sitting outside. Peering in the house, she saw that the khan was still there, so she went around back to wait for him to leave. She took the laundry off the line, tossed the chickens some feed, and paced.

When the khan finally left, Anahita went inside. Her parents, grandmother, aunts, and Shirin were chatting over tea. Pointing to the daybed outside, she asked, "Is the khan leaving that here?"

"It's a gift," Farhad said. "And so are these." He pointed to the pile of items on the floor, including cookware, silver, and fabrics.

"What for?" Anahita asked, though she knew. She looked at her father and mother and grandmother.

"You," they said together.

Anahita slumped onto a cushion.

"It is your bride price," Farhad said.

"But, Baba!" Anahita narrowed her eyes. "How could you?"

"My sweet, Anahita. You have so little faith," Farhad said.

"Your father has not accepted these gifts, Anahita," Mojdeh said. "The khan has left them here for us to think things over."

"Oh, how *thoughtful* of him," Anahita said, catching Shirin's eye. *What is she doing here?* Looking at her again Anahita thought, *She isn't smiling. She looks sorry for me.*

"If he is made to solve your riddle, these will not be ours to keep," Farhad said.

"Here," Maman Bozorg said, handing Anahita a beautifully woven *chanteh* stuffed with something soft. "He sends this to you with his regret that you were not here to receive it."

Anahita set the satchel aside.

"He has also offered fifty camels and half as many Arabians," Farhad said.

Anahita whipped her head toward the door, and looked across the lane to the village square. *All those camels!* "Where will we keep them?"

"The khan has left men to care for the animals until he returns for your contest. Unless, of course, we accept his offer in the meantime. We shall corral them on the other side of the stream."

"They would fetch good prices in Mashhad, I'm sure," Anahita's aunt said.

"Local tribes would buy the horses. They are in top form," her father added.

The conversation made Anahita feel awful, nervous, and guilty. She knew that the men of Hasanabad, when they saw these fine animals, would convince Farhad to take the bride price. *Ooh, the khan is so slippery,* she thought.

"Baba," Anahita said, her voice shaking. "The khan knows that our people would accept no other *kadkhuda* than you. His only power is his conniving mind. He purposely brings these gifts for others to see. He is trying to buy our tribe's favor so that they may influence you!"

Anahita looked at everyone in the room. Their silence told her she was right.

"Can't we just exclude him from the contest and be rid of him?" Anahita nearly shrieked.

"Absolutely not," Farhad said. "I've no wish to increase the conflict within our tribe. I intend to run a fair event. Him winning is one of the possible consequences of your contest that perhaps you did not consider. But as I've said, should he guess your riddle, I will give him your hand."

Farhad picked up a copper vessel and felt its weight. "You could use one of these, Mojdeh, could you not?" Putting it down again, he went out the back door.

Anahita picked up the pot and threw it against the door behind her father. To her surprise, no one reprimanded her. Maman Bozorg retrieved the vessel and placed it carefully on the stack of others.

"Anahita," Mojdeh said, in a strained but soothing tone, "are you not going to open the *chanteh* the khan sent you?"

Anahita glared at her mother and pushed the gift in front of Shirin. *She's probably more curious than I*, she thought. *I'll let her have the pleasure.*

"Are you sure, Anahita?"

"Yes, and you can keep whatever it is."

Shirin looked at her mother and aunts. "Thank you, Anahita. But I cannot accept this. The gift is not meant for me. I will open it for you." She reached into the satchel and pulled out three imported cashmere undergarments.

"Oh!" Anahita said. "Wherever did he find such, such . . ." The intimate gift made her stomach lurch. She ran out the front door and retched.

Shirin followed her. Mojdeh stood in the threshold.

Curling one arm around her cousin's shoulder, Shirin said, "I'm sorry, Anahita. I take back what I said this summer. I would not want to be wed to him either. At least my husband is not so old, and . . . and *creepy*."

Anahita retched again, a dry heave. She pulled the hair out of her face and looked at Shirin. "That's the nicest thing you've said in months—the khan *is* creepy!" A raspy laugh caught in Anahita's throat.

"I know what to do," Shirin said.

"What?"

"Give them to the clothing cart."

The two grinned at each other like they used to when they spied on the village widow.

"Shirin," Anahita said, "you won't believe the story Fatima just told me . . ."

ZEMESTAUN
BAUFTAN
Winter Weaving

Warp, Weft, and Wishes

Outside Anahita's home, the family's red wagon sat on the frost-covered grass like the last ripe apple on a bare winter tree. Steam from a nearby dung pile rose in the cold December morning air.

In an alcove just off the main room of their home, Anahita, her mother, and Maman Bozorg erected the vertical loom on which Anahita would weave her wedding carpet. It stood nine feet tall and six feet wide and consisted of an upper and a lower crossbeam held taut by the two sides of the frame. A bench fastened to a pulley system allowed the weaver to be raised as the rug progressed from the earth toward the sky.

The three women spent the next two days preparing the continuous—and seemingly endless—string of yarn that they would wind around the crossbeams of the loom to create eight hundred and sixty vertical warp threads. This warp would be the foundation of Anahita's carpet.

The warp needed to withstand repetitive pounding from the

lead combs that packed weft threads into place. Pounding that would last as long as the sun was in the sky each day, for the four or five months Anahita, her mother, and grandmother would weave this carpet. Thus, they spun and plied the woolen warp, making it six strands strong and less likely to snap. If a warp thread happened to break, they would have to graft on a patch of yarn, which nearly always resulted in a noticeable lump in the *qali*. And Anahita hated how stopping to repair a warp disrupted the flow of the weaving.

She secured the end of the warp thread onto the lower cross-beam with three square knots, then slipped a smooth stick between alternate threads to create a space or "shed" so that she could pick each warp with ease. Then the women hung two dozen balls of freshly-dyed yarn across the top of the loom. From where she would sit, Anahita could easily reach each color.

When the loom was ready for weaving, Mojdeh reached for an amulet to hang from the top of the frame to protect their work from *chesmeh bad*, the evil eye, and envious onlookers. As she tied the large, ceramic blue bead among the skeins of wool, she recited a prayer:

> In the Name of the Compassionate and Merciful,
> I seek refuge in the Lord of Daybreak from the mischief
> of His creation; from the mischief of the night when she
> spreads her darkness; from the mischief of conjuring
> witches; from the mischief of the envier when he envies.

The women stood back to inspect the loom. Maman Bozorg plucked several warp threads to check for tautness. The tighter the better, Anahita knew, as the threads would stretch some in the process. The tighter the better, so her designs would weave up crisply.

Anahita ran her hand across all the threads on the loom. She loved the feel of them against her palm. *The feel of anticipation,* she thought. *The loom is like a canvas of wool, a desert of sand, a clean expanse where patterns are shaped by the same wind that blows over the plains.*

The women tossed cushions on the bench, now at the bottom of the loom, and sat down. Anahita chose a natural brown wool for the selvage of her carpet. Starting on the lower right side of her loom and working toward the middle, she tied soumak knots by threading two strands of the yarn behind, in front, and around pairs of vertical warp. Her selvage would soon withstand the pounding-in-place of all the threads above them, preventing all the knots she would weave from slipping off the bottom of her *qali.*

As Anahita worked, she thought about how she felt as if she'd always known how to weave. Like many girls in her tribe, she had been taught by her mother and grandmother when she was only five years old. Seated beside them with her own little loom—its frame of sticks the length of her arms—she practiced weaving kitten-sized carpets. Often she had woven salt bags, straps for satchels, and *sofrehs* for her family's use, her little fingers making the delicate knots.

Anahita smiled as she remembered the first weaving she brought to the market, and how proud she was that her work had finally become good enough to sell. She was nine years old and what a fuss the merchant had made over it. She pictured herself then, hidden behind her mother's *chador* as the merchant spoke to her parents. "I cannot believe that the weaver of this lovely *jajim* is only nine years old. Just look at the original pattern and the delightful choice of colors in the stripes of this fine satchel."

Reaching for her new weft comb with its dangling charms, Anahita's smile deepened when she felt the heavy lead implement fit snugly into her palm. *Perhaps it's the comb that chooses the weaver and not the other way around.* As she pounded the weft, the tool sang—*Jing, jing. Jing, jing*—locking her knots into place.

Anahita would weave seven borders for her carpet—her tribe's customary signature. For the first border she chose a dark brown yak wool. She switched from making the soumak knot, which she had formed with two strands of thread, to a plain weave, which she made with a single thread. With this plain knot she could weave intricate designs. Mojdeh and Maman Bozorg followed her lead, moving their yarn in and out of each warp thread.

In and out. In and out.

Jing, jing. Jing, jing.

The three weavers' hands brushed against one another when they met on the loom.

Soon a dark narrow band with small beige squares crept across the bottom of Anahita's wedding *qali*. How wonderful it felt to be weaving again!

Next came a cloud band border—the symbol for life-giving rain. Maman Bozorg got up to stretch and make *chai* for the women to drink. Mojdeh helped her daughter with this more difficult pattern. It was a stair-stepped design that made the clouds appear as if they were blowing east across the carpet.

"With what colors do you wish to celebrate the rain?" Mojdeh asked.

Anahita chose apricot, orange, rust, scarlet, and violet—all made from madder root. "This pattern not only celebrates rain," she said to her mother, "it celebrates the dyemaster's talent, getting all these hues from one plant."

Mojdeh smiled. "Yes, he could look at an ancient wall covered with crusty old lichen and find a rainbow among them."

Anahita bit her lip, concentrating. While she worked, she wondered what riddle she might weave into her carpet, and who would be the one to solve it. She shuddered that the khan might win her contest. An image came to mind of him at the school's second grand opening. He stood before a handful of people showing off the huge carpet with his face woven into it—a noticeably younger countenance, with dark hair and no bags beneath his eyes, the weavers likely having worked off a portrait of him that was twenty years old. *Poor Reza*, she thought, *having to paste on a smile for the occasion.*

Maman Bozorg served her granddaughter a cup of *chai* at the loom. As Anahita blew on the sage-scented liquid, warm thoughts of Dariyoush pushed away those of the khan. Then, catching a glimpse of the blue bead dangling from the upper crossbeam, her thoughts turned back to Reza, her very own teacher for nearly two months now. From this day on the bead would always remind her of Master Reza's eyes. *How lucky Reza is to have been born with amulets for eyes.*

"Maman, have I told you the schoolmaster keeps lovebirds?" Anahita said, resuming her weaving while her *chai* cooled.

Mojdeh looked at her daughter, smiled, and said, "Several times."

Jing, jing. Jing, jing.

"He keeps two of them. You see, they must have a mate or they will perish. They're from Africa. Imagine! He knows *everything* about birds. He can tell me the Latin names of the ones in the trees in the village square."

Maman Bozorg, who had resumed her place at the loom, paused from working. "You know, your grandfather once brought a parrot home all the way from Mashhad."

"He did? I shall tell Reza."

"He tried to teach it to talk but all it could do was snore, like your grandfather."

"You're joking, are you not?" Anahita said. But her grandmother just smiled at the memory.

The three wove quietly. Anahita never tired of watching

Maman Bozorg weave. Her fingers moved across the warp threads like Dariyoush's would across his lute strings. Only faster. Her soothing cadence spread to Anahita's own fingers. Even though her grandmother's eyes failed her, she seemed to see in another way.

"Reza's also explained to our class about the Assembly of the House of Consultation—how this government body is a stepping stone to a more representative type of parliament—like in Western countries. Baba asked him lots of questions. Imagine demanding the shah to give up some of his power! They say, 'A king must reign, not rule.'"

"My, my . . ." Mojdeh said, reaching for the yarn above her head. "Reza has taught you much more than the calligraphy and rudiments of the *Quran* that is taught in most *madrasas*. No wonder your father is greatly enjoying his lessons."

"Perhaps we should pray that such notions of reform, should they come to pass, do not cause bloodshed among our own people," Maman Bozorg said. The three wove in silence for a few moments, except for the sound of Anahita's comb.

Jing, jing. Jing, jing.

Jing, jing. Jing, jing.

Anahita then told them how Reza had been reading to her class from *Gulestan*. She described everything she had been learning as if she had not seen her mother or grandmother in a month.

"Anahita, what is that leather book I have noticed you reading? Is this one of your teacher's as well?" Maman Bozorg asked.

"You can read now?" Mojdeh said, a hint of surprise in her voice.

"Yes, Maman. I stumble a little, but Reza is a good teacher. He tells me if I read slowly, the meaning of the sentence will help me discover each word. He says I'm learning quickly."

Turning to answer her grandmother's question Anahita said, "The book is mine. But . . . it's not mine for keeps." She had become so wrapped up in her life with Reza that thoughts of the man from Marv or Bukhara had settled into a remote place in her mind. This man, Arash, with whom she seemed to share a certain connection, coming at times like little currents from inside and outside of her.

She looked down, hoping to hide her flushed cheeks from her mother and grandmother. *Surely they will see the longing for him in my face should they look at me!* Keeping her eyes on her hands as she wove, she asked herself, *From where do these feelings come? We have met only twice—yet this yearning is so strong.*

Anahita said, "Oh, someone in the crowd who watched the dervish dance gave it to me. I mean, he dropped it and I picked it up and then this camel took off running and he chased it and then somehow I forgot." She peered under her lashes to see both Mojdeh and her Maman Bozorg watching her as if they knew there was more to the story. "It's a book of poetry—by Jalaluddin Rumi."

"Poetry?" Mojdeh said.

No one said anything. *They contemplate my new interest in poetry,* Anahita thought.

"Do you find poetry a bit like riddles?" her mother pressed. But Anahita didn't answer. Not because she meant to be rude, but because she did not hear her mother. Stanzas from the poem "A Great Wagon" rushed to mind. Each knot she wove became a word. Fifteen in all, appearing from right to left across her loom—angular—the way she learned to write them with ink in the linen-bound book of blank parchment Reza had given her. It was a gift she kept secret so that she could write down whatever thoughts she pleased, and practice her letters more easily than she had been able to do by scribbling them into the dirt with a stick, or embroidering them onto *sofrehs* and scarves.

> In your presence I don't want what I thought
> I wanted, those little hanging lamps.

"Anahita, do you find poetry like riddles?" her mother repeated, but Anahita was still lost in Rumi's poems. The ones she had been reading this winter, over and over, so that the pages in Arash's book became worn from her touch. *All these poems. Lucky the woman who received them.* Then it dawned on her that Rumi had written thousands of poems. No man could fall in love with thousands of women in one lifetime. *"His poems push my perception beyond this world . . ."* She heard Arash's voice, his soft consonants. She wondered, *Could it be that Rumi's poems speak of some other kind of love?*

Thinking of Arash, Anahita reached for a gold-brown thread—the color of wet sand after rain. She wove this into the cloud band. Doing this seemed to bring him closer to her.

Anahita adjusted her head scarf. "Speaking of riddles, I *must* think of one to weave into my *qali*." Running her finger over the last cloud she had woven, she noticed a mistake, an extra knot on the wrong warp thread. She rewove it to make a more precise stair-step. "Though I can't seem to focus these days. I don't know what's come over me. I've never been wanting for a riddle."

She stopped weaving and massaged her fingers and hands. Her grandmother said, "I'm not surprised, my child. Every day you are so very busy."

"Yes, Anahita," her mother added. "I hardly ever see you. How am I to know you are still saying your midday prayers?"

I'm stretched thin as a silk thread, Anahita thought. But she didn't want to give anything up: helping her father with the animals since Dariyoush left, working with the dyemaster, going to school almost every afternoon, the clothing cart, weaving her wedding *qali*.

"Only in stillness will an oasis flower."

Anahita looked at Maman Bozorg. Her grandmother's words unleashed a wave of anxiety deep inside her that rolled through her body. "I guess I'm afraid to weave a riddle into my *qali*. What if I give the wrong suitor some clue that allows him to guess the answer? Then I'd be stuck with that man for life!"

"It's quite overwhelming to think about, is it not?" Mojdeh said.

Anahita slammed the weft comb on her row of knots. *JING!*

"Is there someone you would hope to marry?" Maman Bozorg asked.

Anahita wrung her hands. "I'm just so confused and exhausted. I don't know what to think. I am fond of Dariyoush, and Reza, and this man from Marv . . . I feel frenzied . . . like . . ."

"Like a camel in heat, running aimlessly in the sand?" her grandmother offered, a smile bringing out two dimples through her wrinkles.

"Maman Bozorg!" Anahita said, blushing hotly.

"Marv?" her mother said, pausing from her weaving.

"Yes, Marv, or possibly Bukhara," Anahita said. "The man whose book of Rumi I have. And *who* knows how many others out there will come for the contest. Oh Maman, Maman Bozorg, I don't know if I can do this!"

"Marv?" her mother said again. "Bukhara?"

"Anahita," her grandmother said, slipping an arm around her granddaughter's shoulders. "You know what I think whenever I'm faced with a decision that seems insurmountable?"

Anahita's nerves settled some when she heard the light-hearted tone of Maman Bozorg's voice.

"I believe that if you can't be *absolutely* certain of the outcome of your choices, then what difference does it make which path you choose?"

The three of them giggled at the absolute truth of her statement.

A Riddle in the Weaving

When weaving her carpet, Anahita needed no pattern as the women who wove in the workshops at the Mashhad bazaar did. A picture of her finished rug seemed to come to her all at once, as if hidden in her heart all along.

Her life would soon change, and she wished to bring her fondest memories with her. So she wove them into her rug. Within its borders they would keep—each day and forever.

Anahita wove a curly-haired goat and her favorite fat-tailed sheep, the animals that gave her clothing, food, and shelter. She wove a spindle and the shearing tools she used to help her father.

She wove her winter and summer homes and the mountains of the high plateau; a map of the villages where the tribes who once roamed were forced to settle; the market, the mosques, and the modern buildings of Mashhad.

Anahita wove a toddler bundled in blankets and perched upon a camel, herself on her first migrations. She wove a lute to remind her of her favorite lullaby, and of Dariyoush strumming by the fire on summer nights.

Sprinkled here and there in her rug were small roosters, amulets that protected against evil. Anahita wove other winged friends too: peacocks, starlings, and Reza's lovebirds.

Late one evening while weaving alone to the murmur of her parents' talk and the winter wind outside, Anahita wove a dervish and a book. They would remind her of Arash, and of their appreciation for other ways of seeing: Arash and his poetry, herself and her weaving. *Keep your eyes turned to the invisible*— her father's words came to mind. Anahita wove a snow leopard and footprints of the little creatures in the night.

The next morning, as if she could knot together her own destiny, Anahita wove the caravan in which she loved to travel each spring and autumn.

Each of these designs stood out in a deep indigo sea.

"Indigo," Mojdeh said, stepping into the alcove to watch her daughter work. "The color of eternity. Perhaps your love for each other will last for all time."

"My love for *whom*, Maman? Perhaps this blue is for our nomadic ways, which will last for eternity, Allah willing." Anahita finished the last knot of a camel in her caravan.

"The migration will be our stability in these times of change," Mojdeh said.

"Stability?" Anahita spun around to face her mother. "That might make a good riddle—stability and change. Hmm. I could challenge my suitors to guess which two opposing forces in life I have woven into my *qali*."

Mojdeh arched an eyebrow.

"You must keep this a secret in case I use it. Shall I weave a red medallion in the center?"

"The color of happiness? Most certainly," Mojdeh said.

"I will weave my name inside the medallion in a bed of happiness. And I will leave room beside it for the name of my betrothed."

With an idea for her riddle taking shape, Anahita worked effortlessly.

One day while Anahita and her grandmother wove together, she confided, "I've been thinking. Something about my conversations with Reza leave me wanting more."

"More of what? I should think this would please him, this wanting more."

"Well, I'm not sure. I like hearing everything he tells me. And I can see in his face that teaching brings him joy—watching me learn—my alphabet, my reading, my sums. He seems as happy as I am with everything I take in.

"But somehow he doesn't talk to me about things I wish to discuss."

Maman Bozorg tilted her head to listen, her hands still at work.

"Sometimes when I sit among the birds in the village square, it is the colors of their feathers and the sounds I follow in their chatter which speak to me. Not their common and scientific names, their migration patterns, or breeding habits.

"And those little black-feathered sparrows in Abadi-eh-Golab that sit on the backs of the sheep and warble—the ones that sound like underwater chimes, I hear an oasis in each note they seem to chirp and swallow."

Anahita picked up the design her grandmother had started on the right side of the loom and continued it on the left, weaving one flower for every three of Maman Bozorg's.

"There are different ways of experiencing this world, are there not?" Maman Bozorg said. "Not all that is worth knowing flows from books."

Anahita stopped weaving and looked at her grandmother. Maman Bozorg smiled. "Yes, Anahita. Some of us prefer the unpredictability of heaven to the order of man."

That cold afternoon, Reza visited. As he neared Anahita's house, a husky chained beside their shed growled. He walked a good distance around it. *If it weren't for the dogs,* he thought, *Hasanabad could be paradise.* Looking about for Farhad, he spotted him in the barn carrying a large sack of grain in his arms.

Reza picked his way across the pen through chicken manure, and around the sheep dung pellets, trying not to soil his shoes. He hoped to make this pair last the winter here in the village. When he stepped into the barn's dim light, he smiled at Kadkhuda Farhad.

"Schoolmaster?" Anahita's father said. "What brings you here? Is my daughter not performing her lessons well? Or has she posed you a riddle for which you've come for hints?" He winked. Light from cracks in the thatch lit cylinders of dust here and there. Little puffs of breath from sheep's nostrils, steady as heartbeats, warmed the place. Reza cupped his hands to his mouth, blew into them, and rubbed them together.

"Sink your fingers into one of these fleeces," Farhad suggested. "They'll warm your hands in no time."

Reza gestured no, and then folded his arms for lack of anything to do with them. "I came, sir, not for riddles, nor to report on Anahita's progress. I wish to discuss this test of wit, if you will. You see, I . . . I would be honored to win her hand in marriage."

"What do you suppose Reza is here for, Maman? I must go and see."

"Anahita, if he wanted to speak with you, wouldn't he have come to the house?" her grandmother said.

"You know," Mojdeh said, sitting down to join the weavers at the loom, "I've noticed Reza feels quite uncomfortable among the sheep. Did you see the way he walked into the barn?"

"Maman, what do you have against him? I thought you liked all that I'm learning. Your loyalties have always been with Dariyoush. You would like to see me married to Dariyoush."

"Please don't misunderstand me. I am thrilled with all your progress in school, Anahita. I would have liked to have had the same opportunity when I was your age." Her mother cut a red thread with a knife. "My only concern is that times change, as we are witnessing now. Perhaps the next shah or emir, or whatever title he will go by, will see no need for education and close the schools. Where will that leave your teacher, Reza?" Making several more knots, her mother continued, "Sheep are life for our people,

Anahita. If this man Reza were to be your husband, he would need to feel more kin with sheep, and I don't mean the vellum he handles in those old manuscripts he studies."

"And where is Dariyoush now?" Anahita snapped, pounding her weft. *JING!* "Surely he cares little about me. He's gone to fight—and without even saying good-bye." She didn't know if her anger came from feeling slighted or from her worries about him— that he might be hurt, that he might not come back from the war. Ever. How could he just walk away from everyone and everything he knew in life?

As the women wove, their calloused fingertips made soft sounds against the warp.

"I know you have strong feelings for Dariyoush, and how you must feel let down by the way he left. But he did stop in with his brother Mehdi to say good-bye."

"Two times," Maman Bozorg added.

"You weren't in," Mojdeh said. "You know he isn't one for good-byes, or fanfare of any kind . . ." She paused. "I think you forget that he was required by decree to join the army."

"Couldn't he have waited until the fighting is upon us?"

"So that he could marry you and then desert you?"

"But his parents never asked for my hand!"

Anahita wove the last sliver of a blue thread into her carpet and reached for red. The color of blood. *Of war,* she thought. This afternoon she decided red stood for hate, not happiness. *Everything, it seems, is comprised of their opposites. Even colors.*

When Mojdeh had left the loom, Maman Bozorg said to

Anahita, "Your mother speaks from her heart. She knows Reza will someday leave this village, whereas Dariyoush, should Allah bring him home to us safely, will not. She has seen her sisters suffer when their daughters left us to go to their husbands' families—Afshars as far away as Isfahan." Maman Bozorg rubbed her wrists. "Your mother believes the old saying about women who marry out: *You leave in a white dress, you return in a white dress—your death shroud.* Mojdeh only wishes to keep you close to her for as long as possible. She will miss you terribly."

As they wove, a chilly breeze from the partly opened window wafted through the weaving alcove, chilling Anahita's fingers. If they listened closely, they could hear the chatter and jokes that erupted through the door of the carpet repair shop across the alley whenever someone came and went. Along with the conversations, bits of threads escaped—the village's only litter.

This afternoon Anahita heard someone shout, "These dreaded cotton warps! I cannot repair them."

Anahita and Maman Bozorg laughed. It was a complaint the carpet repairers made time and again. "They fray like lint! Only unwise weavers use cotton warp."

Above the din Anahita heard the clatter of hooves and saw horses through the window. Two men and a boy riding Arabians dismounted in the village square. Each with a curious leather pouch fastened to one side of his saddle. Women huddled in doorways. Men strolled toward the visitors.

On that cold afternoon in Hasanabad, the smoke from each chimney seemed to signal to the others, "Who could this be?"

An Alchemy of Color

Slamming his fist on his desk, Arash said, "So all of the weavers named Anahita accepted the dye?"

His men flinched, even Ismail. They'd never seen Arash behave this way.

"All except for one, sir. She accepted only half." Pirouz said.

"Half? How does one accept half a gift? Did she keep one bottle of blue, or one of red?"

"Not exactly. You see," continued a man who had ridden with Ismail and Pirouz to Anahita's village, "we met her father, Kadkhuda Farhad, who took the dyes into their home across the village square. He stayed inside for quite some time, and this woman, Anahita, poked her head out the door once or twice to have a look at us."

Pirouz held up three fingers. "Three times."

"How do you know this woman looking through the door was Anahita?" Arash asked, the slightest trace of irritation in his voice.

"Because, sir, her cheeks were the color of pomegranates." Ismail smiled and the other man added, "She was quite beautiful."

239

Arash looked out one of the star-shaped windows of his office. His irritation deepened hearing them compliment Anahita this way, if it was his Anahita. He felt a mix of anger, jealousy, and, most of all, of wanting. Anger that his responsibilities in Marv held him back. Jealousy toward his own men who had perhaps seen her just days ago. Wanting to have been the one to greet her in her village, wanting to have been the one to have seen her. To make matters worse, he felt guilty for having these bad feelings toward Ismail and the others who had done him the favor of riding to the ends of the kingdom in treacherous winter weather. *Feelings to purge,* his dervish friend would say. *Practice only fraternity, humility, tolerance.*

"Go on," Arash said.

Ismail continued. "When Kadkhuda Farhad returned to us, he thanked us for our generous gift and said something about Anahita wishing to give samples to her granduncle."

"Granduncle . . ." Arash drummed his fingers on the back of his chair.

"And, sir, I found this *elameih* in my saddle bag when I returned to Marv." Pirouz held it up.

Arash unrolled the flower-sprinkled parchment, which the boy had placed in his hands. He began to read it aloud.

> The Kadkhuda Farhad of the Province Khurasan
> cordially invites suitable suitors
> to participate in a Test of Wit
> for the hand of his daughter . . .

Then, realizing it was just like the parchment that had clung to his leg in Mashhad, he stopped. "Where did you get this?" His eyes darted from Pirouz to Ismail and from man to man.

"I believe, sir, in Hasanabad. As you recall, Anahita's father's name is Farhad," Pirouz said.

"No one gave it to you directly?"

"Not exactly. There were children. They swarmed around us in the village square. Some shined our stirrups with their sleeves. Others oiled our saddles and girths. They fingered our sabers. I did a few magic tricks for them. We didn't notice anyone slip the *elameih* into my saddlebag."

"I remember seeing a gray-haired braid beneath one of those 'children's' kerchiefs," Ismail added.

Arash felt the smile forming on his face spread through his whole body as he realized the good news that his men had brought him. "She's not married!" he exclaimed. He tore the turban from his head, tossed it high into the dome of the ceiling, and shouted. "She's not married!" His men congratulated one another, patting one another on the back for a search well done. Amidst the hoopla, Ismail caught Arash's headpiece and tossed it back to him. The men kissed their prince on his right and left cheeks.

While this news brought Arash a minute's thrill, it swiftly twisted into anxiety. He imagined hundreds of suitors vying for Anahita's hand. The faces of the many men he had met across the kingdom would surely haunt him until the day he would either win or lose this test of wit.

After dismissing all his men except for Ismail, he said, "I can't believe I didn't put the two together—the parchment that wrapped about my leg in the bazaar . . . And, what about her village? Is it called Deh-eh Hasan?"

"It's Hasanabad. A day's ride from our beloved Attar's home, Nishapur."

The delicate lines on Arash's brow knit together as he sat in the chair behind his desk. An endless puzzle this seemed, trying to find one woman among so many throughout the land. "Who sanctioned the custom of naming villages after deceased relatives? All of the similar names make for too much confusion."

"Perhaps you should bring this issue to the Assembly of the House of Consultation." Ismail said, wearing a wry smile. "I am sure they will place it on the top of their agenda, and see to it that such practices cease."

Arash laughed. He appreciated Ismail's knack for making light of his grievances.

Later, alone in his office with his feet up on his desk, Arash wondered why Anahita had accepted only half the gift.

"But of course, Anahita. I should be most interested to experiment with these synthetic dyes," the dyemaster said. "I have become an expert at checking flower petals for possibilities, so why not dyes such as these? And from a prince no less!"

"I do not understand how this man, this prince, learned of me and why he sent these lavish dyes. He reminds me of the rug merchant from Mashhad who judges worth by cost—you know, the one for whom Dariyoush has repaired carpets?" Anahita continued without waiting for the dyemaster's reply. "The messenger on horseback allowed me these samples. I knew you would like to try them." She handed the bottles to her granduncle, who removed the stoppers and immediately crinkled his nose and closed his eyes against the sharp smell and smarting vapors.

"Whew!" he exclaimed. "Perhaps the prince seeks dyemasters for the royal workshops. When I was young I dreamed of an opportunity such as this."

"That kind of work is not for me, working to someone else's specifications."

"My dear Anahita, any apprentice of mine will have to get used to dyeing according to the wishes of local weavers—this is a business. I can assure you each dye lot brings its own challenges and rewards. Otherwise, I would not have kept at it for all these years."

Looking at the turban her granduncle wore today, and hoping to change the subject, she said, "How did you discover that color?"

The dyemaster laughed. "By mistake. I do not think I could repeat it if I tried." The turban stood out against the gray sky, its shade somewhere between green and blue with a splash of purple. The only man in town to wear outlandish colors on his head, her granduncle never appeared to Anahita to feel the slightest bit ridiculous. Many of the dyemaster's turbans folded several colors into one, because he often dipped an edge of an unraveled head piece into a pot to test the hue rather than waste the women's hard-won homespun.

Flakes of wet snow, the kind that fall near winter's end, melted in the three cauldrons that the dyemaster had placed to simmer on the fire. In each, he would brew walnuts into a thick, brown, syrupy dye. He put every part of the nuts into the pots of water: the shell, the skin, the kernel, and the oils hidden inside. "This is my secret, Anahita. Many dyers feel it's only the tannins on the shell that color the dye. And they are right. However, it's the oil inside the kernel that brings luster and sheen to the wool. Always remember this. Look for the source."

"Oh yes," Anahita agreed. "This is advice Maman Bozorg has given me: those who, like moths, seek the flame and not the wick will only get burned."

"Your grandmother is most wise. It is no wonder we are brother and sister, is it not?" He winked.

The dyemaster hummed as he sidled over to a stack of small pots. "Ahhh, yummm, ahhh, naa, yaa, yaa, hummm." He picked up three and took them to the well in the center of his courtyard. As he fetched water, Anahita stoked the flames over which the walnuts simmered, then joined him.

"Hmm," her granduncle said when his bucket came up one third full. He peered deep into the well and scratched his temple. At last he managed to fill each pot and Anahita helped him carry them into the dye shed, where the master shook the synthetic dye powders into them and stirred.

Poof! Red. Blue. Yellow.

"I see these new dyes are not like a good mare's milk, requiring fermentation." Dipping a piece of yarn into each, the dyemaster said, "And I see no *abrash*—no variations in hue to tease the eye."

"These colors are dead," he said, lifting the dyepots from his counter. "I can make no likeness for them among the living."

Anahita followed him outside to the crumbling stone wall behind his shed, where he poured the liquid over weeds and a few blades of grass. They would see the plants wilt that day and die the next.

Aub, Water

Beside the stove in the center of Reza's crowded classroom, Fatima pretended to pour invisible tea from an empty kettle into a cup while the dyemaster held up his dry cauldron. Together they said, "We have no water," to the men who now filled the school for a public meeting. The talk grew louder as others made the same complaint.

"There are enough cushions for all," Reza said as he ushered people inside. Folded under to fit inside his classroom, the carpet the khan had donated now comically allowed people to sit on different parts of the diplomat's face. "We'll get to the bottom of this if we have to stay the night," Reza continued. "Everyone's concerns will be heard."

While the villagers found places to sit, he caught a glimpse of Anahita through the window as she crouched down, out of sight. Reza smiled fondly as he watched her. Then he said to the people inside, "Please remember to keep your comments brief."

Fatima spoke first. These days, no one seemed to question her attendance at public meetings—the realm of men. They had long since accepted the fact that by moving her ovens into Ali's tea-house, she had declared herself a part of matters of local business. Besides, they all loved her breads and enjoyed being around some-one whose laugh shook her whole body.

"I'd first like to thank all of you again for your help in rebuild-ing our teahouse roof after the fire. But Ali and I have noticed that the well is running dry in the village square. We need water to run our bakery." Her quick eyes circled the room, grabbing people's attention. "What are we to do?"

"My well is deep," the dyemaster said. "I have never run dry. Yet, I can draw only two buckets a day. This is not enough for my dye vats."

The third to speak was the mullah. "My joints have felt won-derful for at least a fortnight as we've had no rain. Perhaps we worry too soon. A sudden change in weather could rectify things."

"What of the cisterns on your roofs?" Reza asked, his love-birds chirping at the sound of his voice. "Has anyone measured their contents this winter? Have they been unusually low?"

"No." Farhad said, crossing his arms. He looked at the mullah. "Even though it seems drier, we have had normal snow and rain this winter. However, my well is giving less water, too. I did not realize others experienced the same."

"The women have noticed that the water in our stream and the qanat is half its normal force for winter's end," Fatima said.

A buzz spread through the room as men put their heads together.

"Do both the stream and the man-made irrigation system flow from Mount Binalud?" Reza asked.

"Yes," Dariyoush's father said. "The government controls the *qanat*; the landowners own portions of the streams."

"Would it merit a scouting mission upstream? Perhaps something has clogged it."

"I have already looked, Master Reza," Farhad said. "Nothing seems to be blocking our branch of the stream."

"What about the west fork?" Dariyoush's father said. "Could we inspect that?"

"Our khan has yet to secure our right of passage through that land. This is why we typically migrate east and north through Abadi-eh-Golab," Farhad said.

"Could we send word, through courier, and tell them our wishes to inspect the river?" Reza offered.

"Courier? There isn't a scribe in Hasanabad, much less a courier," someone said, chuckling. "Schoolmaster, you forget you are not in Mashhad." Several more people laughed and began to talk among themselves.

"My people," Farhad waved a hand to silence everyone. "I am reluctant to raise this idea because I know how many of you respect our khan. But I fear he has taken unkindly to my agreement to allow Anahita's wedding riddle contest. As you might have heard, he has increased the pressure on me to offer him her hand."

There were knowing nods.

"Our feet still ache from the long journey home," someone said.

"We've noticed the new camels and stallions," another volunteered, and several people laughed.

Reza shot them all dark looks.

"The khan warned me that if I refused him my daughter's hand," Farhad continued, "he would cease to intervene on our behalf with landowners for migratory and water rights, or to represent us in the government in Mashhad. Last summer, I thought his threat a bluff, but again he's proved me wrong."

So the khan makes a habit of threatening people besides me, Reza thought. Looking down at the dignitary's face on the carpet, Reza felt as if the khan were eavesdropping.

"The khan said that?" Ali asked. "He would refuse to represent our tribe because of a personal matter between you and him, Kadkhuda?"

Another man asked, "If the khan *is* involved with this restriction of our water rights, why would he have acted favorably toward us by paying for this school?"

"Yes, that's odd." Reza fingered his eyeglasses. "It's rather contradictory behavior."

"The khan has never been known for his *consistency*," the dyemaster said. "For someone who is trying to build a consensus among the people of this land in order to demand reforms of the shah, you would think he would not choose a time like this to threaten his own tribe."

"So you confirm my suspicion, Dyemaster?" Farhad asked.

"Unfortunately, I do. He's purposely meddled, or has 'forgotten' to secure our water rights this *Nooruz*."

"He's trying to dry us up!" someone shouted, inciting other exclamations and upsetting Reza's birds. They fluttered and screeched at the noise, sending feathers flying out of the cage.

"With all due respect, Kadkhuda Farhad," Dariyoush's father said loudly, "the marriage of your daughter—of all the young women in this tribe—is an important opportunity to bring peace in these lands. I question the . . . the . . ."

"The *sense*," someone offered up the word as the chatter in the room subsided.

". . . of continuing with the wedding riddle contest, given our current circumstances."

Farhad uncrossed his arms and stroked his tightly cropped beard.

"But his last three wives died!" Fatima whispered to her husband too loudly and everyone hushed.

Reza thought, *These people actually believe in that evil eye stuff!*

"Without water, we'll be forced to migrate early," Dariyoush's father pointed out. "We'll risk depleting our summer pastures before our fodder and grains can be harvested in the village. We will lose any possibility of a profit this year."

The room became silent again.

"You are suggesting I marry Anahita to the khan in hopes that he will continue to secure our water rights?"

"It seems, Kadkhuda, from what you've told us, this contest is what has pushed the khan over the edge—his justification for such irrational behavior of late."

Debates sparked. Reza unhooked the birdcage from its stand

and placed it outside, around the corner of the schoolhouse, where it was quiet. In doing so, he startled Anahita, who still knelt beneath the window.

"Are those tears I see in your eyes?" he asked, squatting beside her.

Anahita wiped her face with her sleeve.

Reza laid his palm on her back. "You must not take what these men say to heart. They speak out of fear."

"I should have agreed to marry the khan a year ago, Reza. I've caused nothing but problems for everyone— 'the march,' and now this, no water."

Reza was surprised to hear her refer to "the march" in the same mocking way he had heard the villagers speak of it. Her tone seemed too defeated for her nature. "Had you agreed to marry the khan, where would that leave me? I have every intention of competing for your hand, Anahita," he said, "if you'll have me." He took her hands into his. "We will explore faraway places. We will discover exotic birds and treasures of lost cities!"

Anahita looked at him. "You will enter my contest?" She cast her eyes to the ground. "Surely you have a woman more educated than me waiting for you in Mashhad."

Reza tilted her face toward his. "Your intuition fails you today. It is no happenstance that I am here. After seeing you last summer in the mountains, I wanted to be your teacher. When the clerics in Mashhad established the Rural Madrasa Servanthood, I signed up to come to Hasanabad." He touched the tip of her nose with his finger. "It is only you that I see."

"Reza, you make me happy. But I do not know that this contest will ever take place. I must go now, before Baba sees me here."

Back inside, Reza raised his hand to still the crowd. "May I pose something?" he asked. "I realize that I speak from my own self-interest when I say this, because I intend to participate in Anahita's test of wit." Several favorable gasps arose from the group. "But I believe that by giving in to the khan's wishes, it only shows him you are clay in his hands."

"Hear, hear!" the dyemaster exclaimed.

Fatima nudged her husband. "Yes, my wife and I agree," Ali spoke up. "But how will we see that our water rights are not denied?"

"Our water is not something I wish to gamble with," Dariyoush's father said, holding Ali's gaze. Turning to Farhad he said, "Our fellow tribes could use these stallions the khan has left us. Our scouts are traveling double distances on the lookout for Russians. Allah forbid if war comes to our own village . . ."

"Permit me to pose this question to you all as food for thought," Reza cut in. "Is there anyone in this room who would trust their life to the khan above Kadkhuda Farhad?"

The room fell into utter silence.

"As I thought," the schoolmaster said. "Let your answer guide your loyalty."

The mullah made his way to the center of the room, his black robes brushing against people's legs. Sweeping one hand in an encompassing arc around the room, he began, "I hate to see this community split into factions." Then, closing his eyes, he let the words of the *Quran* flow from his lips,

"In the name of God, the Compassionate, the Merciful . . . God sends down water from the sky with which he quickens the earth after its death. Surely in this there is a sign for prudent men."

"Thank you, Mullah," Farhad said. He nodded to Reza, turned, and left. Most everyone followed him out. A few stayed to talk things over. Reza threw another dung chip into the stove. To conserve water, he offered no one tea.

PASHME
CHINIE
BAHARE
Spring Shearing

Spring Fever

Spring shuffled forward wearing the color of shorn wool. Anahita awakened to the *clip, clip* of Farhad's shears as he sheared their flock. Each snip ticked away the time that was left of her childhood. A year had passed since her father first mentioned that she must prepare to wed. It was now several days after *Nooruz*. Drawing near was the date Farhad had chosen for Anahita's wedding riddle contest.

Her thoughts hovered that morning between sleep and wakefulness. They drifted from her *qali*, now nearly complete, to the suitors who might enter her contest, and whether or not her father would bow to the khan's threat. She worried how she would face her tribe today—another one with scarce water. She couldn't take her people's ostracism any longer. After "the march" last fall, the village women's anger had eventually faded. But not this time.

She must accept the fact that as the *kadkhuda*'s daughter, her wishes were secondary to the tribe's welfare. At last she understood the responsibility of her position—of leading her people.

She realized exactly how much her words and deeds reflected and spoke for them all.

The sun threw shadows on the wall of the room. A warm breeze touched Anahita's face. She lay still. *Last autumn I made amends with Baba. Now I must do so with my tribe.* She realized also that when thanking her father for her contest last fall, she had sought only to be forgiven, a rather selfish act that did not take others' needs into account, much less solve their troubles with the khan. Now she must do something for her tribe, to appease their concerns and prevent any suffering should no rain come.

With this in mind, she dressed. Walking by the ceremonial *sofreh* her family had set out this year for *Nooruz*, Anahita stopped to pick up the tiny carpet, no bigger than her palm, she'd woven as a miniature of her wedding *qali*. She had hoped that by placing this weaving on the *Nooruz sofreh*, it would bring Allah's blessings on her wedding day.

She made a wish as she set the miniature down. She hoped that when she walked outside, she would find the village women sitting with her mother and grandmother, as they had before the water shortage. But no such luck. When Anahita stepped out her front door, she saw the other women and children chatting and playing on the far side of the village square. Her anger rose. It was Ramadan, the sacred season that called on Muslim people to clean their minds and mend past arguments. Her people would celebrate this holy month by fasting from sunrise to sunset. Gathering together was a good way to keep one's mind off food. But it seemed Anahita's family would not be included in any such socializing this year. Only her aunt and Shirin visited with them. Shirin, who hadn't been argumentative since the khan had sent the cashmere undergarments, was now a comfort, a blessing amid all the estrangement.

This morning, when Shirin and her mother came to visit Anahita's family, they talked about the riddle contest and the design on Anahita's wedding rug, but no one dared to compliment its pattern or hues for fear this could curse her carpet.

"The riddle festivities will be such fun!" Anahita's aunt ventured to say. "I'll help with the food."

Anahita exchanged glances with her mother, who said, "Thank you both for your support. We shall see."

Her mother's dejected demeanor weighed heavily on Anahita's mind. Mojdeh had held her head high after "the march," but did not seem to have the energy left to deflect the others' anger this time around. Anahita wanted to make it up to her, to her father, to everyone. There was only one thing to do.

"Please excuse me," she said. "I need to talk with Baba."

She made her way to the back of the house and through the huddle of sheep that Farhad had begun to shear. She saw the pile of fleeces she would have to sort and clean.

"Good morning," her father said, tying the legs of a ram together, the one whose horns they'd decorated with red paint and tassels for luck in fertility. "Please keep your distance; he's feisty."

Anahita nodded. "Baba," she began firmly, but what followed came out half mumbled. "I just wanted to say that I would never want to do anything to jeopardize your position as *kadkhuda*, nor do I desire to disappoint you. From now on, I will keep my wishes to myself, I won't dream up any more contests, or clothing carts that demand so much time, and I will try not to be so outspoken."

Farhad cleaned his shears with a rag. "Anahita, it is not your outspokenness that grieves me of late. You were blessed with this personality—the day you were born, you wailed so that the whole summer camp could hear. Someday this ability may save you." Wiping the sweat from his brow with his sleeve, he said, "It is not even your wish for this contest that grieves me." Her father gripped the ram's horn so that it would not spear his leg. "What *has* grieved me of late is your *khod pasand*."

Anahita's chin sunk to her chest. *My self-absorption!* Her lungs tightened as though her father had squeezed the air out of them. To hear this from him, the person she so admired, so wished to please, and so dearly loved, was the worst kind of punishment.

"It is an unattractive trait in anyone. In fact, Anahita, it is a characteristic that our dear khan possesses. The two of you are more alike than you may care to recognize."

How can Baba say such a thing? Anahita felt as if she'd been bitten by a scorpion—numb and heavy—as though the viper's venom had succeeded in paralyzing her every limb.

She couldn't bear to hear him berate her anymore. "Baba, I understand now that to continue with the contest would be to the detriment of everyone." The ground beneath her feet seemed to sway and her throat felt parched as she prepared herself for what she needed to say. What she *had* to say—she knew there was no other choice. Her voice shook and she felt as if she couldn't get enough air. "I am willing to marry the khan." The impact of her words made her black out for a split second, knowing she must live by her promise.

Coming to, she heard Farhad say, ". . . have no intention of granting the khan your hand, unless, of course, he wins you fairly and squarely." Blurry-eyed, she looked about for a skin of water, something to relieve the awful dryness choking her throat.

"Are you all right, Anahita?"

"I need water."

Farhad handed her the goatskin he had leaned against a fence post. "Cheer up, my sweet. In ten days your contest will be over and you will be wed, and this problem will be behind us all."

Some consolation, she thought. *What a way to think about your wedding day—to wish it away. What have I done? Are not betrothals and weddings supposed to be joyous?*

Anahita turned to leave.

"*Azizam,*" Farhad said. "You have chosen wisely today. You are no longer the child I raised, but a woman I am proud of."

Anahita found her mother and relatives where she had left them, chatting outside the house. Taking her grandmother by the hand, Anahita led her inside.

"Maman Bozorg, I had a dream last night. I don't know what it means, but it seemed so real that I have to tell you."

"Let me find my needlework, Anahita. Something tells me I'm in for a long story." She looked about the room. Anahita knew the shadows on the wall from the bright sun made it difficult for her grandmother to see, so she quickly retrieved the lacework for her and started telling Maman Bozorg about her dream.

"I was traveling in some other land. It looked like Abadi-eh-Golab, but I didn't recognize anyone. I rode a camel with a guide and several others. The land became steeper and steeper until it became so treacherous the guide asked me to get off my beast. Then he asked me to climb inside a grain sack. Without hesitation I did. He carried me on his back high up the mountain—beyond where any goat would venture—to the summit above the clouds. There, he set down the sack on a hard surface, like stone, and helped me out. We stood inside a building of some sort. It looked like a school. He said to me, 'I'm happy you came without questions. It made my task easier.' Then a huge winged bird appeared in the distance, and the guide said, 'The bird of vision is flying toward you with wings of desire.'

"What does it mean, Maman Bozorg? Where is this place on the pinnacle? Why am I having such strange dreams?"

Her grandmother pushed her needle in and out of the lace.

"I think you have these dreams because you are troubled, my sweet Anahita. It's normal before a woman gets married. And your situation is so much more . . . chaotic with this contest. Who would have dreamed of all this happy *harj-o-marj*? I wish your grandfather were here to see it. I believe you and he have much in common. He never did anything the easy way."

"I told Baba that I am willing to marry the khan. That he could call off the contest."

Maman Bozorg smiled at Anahita. "Your father has already

made his decision not to force you to marry the khan. This contest is the best way to attract suitable suitors."

Anahita felt her whole body relax and realized only then how tense she had been.

Her grandmother said, "I think that sometimes our souls must tell us they are having a hard time trying to keep up with all of our worldly festivities and plans. Quiet moments, such as when we weave, or in times of sleep, are when we hear what our inner selves have to say."

Anahita understood. *Weren't all her weavings expressions of her deepest self?*

She hugged a cushion against her chest. "I'm so confused. And restless! I never thought I'd have so many suitors. Reza. He's so smart. He shares what he knows with me: his tales, his maps, his stories of other places. He treats me like an equal, not like some useless girl whose only reason for living is cooking and darning and . . ."

"And loving," Maman Bozorg teased.

Rummaging under her bedding, Anahita pulled out a book. "Reza gave me this gift." She held up the linen-bound book with empty white pages and smiled, thinking of how much she looked forward to seeing him every day at school. "It's for me to practice my own letters. See, I've started with the *alefba*." Anahita opened the book from the back to show her grandmother where she had written the alphabet. "Reza said pen and ink is much faster than a darning needle." She flipped to the page where she'd made her letters with sharp angles and joints.

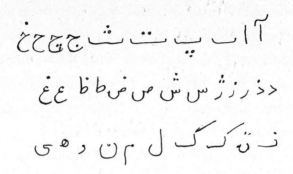

"*And*, Maman Bozorg," Anahita emphasized, "Reza told me he will enter my contest!"

"This is wonderful news. He would make a fine husband."

"But then, I just can't stop thinking about the man I met in Mashhad. You remember, Arash, the gentleman whose book of Rumi I have—the one I told you helped the boy with his camel?"

"How could I forget him?" Her grandmother pulled her thread taut.

"When I think of him, it . . . it's as if heaven is inside me and my heart colors the skies."

Anahita tossed the cushion to the floor and stood up. She peered through the window at the women outside, who seemed to laugh so easily, as if they had no cares.

"But what's the use?" Anahita continued. "I don't know anything about him except where Marv and Bukhara and Samarkand are on a map—and Reza's the one who showed me that."

"Hmm," Maman Bozorg said.

"And there's Dariyoush . . ."

Her grandmother raised an eyebrow.

"And the khan," Anahita rattled on. "Everything about him makes me cringe—his voice, his face, his look-at-what-I-can-do-for-you attitude. Oh Maman Bozorg, when did my life become a . . . a tapestry of men? A tangled skein of suitors?" She clasped her hands to either side of her cheeks. "I'm tired of thinking about all of them." *And I'm scared,* she thought.

Returning to her grandmother's side, Anahita knelt and sat back on her heels. "I do not want to get married this year. I'm happy the way I am. I wish Baba would simply call it all off. It is what our tribe wishes. And I know Maman frets, not knowing who may gallop in here, solve my riddle, and whisk me away."

Her grandmother stilled her needle to lay a hand on Anahita's arm. "Your eyes do not see far. Hasn't your father been good to you your whole life? He will do what is best. Not many girls could say the same and have it be truthful."

Anahita picked at a loose thread in the carpet beneath her. *A wayward thread like myself,* she thought.

Taking up her lace again, Maman Bozorg said, "I think your dream offers some solace in all this. Your bird, like the legendary Simorgh who swoops down from Qaf Mountain to protect all of Persia from evil, has taken you under its great wing. I believe your dream tells you to trust in your journey, even though you cannot see the destination."

Wounds

"*Bia! Bia!* Mojdeh, Anahita, Maman Bozorg," Farhad called, leaning through the threshold. "Bring clean rags. Men arrive on foot, in carts, on camel and horse. Many of them are injured." Before leaving, he added, "Wear your *chadors*."

Anahita groped in the predawn darkness for the oil lamp and lit it. *Why hasn't the mullah called* azan?

Mojdeh hurried into the front room of their home, wrapping herself in a shawl against the early morning chill.

"Allah, have mercy," Maman Bozorg said.

Anahita pulled on her black garment. Grabbing her *rusari* she ran outside, her eyes opening wide at what she saw. Men lifting limp bodies from camels. Others carrying the wounded on stretchers and placing them in rows in the courtyard. Donkeys pulling carts driven by soldiers with one arm or one leg. The dust they kicked up grew thick in the light of daybreak.

Who are these people? Why are they here? Anahita searched for her father among the throng.

Coming upon Shirin, who was tying a clean cloth sling around the bloody arm of a soldier, Anahita asked, "Who are these men? What happened?" She spotted her father with the mullah on the mosque steps across the village square.

The soldier answered her, his voice fatigued. "We fought in the mountains north of Abadi-eh-Golab, not far from Marv. A regiment of Russians came upon us unexpectedly. There was no way out."

Anahita's mind raced. *Is Dariyoush among them?*

"We've come here because we were told Hasanabad had a mosque large enough to shelter the injured." The soldier swallowed. "And because your village has many wells and a stream."

Wells that have nearly dried up, Anahita thought, lowering her eyes.

"What tribe are you from?" Anahita asked.

"I am a Yomut. We moved into this region this winter."

"Were you fighting alone or with other tribes?"

"With a band from Abadi-eh-Golab and some Afshars."

Anahita turned to her cousin. "Dariyoush must be here. Have you seen him?"

Shirin tilted her head back, no. Then she said, "Anahita, we need more rags." Whispering so that the soldier couldn't hear, she added, "We haven't enough water to rinse the bloody ones."

Anahita ran to her house for cloth, glad that Shirin had not berated her about the water—or the lack of it. After finding no scraps in her home, she hurried on to the mosque. The cries of women mixed with the sounds of men groaning, horses snorting, carts creaking. She wondered who could not feel the sudden sadness in the air.

Inside the mosque, Anahita knelt beside the baskets from the clothing cart. She sifted through them for the most threadbare garments and tore them into rags. Stepping into the main room, she was overcome by a putrid smell—a mix of sweat, urine, and blood. But it was the sight of mangled bodies that shocked her most. She gasped and reached for the stone archway to steady herself. The hanging mosque lamps seemed to sway on their chains. Her fingers tingled and her breath came rapidly as the sounds of the room hummed in her ears.

"Anahita, I found Dariyoush," Shirin said, having caught up with her. "He's in the far corner, beside the *minbar*."

"He is?" Anahita glanced toward the pulpit. A wave of anxiety, nearing panic, washed over her. "What about his brother, Mehdi?"

"I didn't see him."

Anahita looked at Shirin's *chador*, streaked with blood, and her arms filled with soiled rags. Breathing deeply against her dizziness, she said, "Shirin . . . you serve these injured men . . . well." Anahita thought she saw a glimmer in her cousin's eyes, a light that she hadn't seen since Shirin's parents told her whom she must marry.

"Are you all right?" her cousin asked.

"I'm feeling sick."

"Would you like me to help you outside?"

"If I just stand here a minute, I'll be all right."

"Anahita, Dariyoush needs you."

"*Needs me?* What skills can I offer him? Isn't his family with him?"

"His family is gone visiting relatives. Your father has sent for them. We need Dariyoush's father here to set bones."

Shirin's voice softened. "When I sat with Dariyoush, he called your name. Go to him. He shivers as though he has a fever."

"Shirin, I can't go in there."

"Think of the love he has shown you over the years. Surely your compassion will overcome your fear."

Anahita glanced around the mosque. Soldiers lay elbow to elbow, cushioned by prayer carpets. In that instant came a flash of truth. How everything in life *must* change. And how quickly this can happen. An oasis dries up in a single rainless season. One awakens in the morning to find a peaceful village a refugee camp. The strong—the soldiers—become the weak. The weak of confidence, like Shirin, become strong. How life calls on us to do what we never dreamed.

Kneeling on the carpet beside Dariyoush, with her back to the rest of the mosque, Anahita trembled. *I can't bear to see him this way*, she thought, eyeing the cloth wrapped around his torso. She tentatively touched the spot on Dariyoush's bandage where deep red blood oozed from a belly wound. His eyes were closed and there was little life in his face. His hair lay matted, his beard unkempt. Death looked near, but the muscular shape of his long limbs told a different story.

Anahita turned to the sound of men hauling a large earthen jar into the mosque, the kind normally used for olive oil. *"Aub,"* one of them said. She wondered where the water had come from.

She looked down again at her lifelong friend. "Dariyoush, it's me, Anahita." But he did not respond. Biting her lower lip, she felt tears well up. "I'm going to shift your bandage a little." With shaking hands she adjusted the cloth around him so that a clean spot on the bandage covered his open lesion. *His wound desperately needs to be sewed up,* she thought. Dariyoush winced but did not open his eyes. She felt his forehead, hot and damp with sweat.

She sat quietly beside him with her arm resting on his. She wondered if he could feel that she was there with him, even though he did not appear to hear her.

Minutes passed. She didn't dare look around the room lest she fall apart. Her mind drifted to the past summer, when Dariyoush had carried her in his arms after she'd sprained her foot. How she wished she could help him as he had helped her. She took his hand into both of hers. *Holding him feels so natural,* she thought. *So right.*

Anahita felt, rather than heard, the footsteps behind her. Soft tremors on the carpet.

"Do you love him?" The question came from over her left shoulder. The accent was unmistakably Arash's.

Arash skirted around Dariyoush's feet to lean on the pulpit beside him and talk with Anahita face to face. "I'm sorry to have been so direct with you, Anahita. But times like these don't lend themselves to superficiality." A shallow conversation was not what he wanted after months of not seeing her. "By the way, my name is Arash. I have never introduced myself properly."

Anahita stood up slowly, as if gathering her thoughts and composure. "I am pleased to meet you." She walked a few steps from Dariyoush and joined Arash in the corner of the mosque.

"Dariyoush is my *doost*," Anahita said, using the word for close friend. "Like family to me. Do you know what happened to him?"

"I am told he took a dagger intended for his brother who fought beside him. He's been fading in and out of consciousness for days now."

Anahita motioned for Arash to follow her out the side door of the mosque where they could be alone. "I do not want to upset Dariyoush with our conversation." She looked down the alley both ways, as if making sure no one could see them.

"Where *is* Mehdi?" she said, glancing back into the room.

"I am very sorry," Arash said. "He died."

Anahita raised a hand to her cheek. "Mehdi had a wife and two children!"

"I am truly sorry."

Looking dazed, Anahita whispered, "Why are you here?"

"I am a Yomut. These men are my people. My father is . . ." Arash began, but then hesitated to tell her the whole truth. He wanted others—and especially her—to befriend him for himself, not because he was a prince. He started again, "My father oversees—well you might say, works for this kingdom. He's asked me to unite our tribes to defend our land against the Russians and nomad bandits."

"Is the fighting near?"

"The skirmishes are sporadic, and we never know where they will erupt. Sometimes we face ambushes by Afghan Tajiks or Tekke Turkmans, other times we dodge Russian cannonballs. Our army, which is a loose alliance of men from various villages and tribes, is not organized enough at this point to do much besides defend itself as we travel around to recruit others." Arash shifted his weight to his other leg. His eyes fixed on Anahita's. "What I'd like is a chance to talk with the northern Turkman, Uzbek, and Khazak leaders, the Iranian tribal khans, and my . . . I mean . . . the shah, to see if there is a peaceful way to protect Marv and the surrounding realm."

"With the Russians so near, why are the bandits attacking other tribes?"Anahita asked.

"I don't know. But they do not seem to realize or care that in doing so they aid the Russians. A weakened Khurasan province can only fall to the czar."

Laying a hand on Anahita's arm, Arash continued, "But, I don't mean to worry you." He knew he shouldn't be touching her, but he wanted to comfort her, feel that she was really here. Anahita didn't draw back. "Your village is safe. The Russian cavalry is having a difficult time crossing the northern mountains. The shah's army in Marv, as small and poorly outfitted as it is, poses enough of a threat that the Russians haven't advanced toward the oasis city. We have come here to bring home your injured, and because we heard your village is equipped to handle all of these men."

"When we had water, perhaps."

"I do not understand."

"As you have said, this is no time for superficialities. I refused to marry our local khan," Anahita said, glancing down the alley. "In retaliation, he has failed to negotiate our water rights this spring. Our wells are running dry and our stream flows at one quarter its normal strength."

"I see." Arash tried to hide the look of concern for his men tugging across his face. Anahita peered into the mosque at Dariyoush. Watching her, Arash wondered, *Will she tell me about her wedding contest? Or does she not like me enough?*

He pressed on. "Not many women would refuse to marry a khan." *Will she refuse a prince?* he wondered.

"Perhaps not all khans are like ours. He does not appreciate that he must test his wit against other suitors in a wedding riddle contest which my father agreed to let me hold."

Arash noticed the blush that crept across her face. "A wedding riddle contest?"

"Yes, I told my father I could not live with a husband who did not enjoy riddles. Only the man who can solve the riddle I have woven into my *qali* will be my, my . . ."

"*Yar*," Arash offered her the word for "inseparable lover."

"You know about *yar*? I thought only silly girls dreamed of this."

"No, Anahita. It's what most everyone seeks in another. A kindred spirit. You never know if or where you will find such a person. Some people never find their *yar* in this world. Perhaps this is why Rumi looked elsewhere."

"And perhaps this is why his poems read as love poems to a woman."

"You have enjoyed my book?" Arash smiled. "I have hoped as much."

As if embarrassed, Anahita covered her mouth with her hand and said, "I should return your book to you . . ."

"Please keep it."

She smiled and looked at her hands. "My schoolteacher says Rumi lives in the Persian language. But, when I think about Rumi, I think how he cradles my heart."

"As he does mine," Arash said. "He warms my soul and brings me closer to myself." Stepping within inches of Anahita, he leaned his face close to hers. "He kisses on the right cheek, and then the left." Arash kissed both Anahita's cheeks as he spoke. Then, taking her into his arms he said, "He wraps his arms around you and holds you close. He will never abandon you."

Drawing her against him, Arash felt her face settle easily into the nape of his neck. Her veil slid down, leaving the tip of her nose and her warm breath brushing his skin. Inhaling, he held something of her inside him.

"*Aub,*" a soldier inside the mosque called out.

"I must tend him," Anahita said. She slipped from Arash's embrace and straightened her *chador*.

Through the wide-open doors he watched her walk to the large earthen jar. She dipped a tea glass inside and brought it to the young man. Her hands trembled, and she spilled little splashes of water from the cup onto her clothing, blackening it in spots. Raising the back of the soldier's head, she held the cup to his lips. The man sipped feebly and lay back down. Anahita stopped to touch Dariyoush's arm and walked back to Arash.

More women from her village had come to administer to the sick. A pile of dirty rags grew in the center of the room.

"This is hard for you, isn't it Anahita?" Arash said.

"Yes. I wish I had the strength of my cousin, Shirin." She pointed to a young woman moving from one wounded soldier to the next. "But, look at me. I'm trembling." Anahita held out an unsteady hand.

"Whenever I am uncomfortable somewhere, I try to impose my own vision upon the place, rather than accept images from it," Arash said.

"How do you mean?"

He turned Anahita to face the mosque. "Look in there a moment. What do you see?"

"A desert of bloody rags and bones."

"I see brave men whose swords flashed for the love of family and Iran. The *real* Iran, Anahita."

"Tell me, what is Iran anymore?" Anahita looked down the alley to where men crossed, hauling shade tents and shouting instructions at each other. "Khans no longer live with their tribes. Nomads are forced to settle and follow laws made by city officials. Landowners claim Allah-given water. Foreigners grab land in the north."

"The Iran I mean, Anahita, is the people like you and me who cherish these mountains, great rivers, and grasslands."

Anahita nodded. "Yes," she whispered. "I am heartened by the same hectare of yellow-eyed chamomile that I see bloom and wither from migration to migration."

"This is what you must see when you look upon these maimed men. Then you will help them without fear." Arash took her hands into his, her scent of rose intoxicating. *She is a flower among the chaff.*

"I'm sorry I must leave here. I will speak to your father about this problem of water before I go."

"Arash," she said. "Will I see you again?"

"Anahita, it is no coincidence that I am here. When the winds blow, they stir up thoughts of you. I will be at your wedding riddle contest, *inshallah*."

"I do not know that there will be a contest. My tribe is against it. And they are right. Water is life. And now, with all this happening . . . these men needing our help . . . the dead . . ." She looked down.

"What about the water *of* life—that inner nectar of hope? For your love, Anahita, there are men in this room holding on. Myself included."

Before turning to walk away, he traced the curve of her cheek with his finger, her color still high.

Anahita tended to Dariyoush often as she circled the mosque giving soldiers sips of water and picking up unclean rags. She pushed the frightened whispers of others from her ears by holding fast to an image of a field full of wildflowers. *I can't believe Arash was here*, she thought, over and over.

The mullah followed her, his sandals scuffling softly with each step. He blessed the sick and spoke with the coherent. Anahita felt awkward with the holy man so near because she hadn't talked with him since the news about the water.

"Anahita," he said, "your clothing cart has helped us in a new way, with all these rags we so desperately need."

Anahita caught Shirin's eye. "Shirin is more deserving of your praise than me, Mullah. She stitches cuts, makes slings, and tests for broken bones."

The mullah laid a hand on Shirin's shoulder. "Blessed are those who have faith and do good works; blissful is their end."

"Thank you, Mullah," Shirin said. Looking at Anahita, she smiled and knelt beside another soldier.

Turning back to Anahita, the mullah said, "Perhaps also, some of your riddles would be good medicine." Anahita's face lit up. *Of course*, she thought. *Why didn't I think of this?*

Then the mullah said, "I have noticed, Anahita, your reluctance of late to speak with me." He leaned his head to one side. "What has imprisoned your tongue?"

I feel so stupid, she thought, as she leaned down to shift a soldier's arm from the cold stone floor to the carpet beside him. *What can I tell the mullah?*

Straightening again, she said, "I've been feeling bad about our lack of water. The tribe would like to cancel my riddle contest. I don't know what to think."

"I see." The mullah raised a hand to his beard. "Perhaps in this case it would be wise to invite people to be part of this contest. This way, they will accept it."

Anahita blinked. "Then you have no misgivings about my wedding riddle contest?"

"Perhaps, *dokhtaram*, I have consented to this event with someone else's heart in mind."

The mullah's black robes swept across Anahita's toes as he turned and walked on.

Someone else's heart?

She was about to ask her cousin if she needed help, when Shirin spoke. "Anahita, who was that handsome man you led out the side door of the mosque?"

Anahita flushed. Seconds lapsed, then the two broke into mischievous giggles. Anahita whispered, "You must keep this a secret."

"My lips are twice sealed, like a camel's inner and outer eyelid."

That night Anahita tossed and turned. The keen of sorrowful women drifted through her window—an eternal weeping for Hasanabad's swordsmen, for their sweet-natured men like Mehdi. She worried if Dariyoush was comfortable or in pain. *I want to go to him,* she thought, pushing back sleep. She felt in the dark for her shawl and slipped out without waking Maman Bozorg. Heading for the mosque, images of battle camels and earthen jars—overflowing with the blood of sacrifice—filled her mind.

Coming through the side door where Dariyoush lay, she saw him moving an arm. *He's awake!* she thought. As she hurried to his side, he turned slowly toward her, his eyes half open.

"Ana . . ." he said. "I'm sorry . . ." He swallowed hard. ". . . didn't . . ."

"Shh," she said, kneeling on the rug beside him. "Save your strength. Why on earth are you apologizing to me? You're the one who is hurt on behalf of your love for Iran, for our safety . . ."

He closed his eyes again. Anahita sat with him throughout the night until she heard the mullah call for morning prayer.

The Riddle in the Weaving

Days had passed and most of the injured had gone, some returned to the fighting while others were taken back to their own villages to recover. A few men from Abadi-eh-Golab stayed to rest before their long journey home. Dariyoush's belly wound still gave him pain, but he seemed better and better with each day. Anahita traded time between helping Hasanabad's wounded and finishing her *qali*.

After making the last knot in her wedding carpet, she hugged her mother and grandmother. Rather than cut the warp threads to free her weaving from the loom, the women left it to stand in the sunshine beneath the poplars, where they had brought it when the weather turned warm. It would stay in this spot for the competition and festivities.

And today—the day before Anahita's wedding contest—her father told her she must tell the dyemaster and the mullah, the appointed judges, her riddle. These two men would determine which suitor's interpretation of Anahita's woven riddle was the most fitting, and declare the winner.

Morning light bathed her rug. Its seven borders shimmered with the pride of centuries past. Each color complemented the next. The goats, camels, bullocks, and sheep of the caravan that Anahita had woven into her *qali* came to life—migrating from one end of the rug to the other. Magpies fluttered. Roosters shooed away evil spirits. Trees of life and wildflowers swayed. Certain to bring happiness to her home were the joyful shades of red and the sea of indigo.

Anahita brooded over what riddle to tell the judges—making the decision felt so binding, so *final!* Standing back to inspect her work, she thought about the months that had led up to this day. How fast the year seemed to have flown. She thought about the afternoon she had selected the best sheep fleeces and picked them clean, and about the argument she'd had with her father over whether or not she would marry this spring. The wool from those fleeces was part of her carpet now. She thought about Dariyoush's spindle—the yarn it had spun carried the perfume of Abadi-eh-Golab, and formed the warp and weft of her rug. She thought about each time she had met Arash—the brown of his eyes was in her carpet, too. She recalled the laughter and tears she shared with her mother and grandmother as they wove. Riddles with her father. Reading with Reza. The injured soldiers. Mourning Mehdi's death.

All of these things are part of this qali.

Looking at her carpet, she thought, *This rug speaks of more than "stability and change," as Maman suggested.*

While she pondered her "official riddle," Mojdeh came to her holding a package. "This is for you. It came with the last caravan from Mashhad."

"I hope it's not another gift from the khan."

"I can't imagine what else he would send you."

Anahita unfolded the muslin wrap to find a shimmering bolt of white silk. A note inside read,

> *My Lovely Anahita,*
> You will make a fine wedding gown with this, I am certain.
> Fondly,
> *Your Khan*

Anahita began to shake. "Maman, can't you make him stop? He stalks me like a wolf."

"I will speak to your father about this, Anahita. Please, don't let it upset you." Mojdeh hugged her daughter tightly.

Anahita wished she could do something to make sure the khan would lose her contest or not show up. She sat on a rock by her loom and bit every one of her fingernails. She fidgeted with her head scarf. *I've got to decide on a riddle,* she scolded herself. Studying her carpet, Arash's voice came to her, a slice of her conversation with him in Mashhad:

"There are always stories within Rumi's stories."

"Just as there are stories in the patterns one sees on the surface of the carpets I weave, there are stories within the warp and weft . . ."

Contemplating her carpet again, her eyes fell on the snow leopard and the footprints of the creatures in the night. Anahita recalled what the mullah had recently said from his pulpit: *"Everywhere you turn is the hidden Face of Allah."*

She thought how her *qali* had been her refuge this year. Her very own sanctuary. Visible and yet not. *This rug speaks of no other riddle than this.*

Anahita felt ready to relay her riddle to the dyemaster. As she hurried to his workshop, she gave thanks to Allah for the happiness she felt whenever she wove. Palms up, she said, *"I trust that my fate is in your hands. I will accept for my husband whoever wins."*

That evening Dariyoush knocked on Anahita's door and asked to speak with her. Farhad nodded.

The two strolled to the side of the house without looking at each other. They walked slowly as Dariyoush was still weak from his wound. A chicken that had escaped its pen pecked at the ground between them.

Anahita, too, felt sapped of strength, the way she always did after finishing a carpet, having put so much of herself into it. And this, her wedding *qali*, robbed her even more.

Dariyoush hooked his thumb on his waist sash. "Anahita, I've seen so many people, their lives stolen from them in the night by a stranger's sword. When my brother Mehdi died, I vowed that when I returned I would tell you my feelings."

Anahita did not want to hear this now. She hadn't yet sorted out her own feelings for him. Closing her heart tight as a pistachio shell would be her only protection, the only way to face this wedding riddle contest.

Dariyoush pulled at his beard. "I guess I just always thought we'd be married someday. I never could have imagined such a thing as this wedding contest. I couldn't stay here while you wove your carpet, thread by thread, and then watch you sew the khan's name—or anyone else's name but my own—into your *qali*."

"The khan will not guess . . ."

"He could win, Anahita," he said. His look burned.

She shifted. "You left without saying good-bye."

"I had to go. I couldn't stay here knowing that our fellow tribes were being attacked and slaughtered." In a soft voice he continued, "When my parents heard the khan wanted to marry you, they refused to let me interfere. I figured I was no match for the khan anyway. The only possessions I have to offer are two strong arms and soft carpets beneath you." He touched his wound. "And now, perhaps not even my former strength."

"You will heal, Dariyoush."

"I've not a keen mind like your father and you. Not when it comes to riddles. And Shirin told me she was certain that the schoolmaster will try to win your hand. I'm no teacher either, Anahita—I'm not one for speaking in front of a crowd."

"But you are here now. And you will try?" she said.

The chicken pecked at Dariyoush's toe. He nudged it with his sandal and sent it clucking. A knowing half smile came to his face. "Anahita, despite your unusual ideas, in some ways you are so very predictable. I have heard this question many times before: 'Will you come with me?' To explore the *qanat* when you were five, to climb the eucalyptus tree in the village square when you were seven, to run up the minaret after dark and better see the stars when you were ten. But now I worry that the only reason you had asked me along those many times was to hold your hand. Dariyoush the big brother."

Looking away, as if he couldn't bear to read the truth he might find in her eyes, he said, "Tell me, did you have me in mind when you thought of your contest?"

Anahita felt as if her heart had been stepped on.

"Anahita," Dariyoush said, placing his hands on her arms and turning her toward him. "I have thought of an answer to the riddle in your carpet. If I win, I will consider myself blessed because for as long as I can remember, I have felt that when you are near, there are two suns in the sky. If I lose, I pray that the winner will be from another village, because it would be difficult for me to live in Hasanabad with another man as your husband." Looking past the roofs of the sheep sheds, he continued, "If I lose, perhaps it is because Allah has more in store for me."

Anahita took both of Dariyoush's hands, his strong healing hands. She opened her mouth as if to say something but instead gripped his hands more tightly, then let them go.

She turned to leave, but stopped. "Dariyoush," she said, "please believe me that I did not think this contest would cause anyone pain. I guess I never allowed myself to believe you cared for me except in a brotherly way. To tell you the truth, I think I was afraid to marry anyone. Shirin hasn't been herself since she married, and my cousins were taken away to Isfahan . . . There was a time last summer when I had hoped you would ask for my hand." Anahita took another step toward her house. "Dariyoush, if you win, I would be honored to be your wife."

As she walked into her home, she wished she could turn back the clock to that safe world she remembered before Reza and Arash, before the march and the water shortage. She hadn't stopped to think how deeply her test of wit might affect others. She thought only of the consequences that she herself might have to face, not understanding that the consequences would be shared by so many.

She felt immobilized by a gale of panic that did not seem to be of this world. She wished for divine intervention—to rid her of this fear, to see her through this night, to heal hearts, answer prayers,

> . . . *grant me the beauty of your Face.*

29

Sandstorm

"Ismail, tell me this is a bad dream," Arash shouted to his servant, the sand whipping across his face and working its way into his eyes, ears, nose, and throat.

"That, I'm afraid, would be a lie," his adviser and confidant replied through the cloth wrapped around his head to seal out the storm.

"There's a ruin ahead. Let's take shelter in it." With one hand on the reins of his horse, Arash tightened the cloth about his face, leaving only a slit for his eyes. He slowed from a gallop to a canter. The stallion, jerking its head between gusts of wind, seemed to know what to do next. It walked to the ruin and began to fold itself down on its knees like a camel—low to the ground for its own protection.

Arash and Ismail slid off their mounts. With their eyes shut against the unbearable lashing, they backed into the ruin feeling their way by hand.

"There is no time to stop, yet we cannot expect our horses to continue in this swirling madness," Arash said, still shouting to be heard.

"Let's just hope the messenger you sent days ago has arrived in Hasanabad and has not been stalled by this storm," Ismail yelled. "Otherwise, what will you tell this Kadkhuda Farhad? When a prince misses an engagement as important as a nuptial celebration, should he not have a better excuse than a sandstorm? How about something a little more glamorous, like a battle or a rock avalanche—like in an Arabian tale!"

Arash smirked. He appreciated the light humor his companion tried to cast on the hour. "Only you could make a romantic story of this. Doesn't all that sand in your pants kill the illusion?"

Ismail laughed.

"*And dear adviser*, you assume too much—my nuptial celebration? What makes you so certain I will be the lucky one? A thousand men must have ridden to Hasanabad to announce their intentions to enter this test of wit . . . Not to mention, I haven't yet laid eyes on Anahita's carpet. How am I to solve . . ."

Like the wind, his thoughts changed direction. "Luck, my friend, comes only to the one who doesn't expect it. If you boast about the winning, it will flee. If you concentrate on the process, it will come to your aid like a bird."

Arash's horse gave a low, nervous whinny.

The storm howled.

The mud bricks of the ruin reminded Arash of his Yomut tribe's winter village. He missed the gazelles and the bighorn sheep who came to nibble on trees there.

He took a drink from his water bag. Pirouz had tied pieces of ram horn to its tassels for good luck. Wiping his mouth, Arash thought, *Marv is not the life I am meant to lead.* He found little joy in his role as governor. Sorting through months of unfulfilled work orders—signed by the former prince, who spent royal funds on himself rather than his realm—seemed a waste of his skills and energy. Especially since he had no promises of money from the shah's treasury to meet such building plans. *I should be with my Yomut family, my tribe who flees from the Russians' guns. Or forging more tribal alliances to safeguard our borders.*

"Ismail, how do you think the shah would react if I requested to step down from my position as governor?"

"Step down?"

"You sound incredulous," Arash said.

"No one has refused an appointment by the shah."

"What if I were to convince him my demotion is his own idea?"

"How?"

"I will convince my father that he needs a confederacy of united tribes to fortify the villages on our frontiers against the Russian armies and bandits, or he will have no kingdom to rule."

Ismail leaned closer to hear above the gusts.

"This is where my heart is." Arash said. "I'd rather defend Iran from external strife than to wallow in internal politics and greed."

"So, you will suggest to the shah that you be assigned as a sort of diplomat or an intermediary for the tribes?"

"Something of this nature." Arash took another sip of water. "I could be an intertribal diplomat."

"It may work."

"It has to. I can't go on shuffling paper when Iran needs to defend itself," Arash said. "The nomads might not like the shah's push for them to settle, but the Turkman tribes who are raiding our villages must realize that they are essentially rolling out the welcome carpet for the Russians. I will ask these nomads: Whose laws would you prefer to live by? Ones that are spoken to you in Farsi and your own Turkish dialects, or those of an alien Russian voice, in a language you cannot understand?"

The two held each other's gaze.

Looking south, the direction in which they should ride, Arash spotted a thin, clear line on the horizon. He shook sand from the folds of his clothes and remembered how it felt to hold Anahita in his arms. *This woman who loves this land as I do is my* yar, he thought.

"*Rafigh*, my good friend," Arash said, "when we get to Hasanabad please do not tell anyone I am a Qajar prince. People get excited when royalty come around. The men dream up all kinds of public projects that their village needs. The women fuss." Arash looked at Ismail, hesitating before saying what he really wanted to say. "I just want Anahita to love me for who I am."

Because his colleague's face was covered, Arash could only see the little crinkles around his eyes. Ismail was smiling.

30

Unweaving a Tale

The morning of her wedding riddle contest, Anahita
awoke to a nervous stomach. Her hands trembled when
she picked up the clothes she and her mother had laid out the
night before—a two-layered indigo skirt, a blouse, a multicolored
waistband embroidered with flowers and birds, and a rust-colored
head scarf dyed with madder. *Will many people be watching?* Anahita
worried. *Has anyone forgiven me for asking for this contest?* She could not
bring herself to dress just yet, so she went to look for her mother
in the back room.

She found Mojdeh and Maman Bozorg fixing her a plate of
goat cheese, bread, and honey. "I can't do this," Anahita
announced, turning down the food with a wave of her hand. Her
mother and Maman Bozorg looked at each other.

"Couldn't we hold a silent contest? People could submit their
guesses on parchment. Forget the feast, divide up the food among
the villagers . . ."

"A bath will help," her mother said.

"Is there enough water for a bath?" Anahita looked at the sky but saw no sign of rain.

"Maman Bozorg has taken care of everything. For weeks now the bathhouse keeper has been funneling all the water into a single cistern that serves one fountain in the bathhouse. She did this for you, Anahita, as a gift for today. Your grandmother works miracles, at times, does she not?" Mojdeh winked and led Anahita by the hand. Maman Bozorg followed with Anahita's clothes.

Rubbing the filthy dry skin on her arms and thinking how she hadn't bathed in weeks, Anahita realized a bath *would* feel delightful.

They entered the bathhouse's blue-and-white tiled stairway. Absent was the attendant who would massage moist bodies, and the usual steam that made the bathers look as ghostly as a mirage.

Anahita chose a dressing alcove, cleansed herself with the cloth folded beside a ewer and dish, and emerged wrapped in a muslin sheet. The room smelled of the oil burning in the hanging lamps. Only one of seven fountains spouted water from thick stone walls. Beneath it lay a marble basin, deep enough to wade in. Anahita dropped her sheet on a stone bench and knelt down to duck her head under the spout. Mojdeh washed her hair, kneading fingers against scalp, using the soap she had made last summer in the mountains.

Be melting snow. Wash yourself of yourself . . .

Anahita smiled as she recalled these words of Rumi's that Arash had shared with her in Mashhad.

Suds ran down her back. She thought about floating in the

deep pool on the men's side of the bathhouse. *Why hadn't the older women in her village ever insisted on this privilege? If they only knew what they were missing!*

Mojdeh's hands stayed in Anahita's hair, relaxing her, while she voiced fond memories from the last seventeen years of her daughter's life.

Maman Bozorg lifted a large clay pitcher above Anahita's head and poured more water on her. Anahita felt a sense of love flowing over her. Her grandmother then patted her hair dry with a towel, combing it until it rippled and shone like starlit sand.

Anahita slipped into her indigo skirt and blouse, wrapped herself in her embroidered waist band, and put on her headpiece. Its multicolored tassels cascaded with her hair to the middle of her back.

The village square bustled like a marketplace, the curious coming from near and far. Farhad held court under the poplars by Anahita's carpet. Having borrowed a low bench from the teahouse, he invited the contestants to sit on it. Fatima served each suitor *chai*, made with water brought from the village of Kemesh. Men threw rugs on the dirt and sat down. Women rushed from house to house, where they would eventually settle in with friends or family and watch the contest from doorways and windows.

Anahita's mother, grandmother, aunts, cousins, and their toddlers gathered in Anahita's house to wait for the festivities to begin.

While her relatives talked, Anahita crept outside to see the contestants gathered near the bench. There were at least a dozen. None, thankfully, caught her inspecting them. She saw the back of Reza's head. And she knew Dariyoush was about. She felt awkward that he would participate even though his parents had never consented. Nowhere did she see the khan. Her spirits soared. Then, searching every face on every turbaned head, she realized she did not see Arash. She went inside, her emotions a shifting dune.

"Did the Yomut come?" Shirin whispered.

Anahita tilt her head back, no, and stood in the doorway beside her cousin.

"Welcome my fellow tribesman, my distinguished guests from Abadi-eh-Golab, and all who have come today to participate in this event." Farhad smiled at the crowd and the eager young suitors.

Clearing his throat he continued, "In the deep places of the heart, two forces, fire and water, struggle together. To the man among us here today who can determine which opposing life forces Anahita has woven into her *qali*, goes my daughter's hand in marriage, and . . . my blessing. To those who fail, I bid you to take your leave in peace."

Murmurs ran through the audience. Farhad raised a hand to silence everyone.

"Please, listen. These are the rules. Contestants may inspect Anahita's *qali* before giving their testimony. We will hear each man's guess. No two men may give the same answer. After all the players have had their turn, Anahita will reveal the answer to the riddle woven into this carpet. The man with the closest match is the winner."

Murmurs grew.

"The riddle's answer is written on parchment in this vessel I hold." Farhad held up an upside-down turban. "It has been signed by our respected judges, the dyemaster and the mullah. No changes will be made to the riddle during the course of this event."

"How long will the contest last?" a man shouted above the others.

"As long as it takes." Farhad smiled. "A dozen men have entered the competition."

The onlookers' chatter rose to full volume while the suitors paced back and forth in front of the carpet, scratching their heads, and crossing their arms. After some time, three young men from nearby villages mounted horses and left without taking a turn at solving the riddle. Only nine suitors would now accept the challenge.

"Is there anyone among the contestants who wishes to begin the contest?" Farhad offered. "Otherwise, we shall proceed in the order in which you were registered."

A young man from Anahita's tribe volunteered to go first. She was surprised to see him step forward. She had heard no rumor of his interest in marrying her and was intrigued because he had kept it to himself. Is this who the mullah meant when he said, "Perhaps it was someone else's heart I had in mind when consenting to your riddle?"

Anahita knew Ahmed to be fiercely loyal to their tribe, but he would also give absolutely everything away in one grand gesture. Anahita wasn't sure this was a desirable quality in a man. Especially if someday he had children to feed.

"My name is Ahmed, and I thank you for this opportunity. I believe this *qali* speaks of good and evil. Its seven borders are the symbols of our tribe, and we are good people. While the roosters and tassels—the amulets against evil—remind us of the bad forces in the world."

Farhad repeated the answer so that all the people could hear. The judges scribbled notes on separate scrolls.

The women in Anahita's house looked at her. *Did Ahmed guess it?*

Anahita glanced at her hands and pretended not to see their questioning eyes. She had promised her father and the judges that she would not reveal the solution to anyone until the contest ended.

The young tribesman thanked Farhad and took his seat. The villagers patted him on the back for his effort.

An injured soldier from Abadi-eh-Golab volunteered to go next. As he stood up on his only leg, the crowd parted for a horse and rider. The khan rode into the center of the village square— the gold tassels on his woven saddle blanket swinging wildly. He greeted everyone he knew. The young man from Abadi-eh-Golab wrestled with his crutches and sat back down.

A disturbed expression spread across Farhad's face as he watched the khan climb from his Arabian. The crowd followed Farhad's stare.

"Will he enter?" someone asked. "Or did he come to watch?"

Several people greeted the khan with kisses on both cheeks. "You have every right to roll Anahita up like a carpet, sling her over your saddle, and ride off," one spectator said.

Anahita, sliding her back down the frame of the door, sank to the floor.

"What is it?" Mojdeh asked.

Anahita couldn't speak. She sat with her chin to her knees, curled up like a babe in the womb.

"I've come to enter Anahita's contest," the khan said. "Where do I sign up?" Anahita noticed a magisterial-looking parchment tucked under his arm. *Whatever documents he has cannot be for our benefit,* she thought.

Farhad glanced at the khan's scroll. "My dear Khan, registration closed yesterday. This gentlemen from Abadi-eh-Golab has been granted the next try. It is up to our judges if you may enter."

"Registration closed yesterday?" Anahita searched Shirin's face to see if she understood what this meant for Arash.

"Don't worry, Anahita," Shirin whispered, but her encouragement didn't slow Anahita's heartbeats.

The crowd sat as quietly as a mosque congregation while the mullah's and dyemaster's turbans touched, discussing the request.

The khan glared at Farhad.

Swaying on his crutches, the suitor from Abadi-eh-Golab stood back up.

Distraught, Anahita did not see the mullah give a nod of consent. Neither did she hear the answer given by the young man from Abadi-eh-Golab. She was too busy chastising herself: This contest was a bad idea. *A foolish, foolish idea.*

"Anahita," Mojdeh said, noticing her anguish. "I agree that it is galling for the khan to show up here today. But in his own way he shows humility by asking permission to play your game. Most men of his age and standing wouldn't bother."

Closing her eyes, Anahita sucked in her breath, and prayed, *Please don't let me become his fourth dead wife.*

Surprises

$\mathcal{A}$nahita recovered her spirits with the thought: *Surely the khan is simply too stupid to guess my riddle.* She asked the women in her home, "Did anyone hear what the suitor from Abadi-eh-Golab answered?"

"Something about love and war," Mojdeh said.

An entourage of merry merchants on horses, towing donkeys laden with textiles and vessels, clinked and clanked their way into the village square. They walked in circles in a manner suggesting they were discussing the possibility of turning back.

"*Na!*" Anahita gasped. "It's the carpet merchant from Mashhad. Surely *he* does not wish to marry me, Maman."

A child led the merchants' animals to the thin ribbon of water running in the dry streambed. The rug merchant, looking clean shaven, joined the others under the poplars.

When Farhad called for the next suitor to solve the riddle in the rug, the merchant sprang to his feet. His baggy clothes rippled in the mounting breeze. Checking the list of contestants, the *kadkhuda* found the merchant's name at the top.

The merchant approached the carpet. He fingered the colorful tassels and looked closely at the knots. Then he sniffed the rug. "Plant dyes, as I would have guessed!"

"Look at him, Maman. He mocks me!" Anahita said as she peeked through the door. "He hasn't any idea of what to say."

"I think he's rather charming," her mother said. Her aunts nodded and giggled.

Anahita crossed her arms. With the merchant standing there next to her carpet, Anahita felt as if she, not her *qali*, were on display—for sale like one of the weavings hung in his booth at the bazaar.

A gust of wind kicked up dust, tossing the leaves on the trees.

"Such an exquisite *qali*," the merchant said. "Its shades of *abrash* shimmer and bring the carpet's motif to life. The patterns are effectively outlined, indicating the weaver's expert planning and sharp eye for color."

He held the crowd in the palm of his hand. "I believe the two forces in life which dear Anahita speaks of are the bitter and the sweet. The sweet is represented by her whimsical design and her glorious floral patterns. The bitter is the smell of the plant dyes she has used to color her rug, and the taste of my tears should I not win her hand in marriage."

People chuckled as they clapped. "Who is this fellow?" they asked, shifting in their seats and turning their backs to the mounting wind. Again the women in Anahita's house searched her face for some indication of whether the merchant's guess was correct.

The merchant bowed to the crowd and sat down.

Farhad shielded his eyes from the sand particles blowing more steadily across the village square. "Yet to test their wit today are our distinguished relatives from Isfahan, our very own tribe's Dariyoush, and our schoolmaster Reza."

"Isfahan!" Mojdeh exclaimed. "Farhad didn't mention anything about them to me."

"He knew you'd lose sleep over it," Maman Bozorg said.

Collecting her daughter into her arms, Mojdeh said, "I won't let you go to Isfahan." Silence fell over the room. Everyone understood, especially Anahita's aunt, whose daughters were married and gone.

"Shh," Shirin said, loudly. "I can't hear Farhad."

All heads turned toward the silencer. Anahita was surprised by her cousin's not-wanting-to-miss-a-word enthusiasm.

As people began to seek shelter from the blowing sand inside the teahouse and nearby homes, Farhad said, "We must try to hurry and finish before the storm is upon us."

Anahita looked outside and noticed a man tethering his dappled gray stallion to a tree on the far side of the square. He approached Farhad with something in his hand.

"Pardon me for coming to this honorable event with no invitation," the newcomer said. "Forgive my appearance. The road has been rough, the wind strong. I represent a most respected man, Arash, the Yomut who brought the injured soldiers to your village.

This gentlemen wishes to take part in these festivities but he has been detained with royal—I mean—business in Marv. He is riding this way as we speak but sent me ahead to ask for your permission to compete. He hopes to arrive any hour now."

Anahita's hands flew to her cheeks. She scanned the sky. *But this storm . . .*

The messenger gave Farhad a small pouch made with a tied-up scarf. "For your daughter," he said. Farhad fingered the madder-red tassels and lifted it to his nose to sniff. "This is my daughter's scarf. How did this gentlemen you represent get this?" Farhad pushed up his sleeves and squared his body with the stranger. He looked at the man's plain clothes, then at his fine horse. A puzzled look crept across the *kadkhuda's* face.

"He recovered it from the mosque in Mashhad where your daughter had dropped it." The man stepped back from Farhad.

"In Mashhad?"

"I believe so."

"And where is it you've come from?"

"Marv."

"Ah," Farhad said.

"Marv." The crowd murmured. "Hadn't a prince sent bottles from Marv?"

"I see no reason why we shouldn't consider one more suitor." Looking at the horizon, Farhad added, "But we need to finish this contest before the sandstorm descends upon us. Our women have prepared a most wonderful feast. Timing, my wife tells me, is everything."

* * *

The women stood and knelt in a knot around Anahita, who lay on the floor in the front room. Shirin fanned her as Maman Bozorg applied a cool cloth to her face. "You must have fainted," Mojdeh said, holding Anahita's hands in her own. "You should have eaten something this morning."

Anahita looked into the eyes of each of her relatives and felt embarrassed. She'd never fainted before.

"What is it?" an aunt asked.

Anahita stared at Shirin, then at her grandmother, who nodded as if she understood. "It's such a long story. I don't know where to begin. Would you explain for me, Maman Bozorg? I need some air."

Anahita eased herself to sitting, then stood up. She clutched the small pouch that her father sent inside to her, made from her favorite scarf, and in which Arash had stuffed camel treats and a folded square of parchment.

Walking behind the barn, she nestled into the side of a bag of wool. Anahita fumbled as she hurried to unfold the parchment onto which Arash had written a poem.

> Anahita my *yar*,
> Happy is the time when we sit in the palace, you and I
> With two forms, and two faces, but a single soul, you and I.
> The colors of the grove and the voices of the birds will
>   bestow immortality
> The moment we enter the garden, you and I!

The stars of heaven will come to look at us:
We'll show them the moon itself, you and I.
You and I, liberated from ourselves, will be united in ecstasy,
Joyful and with no idle words, you and I.
The birds of the heavens will have their hearts eaten by envy
In that place where we will laugh happily, you and I!
But the great marvel is that, you and I, huddled in the same
  nest,
Are in fact and in this instant, the one in Hasanabad,
the other in Marv, you and I.

Arash

As she walked back to join her female relatives, Anahita watched a new stream of onlookers trickle in to the square. She searched every face for Arash. Then, turning, she saw a suitor step down from her *qali*.

Running inside the house, she asked, "Did I miss a suitor give his answer?"

Shirin said, "Yes. Someone from Isfahan. He answered, 'Sickness and health.'"

"Sickness and health?" This time Anahita couldn't mask her look of exasperation. *How far off could someone be?* She wished it had been the khan's guess.

With the end of the contest drawing near, the women of the village had set about preparing *shirin polo*, sweet rice, a wedding dish for good luck in marriage. It was one of Mojdeh's favorites, made with orange peels, pistachios, slivered almonds, saffron, and sugar. Some of the men fired up spits for the roasting of lamb kabobs. Children snuck treats made with dates, reserved for the feast. Someone shoved a bowl and spoon into Anahita's hand for her to hold.

"Does everyone in Marv have messengers who ride stallions?" a child asked.

Anahita spun around.

"I suspect not," Anahita's grandmother said. "It is quite possible this man, Arash, from Marv, and the prince who sent the bottles of dye are one and the same, is it not?"

"Oh!" her aunt exclaimed.

"Are you certain?" Shirin said.

"A prince?" Mojdeh asked, wearing a concerned expression. Princes were known for their infidelity. They accepted many wives, mostly to broker diplomatic deals with neighboring tribes and kingdoms.

"But *my* Arash did not wear the clothes of a prince," Anahita said. "He dressed like us. He said his father worked for . . . Arash would never have sent those bottles of synthetic dyes. He knows me better than this."

"He does?" Mojdeh asked. All eyes fixed on Anahita.

"Yes, he wore plain clothes, my sweet Anahita," her grandmother said, "but in your love-sick state back in Mashhad, while the dervishes danced, did you not notice the imperial seal on your man Arash's gilded dagger?"

Anahita's legs began to shake. She handed the bowl and spoon to Shirin and sank to the ground. *Arash? A prince?* The man who spoke to her through poetry. The man she contemplated for the last twelve months. *He, a prince of the Qajar dynasty? No wonder he had arrived with the wounded soldiers. But do princes fight battles?*

"Why didn't he tell me, Maman Bozorg? Do you think he'll come here today? I must ask Baba to wait for him."

"He will come, Anahita. Have you not seen the dust devils? Haven't you noticed that each time you and this mysterious man from Marv meet—a dust storm occurs?"

32

May the Fated Gentleman Win

People turned their heads as Arash and Ismail dismounted their stallions in the village square. Sand filled Arash's clothes, and his hair stood tangled. He leaned against his horse and listened to two contestants give their answers.

"So the riddle has to do with opposing forces," he said to Ismail.

Arash's stallion nudged him. Stroking its nose, he said, "You are much the reason I made it here through the storm." The animal shook its head side to side, lifted its hoof, and struck the earth.

Ismail placed a hand on Arash's back. "It's time you win this test of wit, my prince. May luck fly to your aid."

Arash shouldered through the spectators to Anahita's father. He thanked Farhad for allowing him to enter the contest on such late notice and looked around for Anahita.

"I wouldn't dream of turning away a prince of our land," Farhad replied, wiping a tear from his eye caused by a grain of

305

dust. "I've been known to be a stickler at times, to hold fast to my own rules. But, turning you away would be the rudest of gestures, would it not? Welcome to our village."

"Forgive me for my secrecy. I only wish to be judged on my own merits, and I didn't want your people to go to any trouble."

"Apologies accepted and understood. Please sit down. We shall continue at once, for the weather is getting the better of us."

Peering out the door of her home, Anahita spotted Arash. "He is here!" She grabbed Shirin's hands and squeezed them.

Arash scanned the hunched shoulders of the crowd and recognized a few faces among them from his last visit. But he didn't find Anahita. Passing by the merchant, he said to him under his breath, "Deh-eh Hasan, Abadi-eh Hasan? Where the devil is that?" The merchant just smiled and shrugged.

Nodding to Dariyoush, Arash said, "It is good to see you up and about."

"I am proud to have fought by your side."

Arash heard a man whisper that a prince had joined the contest. Heads turned this way and that. "Which one is he?" someone asked.

"The only one sitting among the contestants we don't recognize, you idiot!"

He wondered how fast the news would travel across the gathering of people to Anahita's home, where he assumed she was.

Arash turned to the person beside Dariyoush and introduced himself. "My name is Arash. Are you a spectator or player today?"

"I am Reza. I wouldn't pass up this chance for anything." Reza clasped his hands and straightened his posture. "Who would have better insight of Anahita's nature than her own teacher?"

This man has been with Anahita every day, Arash thought, his body tensing. All those vague faces of Anahita's suitors he had imagined now melted into one: Reza's.

Farhad stood beside Anahita's rug. It glimmered despite the dust in the air. "A carpet, like any work of art, should have things about it that you can go on discovering. And so, I should like to call Schoolmaster Reza to the platform." He signaled to Reza to take his place beside the loom.

Anahita thought about her recent dream—the euphoria she felt when she reached the school on the pinnacle of the mountain. Was it an omen? Did it mean Reza was the one?

The schoolmaster pushed up his sleeves and began speaking to the villagers as easily as he would his students. "Good day to all of you. I'd like to start by noting the shades Anahita achieved with this *qali,* the fineness of degree between colors. She has worked hard all winter with the dyemaster in making these."

"Ah, yes," the crowd murmured.

Knowing Anahita's penchant for the mysteries of life—*"About those things books cannot explain"*—Reza thought he would take that tack, rather than something more literal. He smiled at the crowd. "The images she has woven into this carpet, such as the mosques—the one here in Hasanabad and the shrine of Imam

Reza—are symbolic of Anahita's faith and our people's belief in prayer. The light side of what it means to be human."

The mullah smiled and nodded.

Reza adjusted his glasses on his nose. "Alongside the mosques, Anahita has woven battle scenes representing the plight our fellow tribes have suffered. War. The darker side of what it means to be human."

Anahita lifted her hand to her chin. *He draws his riddle from what he sees in front of him, from what is given to him. He has not sought my secrets from within me. Like the water running through the shallow qanat, our friendship trickles no deeper than the surface. But I suppose if he wins, it could be enjoyable to live in a city like Mashhad, or the other cities near and far to which he travels for his studies. Perhaps I could unlearn my nomadic ways.*

"Prayer and war," Reza said. "The lighter and darker sides of life. I therefore conclude that the two opposing forces that Anahita has woven into this carpet are: darkness and light."

The crowd cheered. People stood to applaud. The merchants rattled their cookware. Reza's schoolboys rushed to the platform where he stood and threw pistachios into the air shouting, "Well done, Master Reza!"

"Reza guessed it, didn't he, Anahita?" Shirin shrieked. "Surely it is Reza; I can tell by your expression. You look pale. Did the two of you conspire to win at school?"

"Shirin, please!" Anahita's aunt said.

A new tremor of anxiety washed over Anahita; it spread

quickly, like a *jinn* slipping out of a bottle. She wished her nervousness away as she avoided the women's wondering eyes.

Again Anahita stood on tiptoes to watch Arash.

"Now let us move on to our next contestant," Farhad said, clasping his hands together and nodding to Dariyoush.

As everyone settled down, the squeal of an infant filled the silence. Dariyoush took his place beside Anahita's carpet. Watching him, Anahita felt warmed, like the way summer earth soothed her bare feet.

Dariyoush glanced at the khan, who stood up in the back. The dignitary's presence suggested the likelihood that he himself would not win Anahita's hand. *It just isn't meant to be,* he brooded. *It's all so complicated, this contest, all these suitors.* Dariyoush's words caught in his throat. "I," he began, "I have had the pleasure of watching Anahita spin and dye much of the wool for this carpet."

Keeping his eyes on the rug, he continued, "In an effort to make this *qali* her best ever, Anahita studied with our local dyemaster, her granduncle . . ." He let his voice trail off, remembering Reza had already said this.

Anahita looked at the buds on the poplar trees. *Little in my life would change if I married Dariyoush. Until his leaving for war, his days rarely differed, except for a few changes in position of the carpets on his floor. Yet,* she thought, *he seems to love me. I would not have to leave my people if I married him, and I could continue studying with Reza and the dyemaster.*

But what had her granduncle said to her last night? *"Your carpet shows that your dye studies are complete. There will be others who will follow in my footsteps . . ."*

"Anahita has woven into this *qali* her own conflict between old loyalties and the life she may lead in the future. She loves her homeland, Iran. She respects the tribe into which she was born. The seven borders indicate her pride of family." Dariyoush ran his finger along one edge of the weaving.

"Yet, we are amidst times of change, and of trouble, as Reza has mentioned. Our merchants and bureaucrats have traded their cloaks for Western coats and thrown away their turbans for felt caps. Freedom-seeking women wish to live without the *chador*." Putting a hand to his wound he said, "A revolution is at our doorstep."

Dropping his hand to his side, Dariyoush continued, "Anahita has woven a caravan into her *qali*. Along with the land itself, this seasonal migration of our people, practiced for centuries, is stability. This camel train serves to preserve tradition while it also may represent a train which will lead us into the future."

Anahita fidgeted with her head scarf.

"I therefore conclude that the two opposing forces in life of which this carpet speaks are stability and change within this Land of the Lion and the Sun."

Anahita gripped the doorjamb to hold herself up. Her legs nearly buckled beneath her. "Dear Allah," she whispered. *It's the riddle I thought of, but . . . and he said it so beautifully!*

A chant rose up among the crowd, "Dariyoush! Dariyoush!"

Others stood to applaud him. Dariyoush blushed.

"Well done, Dariyoush," Reza congratulated him. "You gave a well-reasoned guess."

Arash stood up and paced.

Farhad held up his hand. "Thank you, Dariyoush. Judges, have you taken adequate notes?"

Then he called Arash to the stand and the crowd grew silent. So silent, Anahita could hear the sheep chewing their cud—soothingly and hypnotically—in the pen beside her house. *How oblivious to all this, those sheep.*

"Excuse me. Pardon me." Anahita heard the khan making his way through the spectators. The peacock feather in his turban, wiggling. "I believe I am next, Farhad."

"Na!" Anahita yelled, then covered her mouth. Her eyes darting about for whoever may have heard in the square. *He can't go first! What if he guesses the riddle before Arash has a chance?* Anger, then fear, welled up.

It happened too quickly—the judges' decision and the khan taking his place beside the carpet. The wind caused a steady stir of sand in the air, and the spectators wrapped their garbs about themselves.

Clearing his throat the khan said, "I've come here today with much anticipation."

Even now he sounds like a politician, Anahita thought, her clothes flapping in the breeze coming through the doorway. She couldn't bear to watch or listen to him.

"I've been waiting years to marry Anahita. If this is the path I must take, then so be it." The khan's eyes swept across the crowd, narrowing as they fell on Reza.

"Hey! What about our water?" someone demanded.

"Water?" the khan asked. The expression on his face unreadable.

"Dear Khan," Farhad said. "Haven't you noticed the fountain in the village square?"

The khan looked at the fountain. Droplets of water slipped over the lip of its basin, hugging and darkening the contours in the stone. Birds fought for the few puddles.

"Perhaps there's an explanation for that." The khan dismissed the problem with a wave of his hand. Then he began, "This rug speaks of sadness and joy. The shades of red represent happiness and joy for our tribe. And the buildings of the city depict the modern life that is available to all of us who wish to settle. Yet the caravan represents the toil and suffering ways of the nomad."

Suffering? Anahita stiffened.

The khan pressed on, the scent of a possible prize flaring his nostrils. "And I wish to offer Anahita a more pleasurable life— away from dust and dung."

Anahita covered her ears. *Dust and dung! He insults our tribe so!* She kept her ears covered when Farhad repeated the khan's words for the judges to note.

Anahita noticed Shirin would not look at her. *"How will the khan treat you if he's forced to win you?"* Surely Shirin's remembering her words now, Anahita thought.

The crowd tittered and grew silent. Someone even threw hazelnuts at the khan.

"Perhaps you have misunderstood," the khan said above the noise and wind. He looked in the direction of the nut-thrower. "She will be well cared for. They have doctors in Mashhad . . ." But only snippets of his plea seemed to penetrate the spectators' rage.

"Judges, please record 'sadness and joy,'" Farhad said.

"This is not my answer."

"Perhaps the judges will allow you to revise your guess—at the end of the contest—if our final suitor hasn't already given the answer you have in mind. It's time we move on. We'll be choking on this sand before long."

Farhad escorted Arash to the loom.

The prince spoke. "Good afternoon, my fellow people. I am Arash, a Yomut from a northern tribe, and most honored to be here." He bowed.

His voice made him real, something more than a wish. When Anahita heard his northern lilt and his soft-spoken manner, she stepped outside, closed her eyes, and took a deep breath.

Someone in the crowd said, "Couldn't he have dressed for the occasion? He's a mess. His hair's every which way, his clothes are filthy."

"He rode here through a sandstorm!" someone else shot back.

Anahita wiped a trickle of sweat from her neck with her sleeve and walked behind the last row of onlookers.

✻ ✻ ✻

"Please bear with me for these next few minutes," Arash said. "I have not had the pleasure of watching this *qali* progress from sheep to loom, to see its story unfold. I would like a moment to contemplate it." He turned and faced her carpet. Then he ran his palm across its threads. A lanolin and rose scent anointed his fingers, seeped into his skin. *Allah, help me win.*

33

A Twist of Fate

The crowd grew restless, eager for their last contestant's answer. Spectators wagered money, services, and gifts on the winner.

Anahita paced.

When Arash turned to address them, he caught sight of Anahita. Without her *chador*, and with her hair streaming about her shoulders from beneath her kerchief, she looked radiant. Like her carpet, she glowed in color and form from the inside out. *This is what this riddle is about.*

Recalling Anahita's words in the mosque—*"I am heartened by the same hectare of chamomile"*—Arash began. "This *qali* is a metaphor of the relationship between Anahita and our land. Any carpet is a matter of the senses and the mind. The mind is one with the body, as the body is one with the earth. But Anahita's carpet is beyond the reality of the five senses, beyond colors, and beyond motifs."

Swallowing, he continued, "Artisans like Anahita bring a special energy to their work such as the preparation of materials,

315

and the meditation that goes into a carpet before its weaver even warps the loom. It is the part of this *qali* that does not meet the eye."

He looked up to gather his thoughts. "I would like to recite a poem, by an unknown Sufi poet, to help me make this point:

"Here in this carpet lies an ever-lovely spring;
Unscorched by summer's ardent flame,
Safe too from autumn's boisterous gales,
Midwinter's cruel ice and snow,
'Tis gaily blooming still.
The handsome border is the garden wall
Protecting, preserving the Park within
For refuge and renewal: a magic space."

Arash swept a hand across Anahita's carpet. "On the surface we can look at Anahita's *qali* and see that she has woven her tribe's traditional seven borders. These protect the garden of birds and flowers she has woven into the center, 'the Park within.' We can also see the carpet's *abrash*, how each color harmonizes with those around it, indicating that she has used plant dyes. These details we know from our eyes.

"Let us now ponder the nature of plant dyes which we cannot see. Just as a pine door honeys in color over time, so do the shades and hues of plant dyes mature. Like love, madder-root reds may deepen. These dyes are *alive* in Anahita's carpet, 'gaily blooming still,' whether we notice or not.

"Alive also is the wool in this carpet. Beneath the weight of our footsteps, fibers interlock. They migrate like the caravan decorating the rug's surface, forming a solid piece of cloth—much like felt— yet, all the while, hidden from our sight."

Murmurs from the crowd.

Anahita gripped her left arm with her right.

"The 'ever-lovely spring' the poet speaks of could be the special energy Anahita brings to the work, which lives in the work, 'gaily blooming' for all time. 'The Park within' is a sanctuary for Anahita's spirit. The place to which she travels, as she weaves, for refuge and renewal."

Anahita swirled dirt on the ground with her sandal. She held a mix of happiness and sadness, a strange kind of joy. *I think he's on the right path,* she thought. Then she remembered Arash saying to her, *"Look into the mosque, Anahita, what do you see? . . . I see brave men whose swords flashed for the love of family . . . ."*

He transforms my fear into courage.

Arash paused to collect his thoughts. He noticed the wind calming. He would not look in Anahita's direction because he was afraid he might lose his train of thought.

"Yet," he continued, "this 'ever-lovely spring' may also represent something larger, something immortal that inspires the weaver. As the *Quran* tells us, Allah is the External and the Internal. When the Divine Voice wants to express itself, it borrows the different voices of each spiritual man or woman."

Several nods from the crowd.

"So, I suggest when we search for the riddle in Anahita's carpet, we forsake the images she's woven onto the surface. What she has woven into this carpet is the migration of her soul, the path of her journey for refuge and renewal in the eternal love of Allah—that 'magic space.'"

Arash paused.

"There are stories within the warp and weft of the carpets I weave . . ." he recalled.

Yes! Arash thought. This is her riddle. He looked at his audience and said, "I conclude that the two opposing forces in life that Anahita wove into this carpet are: the seen and the unseen."

Women rushed from their doorways as the crowd gave up a cheer. Villagers and guests stood to applaud Arash. The mullah praised him for his insight.

Farhad looked across the tops of the villagers' heads to his daughter. Anahita nodded back at him.

"Did he win? Did he guess the correct riddle, Anahita?" the women pleaded.

"Yes," Anahita said. "Yes!" Euphoria and relief rushed over her. *Thank you, Allah, for letting him win.* Followed by sadness. *He is a prince. I will have to leave my people.*

Farhad stepped onto the platform in front of Anahita's carpet, his body framed in the evening sunlight by the loom and the vivid colors of her rug. He held up his hand to silence the crowd but they paid no attention.

Reza's students circled their teacher.

Fatima, Ali, and half the village saluted Dariyoush.

When Farhad held the turban high above his head, he caught his people's attention.

"Shh, shh . . ." The signal traveled until everyone listened.

Reaching into the hat, Farhad pulled out the slip of parchment with Anahita's riddle on it. He waved it back and forth for all to see. Then he read Anahita's words: "The two opposing forces in life that I have woven into my wedding *qali* are: the seen and the unseen."

Cheer after cheer rose up. Someone broke out a *santur* and a lute. Children danced among the adults. With the weather clearing, women toted bowls, platters, and cotton spreads for setting up their feast in the village square. The merchant from Mashhad offered his carpets, *sofrehs*, and his friend's cookware to accommodate the crowd. "'All is fair in love and war,' as they say. I'm not a sore loser!"

Anahita, with her mother, grandmother, aunts, and cousins following, made her way through the crowd to where Arash and Farhad stood talking. Arash turned to the sound of Anahita's voice and drank deeply from her gaze.

The khan started toward Farhad with his Arabian in tow, stepping on abandoned rugs, water pipes, and a little girl's fingers.

In the midst of the noise and celebration, Arash stood beside the carpet a second time and held up his hand until the music ceased and the chatter stopped. Everyone wanted to hear this stranger, their prince, speak.

"Please allow me to formally introduce myself. I am Arash, governor of Marv, a prince in the Qajar dynasty."

Farhad winked at Mojdeh.

"I am honored to have won Anahita's hand in marriage. However, it is my intent not to win her hand, but her heart. I must be certain that Anahita loves me, as I love her."

Mojdeh curled an arm around her daughter as Arash spoke. Anahita was glad her mother was there beside her.

"Since Anahita is so fond of riddles, I challenge her with one of my own. Tomorrow at sunrise I must leave for Tehran to attend the Assembly of the House of Consultation. I will bring your concerns to its members, including the notion of a constitutional parliament. I agree with those who call for a voice in the kingdom's affairs. After giving my recommendations, I intend to step down from my post . . ."

"Step down?!" someone said.

"Give up the provincial seat to which you are heir?" asked another.

"Yes, this is what I want. I am first a nomad, second a prince." Arash turned to face another section of the crowd. "My Yomut people need me now. I wish to establish a Council of Intertribal Relations," Arash explained. "In this role I feel I may better protect Iran from its present danger."

Cheer after cheer rang out. Arms and scarves waving.

"It is my hope that my tribe will summer in the same mountains and plateaus as you Afshars. We can no longer risk migrating to the highlands in the north and east because of the turmoil."

Arash looked solely at Anahita. "Should Anahita solve my riddle, I give her a choice. She may marry me, or she may choose to marry another suitor whom she loves, one who may have tried but failed to solve her riddle in this test of wit."

Anahita clutched her mother's arm and broke from Arash's gaze. *He's giving me choice? O Compassionate and Merciful One, I dreamed of this, yet . . . I am frightened.*

"Perhaps with this man you will always have riddles in your life, Anahita," Farhad said. "And perhaps I will have the chance to pose one to you each summer—one that will take you the whole winter to figure out!" A sudden rush of emotion brought a visible quiver to his lips.

Anahita's and Dariyoush's eyes met. During that split-second glance, before his mother hugged him, and his father laid a hand on his shoulder to turn him away, Anahita sensed something—*a wish?*

"Yes, Baba," Anahita said to her father, as she wiped joyful tears from her face and gathered inner strength.

Turning to Arash she said, "I accept your challenge, my prince."

"Your *yar*, I hope. There's a difference, you know." He flashed her a grin for all the world to see! That grin, which on three occasions now had made her melt.

She blushed as the crowd went wild. Shirin nudged her.

"He's as good as family!" A man shouted. "Why, his tribe is molded from the same dunes, fed by the same grasses."

"Perhaps I'll hold off on my wedding gift," the merchant said to his friends. "Maybe she'll choose me after all."

Above all the noise Arash said, "This is the riddle I pose . . ."

Hush spread around the village square until the silence was so complete that anyone could have heard wool sprouting on suckling lambs.

"What is it, besides the caravan, that serves as a foundation for our people? Through this, the old and the new will live in harmony."

Farhad smiled at Anahita. A smile that she knew meant, "You can do it, my sweet." Her father put his arm around her as they walked to their house. "I am certain you will discover the answer to the prince's riddle by sunrise."

For the rest of that evening, everyone in Hasanabad feasted, the women drifting to the east side of the village square, the men to the west.

"Farhad," the khan shouted above the din as he pushed through the festive crowd with his cat curled about his neck. He held documents under one arm and horse reins in the other. People dashed out of his way. "The winner was to be announced after all the testimonies have been given. You never gave me my second chance." The cat's red tail thumped on his chest, as if she too demanded an answer.

"My dear Khan, no one got a second chance. And what difference would it make now? Perhaps you'd like to take the matter up with *the winner*—the prince."

"Prince?" The khan felt his cheeks draw down to his lower jaw and begin to spasm. He looked over his horse at Arash. He vaguely recognized his face from their meeting in Mashhad. *Prince?* the khan thought. *How did I miss that detail?*

"You did not hear the Qajar prince introduce himself?" Farhad said, taking a few steps back, and leading the khan away from the circle of women standing with his daughter.

"I must have been relieving myself at that moment," the khan retorted, scratching his backside. Then he said, "But I did hear him say he was quitting some post or other. I would hope the shah chooses a successor with more backbone than this one. Someone who will take command and live up to his duties, not run away from them."

"I should think you'd be happy that the prince plans to support your constitution." Farhad ducked a slipper someone had thrown into the air. "Wouldn't you agree that Arash's intentions to forgo the provincial governorship, but establish a Council of Intertribal Relations in order to better protect our boundaries, makes him even more a leader?"

The khan felt his face redden. "My dear Kadkhuda, I assure you, princes of any kind are not long for this land." The khan pulled the scroll from under his arm and thrust it at Farhad. "Get your schoolteacher to read this for you. But don't lose heart—I hear the prisons are shaping up these days. Better food, fewer rats."

Farhad stared coldly. He didn't reach for the parchment so the khan let it fall to the *kadkhuda*'s feet. "When the prince returns to Marv to mingle among the nomads, consider yourself left to your own resources. You may as well say good-bye to your water."

The khan peeled the cat from his neck and placed her in a *chanteh* tied to his saddle. "Unless Anahita chooses me tonight, I'll have you arrested, as that document from the *mujtahad*, the religious jurists in Mashhad, gives me the right to do." He pointed to the ground where the parchment still lay. "This wedding riddle contest is against civil law."

"Love, against the law?"

"When did you become such a sentimental fool, Farhad?" The khan mounted his horse in the middle of the happy bedlam and galloped off, his peacock feather horizontal in the wind.

Anahita felt giddy as she watched the khan ride away, but she knew by the tightness of her father's jaw that he was troubled.

"What did the khan say to you, Baba?"

"Nothing with which you need to trouble your riddle-solving mind," he winked. Then he strolled over to where Arash, Ismail, the mullah, and others had gathered at the teahouse.

Anahita sat with Shirin on the fountain wall eating *shirin polo*. Feeling that this was just like old times, she decided she should tell Shirin she was sorry for a year of lost friendship. *If not now, when?*

"Shirin," she said. "I am sorry for having been so busy this last year with my weaving, the clothing cart, and school. I would like to spend more time with you before my wedding."

"It was my fault too, Anahita. I was quite jealous," Shirin replied, just as Anahita said, "When you got married, I felt betrayed . . . and left behind."

The two hugged.

Then Shirin whispered, "I heard Arash and his subject talking about Reza and Dariyoush."

"Shirin! Were you eavesdropping?"

"Of course not—I was serving them kabobs. Anyway, I heard Ismail suggest that Reza should be recruited to write up a proposal to the Assembly of the House of Consultation regarding the need for an Iranian rural education system. Reza is invited to deliver it with Arash to the members of the Council! And Dariyoush . . ."

Anahita squirmed. That someone would play with Dariyoush's fate intensified her own responsibility to him tonight—whether or not she would choose him as her husband.

"They spoke highly of him. How bravely he fought and how skilled he is with animal care. It seems they would like to give him an honor of sorts and ask him to head up a regional battalion."

Anahita looked around the village square for her childhood companion. Her caveman and swim coach. *He has been such a joy in my life.* When she spotted him, he was accepting water from a young woman, the daughter of the man who hauled the urns of water to Hasanabad from Kemesh. She looked a little like Shirin with a fair complexion but her eyes were the color of lapis. Anahita saw Dariyoush's gaze linger on her face ever so briefly, and how he watched the young woman as she walked away.

"Who are you . . . ?" Shirin asked, following Anahita's gaze.

Anahita looked down. She changed her position on the wall and smoothed her skirt. Then she looked back again to make sure Dariyoush wasn't still watching the woman from Kemesh. She felt surprise, disbelief, jealousy, defeat, sadness, relief, and hope all crushed into one. *I am not the only one for him*, she realized.

"Oh," Shirin said. "The girl with the unusual birthmark on her left cheek—a rosette of sorts that sets off her eyes. Don't you think it looks as if an artist painted it on for her? As if some miniaturist chose her skin for his canvas?"

Anahita could only nod. Her cousin really had an annoying way of rubbing things in, even if she didn't mean to.

Shirin looked at Anahita as if expecting a better response. Between mouthfuls of rice she said, "I know who I'd choose for my husband tonight."

Weaving a Mate

Anahita sat beneath a poplar tree with her grandmother, the dust in the air having settled as the storm moved south. Maman Bozorg said, "Second chances are not to be taken lightly."

With her grandmother's words in mind, and while the others feasted, Anahita decided to watch the game of "Leap Over the Camel" that Reza and his young students had organized in the village square. Their antics calmed her. When Reza noticed her, he gave up his turn to speak with Anahita.

"Thank you, Reza, for joining my riddle contest. And thank you for all your help with my studies. I . . ."

"Say no more. I am hopeful that I will be the lucky winner at sunrise!" He smiled. "And if not, at least I will have you until the tribe migrates for summer pastures, yes?"

Anahita looked into the schoolmaster's blue eyes and nodded.

Turning, she walked to where Dariyoush had tethered his horse on the other side of the square. As she approached him, she said to his back, "Beautiful evening, isn't it?" He adjusted the halter on his horse, turned to Anahita, then back again to his horse.

"I want to thank you for entering my contest." She reached out to touch his arm, but hesitated. *This time he is closed as tight as a pistachio shell.*

"It was my privilege."

"Are you leaving for somewhere?" She peered around his shoulder.

"To the stream."

Anahita's eyes moistened. Dariyoush tugged gently on the horse's halter.

"I appreciate your lovely thoughts today about my riddle, and for having told me yesterday how you feel about me, Dariyoush . . ."

"Anahita, the most beautiful words I want to tell you, I haven't said yet."

He nudged his stallion and led him away. Rather than the sound of hooves on cobbles, Anahita heard only the sound of her heart snapping, a brittle twig Dariyoush would discard rather than whittle.

With a riddle to solve, there was no hope of sleep that night. Anahita wrapped herself in a woolen shawl and walked outside to her loom. She sat with her feet dangling from the seat perched halfway up the frame. The moon cast her silhouette against the wedding rug. *Baba is right,* she thought: *Life, like a garden, never stays the same.*

She relived moments of her day, shuddering at the memory of

the khan's answer to her riddle: *suffering toil, dirt, and dung.* She wondered how he could forsake his roots as he did. The only vestiges of his past that the khan kept with him were the rose petals he floated in his tea. If she did not choose him, would Hasanabad suffer without water for years to come? Would they be forced to leave their village? Would Baba remain *kadkhuda*?

Flooding back to her came the deep sorrow she pushed away when Dariyoush professed his love for her.

"Anahita, when you are near there are two suns in the sky . . ."

How long had Dariyoush paced in the shadows, *My very own snow leopard? He understood the riddle I thought of first.*

"You love him only as a brother?" She recalled Maman Bozorg's question. And then the mullah's words—*"Perhaps it is not your heart I had in mind when I consented to this contest."*

Yes, she thought. *I do love Dariyoush, but as a brother. And won't he make a fine battalion leader or* kadkhuda *one day?*

Anahita drew one leg onto the bench and leaned her chin on her knee. Golden-brown eyes and a certain smile crept to mind. *Perhaps Arash is the bird of vision in my dream who flies toward me with desire!*

She thought about all of what she and Arash had talked about in Mashhad. His love of Iran. His poetry. His gentle manner with the boy and his camel.

Like Maman Bozorg, Arash has a special way of thinking that helps me see differently. And he feels comfortable discussing things outside of books.

Anahita turned to a small sound she heard in the tree beside her, but saw nothing.

Even though he hasn't spent years with me like Dariyoush, he knows some-
thing of me that is true. And he guessed my riddle! Knew my riddle, she
thought, as she played with a thread of her hair.

Shirin's words pinched her ears: *"He's a prince. He may not love you.*
Perhaps he only wishes to secure a safe summer pasture for his people." Followed
by her mother's: *"Princes are known for their infidelity, Anahita."*

But the words of her grandmother rang more true to her own
beliefs: *"Marriages of both kinds can be joyful . . . You have always seemed*
happiest when exploring new horizons . . ."

Anahita thought that even though her mother wished for her to
marry and stay in the village, she herself was ready to go.

With her carpet woven and the contest over, Anahita's mind
cleared itself for the first time in months. That quietness, the kind
her grandmother always spoke of—the silence in which an oasis
will flower—overcame her. Still, like the trees beside her, she
could feel the slow movement of the moon as it threw different
slants of light on her back and on her carpet. Cool air filled her
lungs.

She wanted to solve Arash's riddle. To show him she could
match his wit. She wanted the privilege of choosing her husband.

"Arash," Anahita said aloud—a strong Persian name that fit
him so. She liked the sound of it, like the rustle of sage rising in
her. She would always be proud of their melodious Persian and
Turkic languages. No matter what changes the future would hold.

"Language," Anahita said with sudden insight. *Our language is the*
foundation of our people. The refuge of our souls in times of change.

"Arash," she repeated. *My mysterious friend. My* ashena *. . . Happy is*

330

the time when we sit in the palace, you and I. With two forms, and two faces, but a single soul . . .

My yar.

With a confident heart and unsteady hands, she threaded a needle and wove the name of the suitor she had chosen into her carpet beside her own . . .

Arash

Anahita smiled and thought, *Only one short year ago, I argued with Maman that I would never weave a stranger's name into my wedding* qali.

*I*t is in the vision of the physical eyes

That no invisible or secret thing exists.

But when the eye is turned toward the Light of God

What thing could remain hidden under such a Light?

—*R*umi

Glossary

abadi (ah-baa-dee)—a village or settlement

abrash (ah-brahsh)—a term used to describe variations in the hue or colors of yarn in a rug or weaving caused by age, or yarn used from different dye lots. Most natural or plant dyes will yield color variations, whereas synthetic dyes are more uniform.

Afshar (Af-shar)—a semi-nomadic people who reside in southern and northeastern Iran near Kerman and Mashhad, respectively. Some also live in eastern Turkey. They are noted for weaving Afshar soumak rugs with geometric designs.

ashena (ash-en-a)—a casual friend

agha (ah-ga)—sir, a title of respect

aziz (ah-zeez)—one who is closest to your heart (*azizam* is the possessive form of this term of endearment)

azan (ah-zan)—a call to prayer

bagh (bawg)—a garden

Baluch (Bah-looch)—a Baluchi-speaking tribal group inhabiting eastern Iran, western Pakistan, and southern Afghanistan

carding combs—wooden paddles embedded with metal bristles (or long teeth) used to straighten wool fibers before spinning

chai (chah-ee)—tea

chanteh (chan-teh)—a small woven bag

cochineal (cah-che-neel)—an organic dyestuff derived from dried insects thatfeed on prickly pear cacti. Dye colors range from red to pink and violet. It takes seventy thousand insects to make a pound of cochineal. One ounce will dye one pound of wool.

darya (dar-y-a)—sea. Darya Khazar is the Caspian Sea.

dervish (der-vish)—a kind of Sufi who follows a special form of Islamic mysticism. Dervishes are known for their drumming, chanting, and whirling ceremonies, in which they experience a closeness or intimacy with Allah. Some of the first orders of dervishes were inspired by the scholar, poet, and spiritual master Jalaluddin Rumi, who lived in the thirteenth century, in Konya, Turkey.

divan (dee-van)—a government bureau or tribunal; a council chamber

dokhtar (dah-tar)—daughter

dokhtaram (dah-tar-am)—my daughter

doost (doost)—a close friend

duk (duke)—spindle

felt—a cloth made by working together wool fibers by pressure and douses in hot, cold, and soapy water, which shocks and shrinks the fibers into a solid mass

flatweaves—a term used to describe a pileless weaving such as a *gelim* or soumak. Weft wraps are used to make a colorful pattern.

gabbeh (gab-bay)—a style of weaving that has a strong informal flavor. Numerous wefts are used between rows of knots to speed the weaving process.

gelim (ge-leem)—a flatwoven rug in which a smooth surface pattern is formed by the wefts; *kilim* in Turkish

goat hair tent—a black nomadic tent woven in long strips and sewn together

golab (go-lob)—rose water

gul (gol)—a flower; also a term used to describe the pattern of a particular tribal weaving

Gulestan (Gol-es-tan)—an epic poem by the Persian Sufi poet Sa'adi

imam (ee-mom)—a prayer leader or holy man

indigo—an ancient blue dyestuff that has been produced since 2500 BCE with perennial plants from the Old and New World tropics. It is used for dyeing fabrics and yarn, and is also ground up and mixed with clay to make cosmetics, crayons, and paint.

inshallah (in-shala)—God willing

jajim (ja-jeem)—a woven textile that has a colorful, striped design; usually used for robes or blankets of a lower quality than *gelims*

jambiya (jam-bee-ya)—a dagger

jube (joob)—a shallow trench alongside village lanes that carries water from the *qanat*

kadkhuda (kad-khoo-da)—a headman or tribal leader

khan (khawn)—a tribal chief who oversees tribal affairs and represents the tribe with the government. The khan appoints the *kadkhuda*.

khanom (kha-noom)—madam (used for a married woman)

khatam (khat-am)—ornately carved boxes inlaid with thousands of triangular pieces of ebony, ivory, and gold

loom—a device for weaving yarn into cloth and carpets

madder—a sprawling perennial native to Asia Minor and the Mediterranean. The roots produce a dye that gives a variety of orange, red, and brown pigments.

madrasa (mah-drah-sah)—a school

manzel (man-zel)—a small dwelling, like an apartment

masnui (mahs-new-ee)—synthetic

mihrab (meh-rob)—a niche in a mosque wall that points toward Mecca

mujtahad (mooj-ta-had)—a religious jurist who helps to settle civil affairs

naan (naahn)—flat bread

natural dyes—tinctures derived from native plants, insects, and minerals

nomads—people who travel in search of pasture. In the Middle East and Asia these people often travel between mountains in the summer and lowlands in the winter. Stock breeding is their principal livelihood.

Nooruz (new-rooz)—Persian New Year

pile weaves—knots that are wrapped around warp threads and left to project at right angles to the plane of the weaving. They are tied individually in a transverse row and held in place by a weft thread.

qali (ghawl-ee)—a carpet

qanat (ghan-not)—an irrigation channel

rafigh (ra-feeg)—best friend

ruh (roo)—spirit, soul

runas (roo-nahs)—madder root, a plant used for red dyes

saffron—small lilies or crocuses with orange stigmas, grown in the Eastern Mediterranean region and Middle East. In early fall the stigmas are plucked out of the flowers and dried. A yellow dyestuff may be obtained. It is also used for seasoning food.

sama (saa-ma)—a turning dance, a Sufi ritual performed by dervish "monks" who whirl in hope of reaching an ecstatic state or union with Allah

selvage—a specially woven edge that prevents the cloth from unraveling

shuttle—an instrument containing a spool of weft thread that is used in weaving to carry the weft yarn back and forth between the warp threads

sofreh (soo-fre)—a dinner cloth on which food is served and which is used on the floor

soumak knot—two or more weft wraps around a pair of warp threads, a weaving technique that produces a flat weave

spindle—a tool used to spin wool into yarn. It consists of a shaft inserted through the center of a disc, or whorl.

sprak (sprack)—dyer's broom, a plant used for a primary yellow dye that will not fade in sunlight

Sufi—A Sufi is commonly known as a Muslim following a special form of Islamic mysticism, and one who seeks union with Allah through silence, meditation, music, song, stories, poetry, and dance. Sufis are people who live everyday lives and work in a variety of careers, and are devoted to kindness, often poverty, and acts of helping.

synthetic dyes—human-made chemicals that color fabric

tasnif (taz-neef)—a song

toman (toe-maahn)—Iranian money

warp—lengthwise threads attached to the loom that form the structure and length of a rug

weft—also "woof." Horizontal threads worked between rows of knots in a carpet, which secure the knots in place.

weft comb—a heavy comb, usually made of lead, that is used in weaving for pounding weft threads into place

yar (yahr)—soul mate, kindred spirit

Yomut (Yo-mutt)—a Turkman tribe of northeastern Iran

yurt (yirt)—a circular nomadic home, usually made by draping felt coverings over a portable framework

zafaran (za-far-an)—saffron

Reader's Guide

A Q&A WITH THE AUTHOR

Q: Anahita is a remarkably modern character in a traditional nineteenth-century Persian society. How did you come up with her and her story?

A: Anahita's story began with an Afshar tribal rug that I keep in my home, which is full of symbolism and was likely woven as a dowry carpet. There is an inscription on the rug, "Shah live forever," and it is dated around 1936. Thus, I assumed the weaver of this rug was a strong woman who expressed her opinions, and possibly even a political activist. The carpet is made with naturally dyed yarns, which tells me that the weaver appreciated the aesthetic nature of these traditional dyes and that she preferred them over the new synthetic dyes that were available to her at that time. Knowing this led me to develop a character who was progressive yet grounded in her heritage. I don't see Anahita as a remarkably modern character for her time. I believe women in every era have had to strike a balance between tradition and change, as change is inevitable. Choosing her own husband was not all that uncommon among nomads of the period. In many aspects they did not adhere to the same practices as those people who were living in cities, whose lives were governed more closely by the mores of the settled and established culture, or perhaps the ways of Islam. We must remember that arranged marriages were something that women in Western cultures, as well as others around the world, also faced in those days.

Q: What do you want readers to learn from Anahita's experiences?

A: To follow their hearts and minds.

Q: How did you come up with Anahita's suitors?

A: This is a difficult question to answer. I really don't know! I believe I had the khan in mind from the outset as the antagonist, as he is central to the plot which launches the tale. I suppose Dariyoush, her tribes-mate, was there from the start because the "boy next door" as a romantic interest is a universal notion. The schoolteacher, Reza, evolved out of what I knew about Iranian history, that at one point (although later in time) the government set up tents in which to educate nomads. So I was able to send a teacher/suitor to Anahita's village. The merchant from Mashhad materialized on his own, and I decided to have him show up for her wedding-riddle contest while I was writing that section of the book. Arash . . . I believe he arose from the poetry of Jalaluddin Rumi that I was reading throughout the writing of the novel. Perhaps he was a gift to me from this spir-itual master himself.

Q: What research did you do to make the story authentic?

A: I had been weaving tapestry and studying Middle Eastern carpets for years before I began to write this novel. Part of my research included trips to Turkey in which I visited many carpet shops, spoke with dye masters, and stayed with friends in a village of carpet weavers and rug repairmen. Later, I traveled to Iran, where I was able to visit carpet workshops, as well as experience the landscape itself—feel the aridity in the air, the mountains looming over me, the smell of cypress trees—and experience the barrenness of the deserts. I marveled at the elegance of the architecture, ran my fingers across the intricate, blue mosaic walls of their mosques and bathhouses. I climbed their minarets and heard the lilting, haunting chant of the muezzin's call to prayer. I also consulted scholars about Iran's history, classical Persian literature, and nomadic life, which I have explained in more depth in my author's note.

Q: You have traveled extensively in Iran and the Middle East. What do you value most from the time you spent there?

A: I feel as if I have only scratched the surface of my understanding of Middle Eastern cultures, and hope to live there for extended periods of time in the near future. What I value most are the friendships I have cultivated in Turkey and Iran. From these I have acquired new perspectives. I appreciate knowing there are other ways to live and lead a fulfilling life other than the culture in which I grew up.

Q: What is your writing process?

A: I began writing when I was a new mother, and so my writing process has evolved along with my children's maturity. At first I wrote when they napped. Later, when they were in school, I wrote during the day. Soon they will all attend college, and I suspect I will have much more free time in which to travel and write. I try to work on manuscripts in the morning when I am fresh and do research, make phone calls, and e-mail in the late afternoon.

Q: What kinds of books do you read when you're not writing?

A: I read everything: fiction, nonfiction, poetry, journal articles, and newspapers, including those published in other countries (I subscribe to some and bring home others from the places I visit). Most often I delve into the myths, folklore, history, and classical literature of Ireland and of the Middle East. I also like to read translations of modern and contemporary writers from around the world.

Q: You're an accomplished weaver and dyer. How did you get started, and where did you learn the crafts?

A: About sixteen years ago I moved to eastern Washington, which is quite rural, and began raising my own sheep (as my Irish grandmother did). I learned from a local weaving guild how to spin yarn. After reading a few books about natural dyes used by Native American, Scottish, and Middle Eastern weavers, I experimented on my own. Many of the dye plants grew in my yard; others I collected while hiking locally, or in southern Utah, Ireland, and Turkey, places I often visit. Sarah Swett, an accomplished weaver in Moscow, Idaho, taught me the basics in weaving, and I have trundled along on my own ever since. Although my tapestries are riddled with mistakes, I've been told they exude spirit, which is good enough for me. I enjoy the process—working with different textures of fiber and playing with the dyes, whose colors never cease to surprise me in the end.

Q: What message do you want readers to go away with after reading Anahita's story?

A: I hope that readers will see the beauty that I have discovered in Iranian culture.

. . .

QUESTIONS FOR DISCUSSION

1. In many ways this is a story about actions and their consequences. In what way does Anahita take control of her life? Do her actions have negative consequences? Why?

2. Throughout history, and still today in many cultures, people uphold the tradition of arranged marriages. What are your thoughts on arranged marriage? Do you understand the reasons Anahita's father wants to choose a husband for her, and for her to wed at such a young age? On page 5 he says to Anahita, "Marriage is what gives women value . . . To be unwed in this world is to be nothing!" In the world of the story, is this true? Does this system have its merits? If so, what are they? If not, why?

3. There is an emphasis on the tradition of poetry in *Anahita's Woven Riddle*. For instance, Arash consults his book of Sufi poetry in times of need. How else is poetry used throughout the story? Why do some of the weavings include poems?

4. If you were to devise a riddle, what would it be?

5. Do you feel as though Anahita's culture influences her actions and the choices that she makes? Think about your own culture. In what ways do you feel it influences the way you behave?

6. Rug-making plays a central role in this story. What does it mean to be a rug maker? What does the weaving symbolize? Are the weavings themselves symbolic?

Author's Note

CARPETS

The tradition of weaving wedding carpets as part of a woman's dowry continues today throughout traditional communities in the Middle East. Yet, since the end of the nineteenth century, tribal rugs such as those Anahita weaves have become scarce. In the marketplaces, commercial rugs made in factories with synthetic dyes and predesigned patterns have largely replaced folk art rugs made with natural dyes. Iran is one of the world's largest exporters of carpets. Its factory, village, and nomadic weaving enterprises employ more people than the oil industry.

In my story, Anahita, her mother, and her grandmother are shown using an upright loom in their home such as those used in workshops or factories; however, when on migrations, most Iranian nomads weave on horizontal looms, which are better suited for low tent ceilings and maneuverability.

Anahita's Woven Riddle arose from my daily musings regarding the Afshar tribal rug that is in my living room. I wondered about its many-colored tassels, its bird-and-leaf pattern, and its seven borders. I learned that many carpets woven in the tents and villages of Asia have meanings as well as artistic and practical uses. For thousands of years, and before most people learned to read and write, women wove stories, myths, and symbols into their textiles—some of which had the perceived power to bless or protect life. A visual motif such as the "cloud band" in my rug might have celebrated rain, much needed in a desert village like Anahita's. Colors such as indigo (blues), cochineal (purples), and madder root (reds) represented happiness and eternal life. The direction in which a weaver spun her threads could invoke good luck. Thanks to the weaver who wove the rooster and tassel talismans on my carpet, my home is protected from the evil eye.

Perhaps the carpets you walk on tell a story.

HISTORY

At one time, the Persian Empire, today known as Iran, spread farther north and east than it does now to include the cities of Marv, Samarkand, and Herat. This story takes place near the end the Qajar Dynasty (1787–1925), during the reign of Nasir al-Din Shah in about 1885. At this time, Iran was neighbored in the north by the Russians and in the south by the British, who were protecting their access to India. At the same time, Iranian and Afghan tribes fought for possession of the borderlands. A turbulent era, it made travel unsafe, even for caravans like Anahita's.

The call for a constitutional parliament—the representative body of government mentioned in my novel—actually formed under a different shah between 1906 and 1911.

The Qajar Dynasty sanctioned European-style schools to

educate men, and a missionary school in Tehran in 1890 to educate women. But in the 1880s, when this story takes place, a large sector of the population of Iran was illiterate (as were those in most of the rest of the world, including the United States). As early as 1900 there were schools for girls in the cities. A new Pahlavi Dynasty under Reza Shah brought about a national effort to educate women in Iran in the 1920s. Later, Mohammad Reza Shah provided for women's suffrage, and a rural teaching corps around the 1940s. Before that time there were Quranic schools, many run by women teachers, in the villages.

Bathhouses in Iran, such as the one described in the novel, were generally not separated into two rooms, one for each gender, but rather segregated by different bathing hours for men and women. For purposes of my plot, I imagined a bathhouse much like one I visited in Turkey, which had different sides for men and women. Community bathhouses were used in Iran until recently. Today many of these beautifully tiled, subterranean spaces have been made into restaurants and teahouses.

NOMADS

Little is written about the culture or traditions of Anahita's Afshar or Arash's Yomut tribes, which still migrate today in the Middle East.

The political structure of nomadic life varies among tribes, but the similarities are strong. The smallest political division is a single family, or "tent." Five or six tents form a "herding unit." These units make the milking of animals and the setting up and breaking of camp more efficient.

Numerous herding units join during migrations to form a "camp." Each camp is often led by a *kadkhuda*, or headman. *Kadkhudas* are appointed by the khan, the man who directs the whole tribe and represents his people with the government.

Because of its climate and good pastures, the northern Khurasan province of Iran has attracted many nomads and semi-nomads of neighboring areas for centuries. A small number of Afshars dwell near Mashhad—the market city that Anahita visits on migrations—but many live in southern Iran near the city of Kerman.

FARSI LANGUAGE

Many speakers of Farsi helped me with the language used in this story. Because the Farsi alphabet does not translate exactly into English, spellings of the Farsi words can vary. Any inaccuracies within the text are my own. The Farsi language, often referred to as Persian, is an ancient language. In Iran it predated the use of Arabic, which came with the introduction of Islam and the Muslim holy book, the *Quran*. Later, Iran was overcome by Ottoman Turks and others. While many tribal people today in Iran speak Turkish dialects, Iranians retain Farsi as their national language.

I would like to acknowledge Shahram Shiva for his explanation of four words that describe friendship in the Persian language: *ashena, doost, rafigh,* and *yar,* and how these terms also refer to degrees of closeness and intimacy. I have used these terms in the novel, along with his notion that Rumi "kisses you on the right cheek, then on the left, warms your soul and brings you closer to yourself," in a conversation between Anahita and Arash.

RUMI, RABI'A, AND SUFI POEMS

The poems in this story are primarily the work of Jalaluddin Rumi, a poet of the thirteenth century who wrote volumes of poetry, discourses, and letters. I have taken—and in some cases modified—lines or place names in Rumi's poems to fit my plot or to use in dialogue for Arash and Maman Bozorg. Please see my acknowledgments for the original translation sources. Rumi was born in Balkh, Afghanistan, then part of the Persian empire. His father was a professor of religion. Fleeing the Mongol armies, his family traveled through Nishapur near Mashhad—the setting of this novel—where they met the great poet Fariduddin Attar, who presented young Rumi with the *Book of Mysteries*. After traveling to Baghdad, Mecca, and Damascus, Rumi's family settled in the land of Rum—Roman Anatolia—present-day Konya, Turkey. There, Rumi became the spiritual leader of what would later become the Mevlevi order of dervishes, who invented the ritual turning dance. The Mevlana Museum, a mosque in Konya that marks Rumi's grave, has been made into a national heritage site. I have visited this sanctuary. Please visit my Web site for images of it: www.meghannuttallsayres.com.

Rabi'a al-Adawiyya, the woman poet beloved by Maman Borzorg and Anahita, was born in about 717 C.E. and lived in

Basra, in what is now Iraq. In this novel I have used the second two stanzas of "O My Lord," a poem attributed to Rabi'a and translated by Charles Upton. Rabi'a was a freed slave who later in life became widely recognized as a holy woman. She preferred to remain single and spent her time in prayer and receiving others. Her stories and poems were transmitted orally over the centuries before being written down by Sufi writers such as al-Ghazzal and Attar, who hailed from Nishapur, as mentioned in my story.

BAM EARTHQUAKE

On December 26, 2003, while I was writing this novel, a devastating earthquake hit southern Iran and the ancient city of Bam, killing more than twenty thousand people and destroying an international heritage site. I decided then that I would donate proceeds from *Anahita's Woven Riddle* to help the people of Iran in recovery from the quake. Royalties from the sale of this book will go to development enterprises in Bam that serve women and children. Thank you for your contribution.

Acknowledgments

$\mathcal{I}$ would like to thank my friend Kenan Yasurgan of Istanbul, who first introduced me to the carpets of Asia. Turabi Topal, owner of Turabi and Birdem Carpet Gallery in Seattle, who sent me to his relatives in Turkey. The family of Hasan Solak of Sultanhani, Turkey, for opening their hearts and home, and teaching me carpet weaving. Murat and Uzeyir Ozyurt, of Dervish Brothers' Carpets in Konya, Turkey, for their hospitality and expertise.

I cannot express the depth of my gratitude to Hossein "Elvand" Ebrahimi, founder, editor, and translator of House of Translation for Children's and Young Adult Books in Tehran, Iran, for his suggestions on this manuscript and for inviting me on my first trip to Iran. I wish to thank also, in this regard, the Ministry of Culture and Islamic Guidance for making this journey possible, and also express my appreciation of the writers, translators, publishers, poets, children, journalists, museum curators, schoolteachers, librarians, handicraft specialists, weavers, local guides, and the van driver who all helped to make my experience memorable. Others who helped me with Iranian culture and history include Dr. Abbas Amanat of Yale and Dr. Lois Beck of Washington University in St. Louis, for careful editing and first-hand information about Iranian nomadic cultures and languages. I wish to thank James Opie, owner of James Opie Rugs in Portland, Oregon, whose books offered a wellspring of information on carpets and nomadic cultures, for introducing me to Abbas and Parham Sayahi of Shiraz, Iran, who helped with natural dyes. For information about sources of Rumi translations I would like to thank Dr. Fatemeh Keshavarz of Washington University, St. Louis, and Farhad Hakimzadeh of London's Iran Heritage Foundation. Thanks also to Naheed Dareshuri of Ardmore, Pennsylvania, for sewing me traditional Qashqa'i nomad clothing.

My friends Mojdeh Khalighi, Farhad, Farnaz, and Anahita Kashefi of Irvine befriended me years ago and first introduced me to Iranian culture and Farsi language. In Spokane, I thank Ahmad Haghighi for his assistance with Farsi language in my text, Dr. Hasan Ramani for his patience and generosity in teaching me conversational Farsi before my trip to Iran, and Shahrokh Nikfar for his help with Iranian culture and language and for providing Persian music each weekend on his KYRS "Persian Hour" radio show, which helped invigorate some of my drafts.

I give thanks to my consultants on Islam, Fatima Ansari of Spokane, Dr. Freda Shama, and Imam Sayed Mostafa al Quzwini of the Islamic Foundation Center in Orange County.

Thanks as well to Bethany Lutz of the Hogle Zoo in Salt Lake City, my consultant for camel sounds.

I am grateful to my daughter, Maeve, and my writing group,

including Mary Douthitt, Mary Cronk Farrell, Claire Rudolf Murphy, Lynn Caruso, Patricia Nikolina Clark, Betsy Wharton, Marie Whalen, and Lisa Frank, for their generosity, careful reading, and suggestions on this manuscript. Thank you, Sarah Swett and Jaynee Koch for weaving wisdom. I also thank my sons, Conor, for his Photoshop artistry, and Gaelen, for his computer help in a time of need.

Many thanks to my agent, Steven Chudney, for his insights and faith in this novel; my editor, Susan Van Metre, for believing in my characters, and the staff at Harry N. Abrams for shepherding them into the world; Chad Beckerman for the cover and interior art designs; and Jason Wells and Amy Geduldig for their marketing assistance.

Thanks also to the librarians of the Spokane County Library, whose positive attitudes and superb skills facilitated my research; Gail Nadeau, Lora Hughes, and Laurie MacMillan for their ideas and lending an ear; and especially to Laurie for her time and talents in designing my Web pages for this book. A big thank you to Adam Jackman and Mark D. Kelly of University of Washington Libraries in Seattle for finding Rumi translations.

Heartfelt thanks always to my husband, Bill, and my parents, siblings, and friends for their support through the years of *Anahita*'s growth and development.

PERMISSIONS

The poem attributed to Rabi'a al-Adawiyya, "O My Lord," was translated by Charles Upton, and anthologized by Jane Hirshfield in *Women in Praise of the Sacred*, HarperCollins Publishers, 1994. The Rumi poem "You and I," which Arash sends to Anahita, is a version of a translation by Reynold A. Nicholson, *Selected Poems from the Divani Shamsi Tabriz*, Curzon Press, Cambridge University, 1994, p. 153. The Rumi ode that closes the story is an excerpt from "Our Death Is Our Wedding with Eternity," poem number 105, *Mystical Poems of Rumi, 1st Selection*, translated by A. J. Arberry, University of Chicago Press, 1991, p. 90 (however, this excerpt may be closer to a translation by E. H. Whinfield). The Rumi poem "A Great Wagon" and a few other lines of verse by this poet are from *The Essential Rumi*, translated by Coleman Barks with John Moyne, HarperSanFrancisco, 1995. Rumi's phrase "Wool in the hands of a spiritual man . . ." and other Sufi phrases are cited from *The Sufis*, by Indries Shah, Doubleday, New York, 1964. I regret that I cannot find the source of the epigraph poem that opens the novel. It may be attributed to Rumi and quite possibly may be the translation of Franklin D. Lewis, Paul Lamborn Wilson, or Anne Marie Schimmel. Please contact the publisher with concerns regarding the use of this poem. The phrase "Rumi kisses you on the right cheek, then on the left, warms your soul and brings you closer to yourself," used in a conversation between Anahita and Arash, is adapted from Shahram Shiva's *Rumi: Thief of Sleep*, Holm Press, 2000, p. xvi.

References

Amanat, Abbas. *Pivot of the Universe: Nasir al-Din Shah Qajar and the Iranian Monarchy 1831–1896.* University of California Press, Berkeley, 1997.

Barks, Coleman. *The Essential Rumi.* HarperCollins, San Francisco, 1995.

Beck, Lois. *Nomad: A Year in the Life of a Qashqa'i Tribesman in Iran.* University of California Press, Berkeley, 1991.

Cammann, Schuyler V. R. "Symbolic Meaning in Oriental Rugs." *Textile Museum Journal,* vol. 3, no. 3, 1972: 5–66.

Dawood, N. J. *The Koran.* Penguin Books, London, England, 1997.

Greenway and St. Vincent. *Iran.* Lonely Planet, Oakland, CA, 1992.

Gregorian, Arthur. *Oriental Rugs and the Stories They Tell.* Frederick Warne, 1978.

Hirshfield, Jane. *Women in Praise of the Sacred.* Harper Perennial, New York, 1994.

Opie, James. *Tribal Rugs.* The Tolstoy Press, Portland, Oregon, 1992.

Raphaelian, Harold. *The Hidden Language of Symbols in Oriental Rugs.* A. Sivas, 1953.

Shah, Indries. *The Sufis.* Doubleday, New York, 1964.

Shiva, Shahram. *Rumi: Thief of Sleep.* Hohm Press, Presscott, Arizona, 2000.

Thompson, Jon. *Oriental Carpets: The Art of Carpets from the Tents, Cottages, and Workshops of Asia.* Dutton, New York, 1988.

FURTHER READING

Bayat, Mojdeh. *Tales from the Land of the Sufis*. Shambhala, Boston and London, 1994.

Buchanan, Rita. *A Weavers Garden*. Interweave Press, Loveland, Colorado, 1987.

Farmaian, Sattareh Farman. *Daughter of Persia. A Woman's Journey from Her Father's Harem Through the Islamic Revolution*. Doubleday, 1992.

Forbis, William H. *Fall of the Peacock Throne: The Story of Iran*. Harper & Row, New York, 1980.

Fox, Mary Virginia. *Enchantment of the World: Iran*. Children's Press, Chicago, 1991.

Irons, William. *The Yomut Turkmen: A Study of Kinship in a Pastoral Society*. University of Michigan, Museum of Anthropology, 1975.

Ross, Robert Horace. *Ancient Persian Designs in Needlepoint*. St. Martin's Press, New York, 1982.

Taj Al-Saltana. *Crowning Anguish: Memoirs of a Persian Princess from the Harem to Modernity*, edited by Abbas Amanat. Mage Publishers, Washington, D.C., 1993.

Tapper, Richard, and Jon Thompson. *The Nomadic Peoples of Iran*. Distributed by Thames & Hudson, New York, 2002.

Upton, Charles. *Doorkeeper of the Heart: Versions of Rabi'a*. Threshold Books, Vermont, 1988.

Van Stralen, Trudy. *Indigo, Madder, and Marigold*. Interweave Press, Loveland, Colorado, 1993.

Vitray-Meyerovitch, Eva de. *Rumi and Sufism*. The Post-Apollo Press, Sausalito, California, 1997.

ABOUT THE AUTHOR

Meghan Nuttall Sayres is a tapestry weaver who has traveled in Turkey and Iran, where she met with scholars, carpet weavers, dyemasters, and merchants to study the age-old techniques, symbolism, and Sufi poetry that infuse many rugs woven throughout the Middle East. She is co-author of *Daughters of the Desert: Tales of Remarkable Women from the Christian, Jewish and Muslim Traditions* and author of *The Shape of Betts Meadow: A Wetlands Story*, among other books. She lives in Washington State with her husband, three children, two sheep, and a cat. In their living room is a carpet very much like the one Anahita weaves for her riddle contest. For more information about Meghan and this book, including discussion guides, please visit www.meghannuttallsayres.com.

This book was designed

and art directed by Chad W. Beckerman, and
is set in 13-point Centaur, a re-creation of a
font designed in the fifteenth century by the
Frenchman Nicolas Jenson. The display text
is set in Civilité and Requiem.

Keep reading! If you liked this book, check out these other titles.

Cicada Summer
By Andrea Beaty
978-0-8109-9472-0
$15.95 hardcover

Something to Blog About
By Shana Norris
978-0-8109-9474-4
$15.95 hardcover

A Midsummer Night's Dream
Manga Shakespeare
978-0-8109-9475-1
$9.95 paperback

Visit www.amuletbooks.com to download
screensavers and ring tones, to find out where
authors will be appearing, and to send e-cards.

The Hour of the Outlaw
By Maiya Williams
978-0-8109-9355-6
$16.95 hardcover

This Is All
By Aidan Chambers
978-0-8109-7060-1 $19.95 hardcover
978-0-8109-9550-5 $14.95 paperback

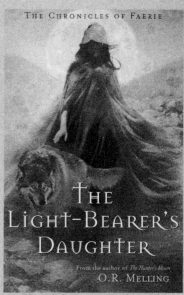

The Light-Bearer's Daughter
By O.R. Melling
978-0-8109-0781-2
$16.95 hardcover